Shadow of an Angel

THE BEELER LARGE PRINT MYSTERY SERIES

Edited by Audrey A. Lesko

Also available in Large Print by Mignon F.Ballard

An Angel to Die For
Angel at Troublesome Creek

Shadow of an Angel

An Augusta Goodnight Mystery

MIGNON F. BALLARD

BEELER LARGE PRINT
Hampton Falls, New Hampshire, 2002

Library of Congress Cataloging-in-Publication Data

Ballard, Mignon F.
 Shadow of an angel / Mignon F. Ballard.
  p.   cm.—(The Beeler Large Print mystery series)
 ISBN 1-57490-433-7 (acid-free paper)
  1. Goodnight, Augusta (Fictitious character)—Fiction. 2.
Guardian angels—Fiction. 3. Large type books. I. Title. II.
Series.

PS3552.A466 S47 2002b
813'.54—dc21   2002010435

Published in Large Print by arrangement with
St. Martins Press, LLC.

BEELER LARGE PRINT
is published by
Thomas T. Beeler, Publisher
Post Office Box 659
Hampton Falls, New Hampshire 03844

Typeset in 16 point Times New Roman type.
Printed on acid-free paper, sewn and bound by
Sheridan Books in Chelsea, Michigan.

For our five loves:
Sam, Helen, Anna, Frances, and Will
(and not an angel in the lot!)

Acknowledgments

I would like to thank Laura Langlie, whom I'm fortunate to have as an agent and friend; my husband, Gene, for his sustaining love and valuable help over the years; St. Martin's' Hope Dellon and Kris Kamikawa, for helping to make Augusta "fly," and my patient family for loving me anyway.

—M.F.B.

Family Tree

Lucy Arminda   Westbrook Alexander

Vesta Alexander Maxwell   Edward Alexander

Elizabeth   Jo Lynn   Otto Alexander

Arminda   Gatlin

(m. Jarvis Hobbs) *(m. David Norwood)*

Lizzie and Faye

Cast of Characters

Minda (Arminda) Hobbs: young and recently widowed, she returns to the family home seeking peace of mind.

Otto Alexander: the ne'er-do-well cousin she finds dead instead

Augusta Goodnight: Minda's guardian angel 'temp'

Gatlin Norwood: Minda's friend and cousin

Dave Norwood: Gatlin's husband and football coach at Angel Heights High

Lizzy and Faye: their children

Vesta Alexander: grandmother to Minda and Gatlin

Mildred Parsons: family housekeeper who raised Otto

Fitzhugh Holley: noted professor at Minerva Academy who died heroically in a long ago fire, and author of a popular series of children's books

Hugh Talbot: his grandson who heads the museum at Minerva Academy

Gertrude Whitmire: Hugh's sister and retired history teacher

Hank Smith: local doctor and friend of the family

Edna Smith: his wife

Sylvie Smith: their daughter, rumored to have been seeing Otto

Irene Bradshaw: Vesta's longtime neighbor

Pauline Satts: Irene's mother and Lucy Westbrook's friend

Annie Rose Westbrook: Lucy's younger sister, who drowned in the Saluda River in 1916

Chief McBride: Angel Height's chief of police

Rusty Echols: his nephew and second in command

Lydia Bowen: Mildred's friend

Mrs. Grimes: school principal who hasn't a clue

Maureen Foster: quilter who does

R.T. Foster: Maureen's husband

Gordon Carstairs: local historian

Peggy O'Connor: who is guarding an old secret

Shadow of an Angel

Chapter One

THINGS GOT OFF TO A ROTTEN START WHEN I found Cousin Otto dead in the ladies' room.

Of course, at first I didn't know it was Cousin Otto, and I certainly didn't know he was dead! All I could see were those big brown shoes in the stall next to mine when I bent to retrieve a roll of bathroom paper making a pathway across the floor. (Apparently the people responsible for the upkeep of historic Holley Hall had never thought to replace the broken tissue spindle.)

My neighbor's shoes were at least size twelve, scuffed at the toes, and obviously not on intimate terms with a buffing brush. I peeked again. Blue nylon socks stretched beneath creased khaki trousers. Had I wandered into the men's room by mistake? Gasping, I drew up my feet before I remembered seeing the tampon dispenser on the wall when I came in. Unless nature had taken a drastic turn, I was in the right place.

The man next door was terribly still. Did he know I knew? He was mortified, naturally. Maybe if I stayed where I was for a few minutes, it would give him a chance to escape.

It was then I noticed the small gold earring—or it looked like an earring—wedged in the corner of my stall. Whoever had dropped it would probably be glad to have it back, and I snatched up the trinket and put it in my shirt pocket, intending to turn it in to the academy's hostess later.

Surely by now the man to my left would realize he'd made a really big "oops!" and vamoose. I sat, afraid to breathe. Go on, I urged under my breath. Get out!

Nothing. Well, I couldn't wait forever. To heck with him!

It wasn't until I was washing my hands that I noticed the reflection in the mirror. Beneath the side of the stall toward the sink, the knuckles of a large hand—a man's hand—hung, barely brushing the floor. I've heard of being embarrassed to death, but this was going to the extreme.

Forgetting decorum, I pounded on the stall. "Are you all right? Do you need help?

"Listen, we all make mistakes," I persisted. "I'll leave if you like, but please answer me. Is anything wrong? Are you sick?"

Still no answer. Beneath the stall's door I saw the feet in the same slightly turned in position, the arm dangled in a most unnatural way. Not a good sign.

"There's a man in the ladies' room," I announced to Gertrude Whitmire, who was at the reception desk that day. "I'm afraid something's wrong with him; he's not moving."

She skewered me with her sharp blue eyes. This woman had taught history to generations—including mine. Wordy Gerty, we called her. She *was* history, and I knew she suffered no shilly-shallying.

"What do you mean, he's not moving?" She was on her feet and halfway down the hallway before I caught up with her.

"In that last stall," I directed. "I can't get him to answer."

The metal door trembled under the pressure of her pounding. "Who's in there?" the woman demanded in a voice loud enough to bring even the comatose to attention, but there was no reply.

"Stall's locked," she informed me. "You'll have to

2

crawl under."

"Me? I can't do that!"

I had come to Angel Heights, the home of my forebearers, to seek spiritual renewal in a peaceful retreat after my husband's sudden death and, I hoped, to smooth an uneasy relationship with my grandmother. This was not what I had in mind.

"Yes, you can. You'll have to." Gertrude Whitmire patted her ample hips as if to explain why I would be the better choice.

Still I shook my head. I didn't care how many years she'd been "yes, ma'amed" at Angel Heights High. I was *not* crawling under that awful booth.

"If we can find something for me to stand on, maybe I can reach over," I said, wilting under her look of utter disgust.

Soon afterward a chair appeared, and I came face-to-face with Cousin Otto. My relative is never one to turn down a drink, no matter how early in the day, and I thought he'd probably tied one on at lunchtime and wandered into the ladies' room by mistake. He smelled of liquor and urine, and I almost gagged until I finally got the door unlatched. My first instinct was to block Gertrude Whitmire's view so she couldn't see who it was. How dare this disgusting man embarrass the family this way!

Too late. "Is that Otto? It is, isn't it?" The woman wedged her head over my shoulder, almost nudging me into Cousin Otto's lap. His head sagged to one side, and he clutched what looked like a balled up handkerchief.

"Ye gods!" Gertrude Whitmire's breath was hot on my neck and smelled of the chocolates she kept hidden in her desk. "Well, Arminda, you were asking for your cousin. Seems as if we've found him."

3

This was my grandmother's fault. If Vesta had stayed at home just this once to pass along the key to the home place, I wouldn't be squashed in this toilet practically sitting on Cousin Otto.

"I'll probably be on the golf course when you get here," my grandmother had told me, "but you can get a key to the Nut House from Otto. He volunteers over at Holley Hall every other Saturday—if he's sober, that is."

Vesta liked to refer to our family home as the Nut House because it stands in a pecan grove, she said, but I suspected this was only part of the reason.

Failing to find my grandmother at home in her newly acquired condominium, I had dutifully inquired after my cousin at the town's one historic site.

Gertrude Whitmire hadn't seen him, she'd told me earlier, but directed me to the upstairs library, where she said he usually spent his time. Finding that room empty, I had taken advantage of the facilities, planning to stroll about the grounds until my cousin returned from what was obviously a late lunch.

"So, what do we do now?" I quickly shut the door and backed away from the pathetic tableau, stepping on my own feet and Gertrude's, as well.

"Get him out of here, of course, and as soon as possible. We can't have people in here gawking. It's a wonder some tourist hasn't stumbled in here already."

The only museum-goers I had seen that day were an elderly couple chuckling over a class picture in the hallway and a handful of young boys tussling over a football on the lawn. On a sunny Saturday in early November, it seemed, people had better things to do than poke about the musty remains of what once had been a school for young women.

4

Gertrude lowered her head, bull-like, and stepped forward, determined to do her duty, no matter how distasteful. "I suppose it's up to us, Arminda, to see that your cousin gets home to sleep it off." She emphasized, I noticed, the fact that Otto was my relative and left me no choice but to follow suit.

But as soon as I touched Otto Alexander's cold, stiff hand, I knew my cousin would be a long time sleeping this one off. I think I screamed, but my cry was cut short by a look from Gertrude that had the same effect as a splash of icy well water.

Later, in the building's austere parlor, we waited for the coroner by a gas fire that wasn't much warmer. Above the marble mantel, a dark portrait of Fitzhugh Holley, long-ago head of Minerva Academy and Angel Heights's contribution to kiddie lit, smiled down at me as if amused by the situation.

His grandson wasn't. Hugh Talbot, florid and fiftyish, bore little resemblance to his ancestor in the portrait. In the likeness over the fireplace, blue eyes gleamed behind rimless spectacles, and lips turned up in a slight smile, as if the subject of the painting might be dreaming up additional antics for his lovable storybook characters, Callie Cat and Doggie Dan. He wore his sandy mustache neatly trimmed above a firm, beardless chin. The portrait had been painted from a photograph, Cousin Otto once pointed out. The professor died in his thirties while saving one of his students from a fire. A pity, I thought. So young and so handsome—like my own Jarvis.

Don't go there, Minda! The thought of Jarvis, whose zany sense of humor and boyish sweetness made me love him from the start, could send me back into that dark pit of self-pity, and I didn't want to go through that

5

again.

"I just can't believe this!" Hugh Talbot repeated for the umpteenth time. "What in the world made Otto go into the ladies' room? What could he have been thinking?" He paced the room, watching for the arrival of the coroner. "Do you suppose he had a heart attack? It was probably his liver. All that alcohol, you know."

He patted his toupee, which was at least two shades darker than his graying reddish hair. A lonely tuft of his own hair stuck out over his forehead like a misplaced goatee. "I'm sorry, Minda," he added, as if in an afterthought. "I know this must be difficult for you after what you've been through and all, but this isn't going to be good for the academy—not good at all. And on the toilet, for heaven's sake! I don't suppose we could move him, could we?"

"Certainly not! You know better than that." Gertrude, Hugh's older sister, stood as if to block the doorway and prevent any foolish action on his part. "I put 'closed' signs on both entrances and gave the couple from Kentucky a rain check. Other than that, we'll have to leave things as they are." Despite her pretense at calmness, Gertrude Whitmire's breath came fast, and her face was almost as flushed as her brother's.

"Why don't you sit down for a minute?" I asked her. "Would you like some water?"

Gertrude shook her head at my offer, but she did sink, still protesting, into the Victorian chair nearest the door. Against the burgundy velvet, her face looked rather like an overripe plum.

Hugh hurried to her side and bent as if he meant to comfort her, but instead thumped the back of her chair. "What on earth's taking so long?" he asked of no one in particular. Then, striding to the mantel, Hugh declared

6

to his grandfather's portrait that he had no idea how to explain this to Minerva's board of directors. "My God, this couldn't come at a worse time! And right before the holidays, too!" He frowned at me. "I suppose it would be in bad taste to host our usual Christmas gala."

"Now wait just a minute!" I said, facing him across the hearth. "My cousin didn't mean to die here! He was only in his forties, and I've never heard of any problems with his heart. I'm sure if he'd had a choice, he'd rather not have died at all." Otto wasn't my favorite relative, but I was tired of having his death referred to as a mere inconvenience. "And what's more, you both seem to have forgotten how many hours he gave to this place." Frankly, I had no idea how often my cousin volunteered at the academy, but it seemed the right thing to say.

Obviously it was.

"You're right, my dear." Gertrude sat upright in her thronelike chair. "My brother isn't thinking, I'm afraid. Unfortunately he only cares about two things: Minerva Academy and the almighty dollar—although not necessarily in that order.

"That was extremely callous of you, Hugh. I think you've said enough."

The chastized one came forward and touched my shoulder with a hesitant hand. "My sister's right, of course. I wasn't thinking, and I apologize. I'm terribly sorry, Minda. Please forgive me, won't you?"

I said I would and meant it. Actually, I felt a little sorry for him.

"Has anyone called Vesta?" Hugh Talbot almost stumbled over the threadbare rug. "I'm afraid this will be a terrible shock to your grandmother . . . her only nephew going like this."

Gertrude seemed to be inspecting the dusty sunlight

7

seeping across the floor. She spoke in a monotone. "They're sending someone to try to locate her on the golf course. It's Mildred I'm concerned about. She dotes on Otto so."

Mildred Parsons had kept house for my great-grandmother until she died, and then for Vesta. When my grandmother moved into a smaller place, Otto made room for Mildred in his quarters behind Papa's Armchair, the secondhand bookshop he owned. Otto was only a child when Mildred came to live with his family in Angel Heights, and Vesta always said Mildred paid more attention to him than his own mother had.

I glanced about me at the narrow, high-ceilinged parlor, at the tall windows shrouded in faded green satin. The acrid smell of old books and musty furniture permeated the room; blue flames flared and vanished into one another behind the brass fender. Another world. Another time. What was I doing here? Did death trail me like a somber shadow? Less than two years ago, without any warning, my husband, Jarvis, had been killed by lightning while we picnicked in the country. A freak accident, they said. And now this.

I had come to Angel Heights, South Carolina, to escape the stirring memories of the home Jarvis and I had built together and lived in for less than a year. We had dreamed of it during our six years of marriage and planned to begin our family there. Now, after the Christmas holidays, I would step in and substitute for a teacher at Angel Heights Elementary School when she left to have her baby, and my grandmother had surprised me by offering the family home to me, still partially furnished, after she downsized to a condominium. But she was still miffed at me, I could tell, for finally accepting my dad's second wife.

I was still in high school when my father remarried, less than a year after Mom died, and I came to live with Vesta. I'm still not wild about Dad's wife, Roberta, but I've come to terms with their relationship. When Jarvis died, Dad was there for me more than he'd ever been when we lost Mom, and I loved him for that. Although Vesta hadn't actually said anything, her displeasure was obvious.

Now she was holding out a tentative olive branch.

"I'm not ready to let it go out of the family," my grandmother had said. "And I'd hate to see the old place empty after all these years; besides, it is part of your heritage, Minda.

"Heritage. Right now I could do without it, I thought. But even here I couldn't escape. My great-grandmother, Lucy Westbrook, and her sister, Annie Rose, who was only sixteen when she drowned in the Saluda River, had both attended Minerva Academy.

While still a schoolgirl, Lucy had written and stitched the school's alma mater that hung, I noticed, to the right of the mantel. A talented artist, musician, and seamstress, Lucy seemed to excel at everything. Our family home was filled with her paintings, and the local paper had published her verses on a regular basis.

The room seemed suddenly silent, and I glanced about to find myself alone. Someone was pounding on the front door, and Gertrude and her brother had gone to let them in. I supposed it was the coroner and I should go as well, but I held back. I couldn't bear to look at Cousin Otto again.

Instead I wandered over to examine my ancestor's handiwork. I had been in this building on several occasions, yet I had never taken the time to read it.

The words were bordered in tiny six-petaled flowers,

9

and at the bottom a larger flower of the same design held a star in its center. It seemed vaguely familiar, and then I remembered where I'd seen that emblem before. It was the design on the gold earring I'd found on the floor in the ladies' room. When I took it out to examine it, I found it wasn't an earring at all, but a pin. The gold six-pointed star in the center sat on a tiny circle of onyx; this was surrounded by six mother-of-pearl flower petals on an onyx circle rimmed in gold.

This was no ordinary bauble. I dropped it back into my pocket. Obviously it had significance or my great-grandmother wouldn't have incorporated it into her handiwork. But what was it doing here now almost a hundred years later on the floor of a toilet stall!

My great-grandmother had stitched her name, LUCY ARMINDA WESTBROOK, neatly at the bottom, along with the date, MAY 21, 1915. She would have been about sixteen or seventeen when she wrote it. I had inherited her middle name, but shared few of her talents, it seemed.

The verse was written in the style of the period and was sung, I'm told, during assemblies and other school functions, but the tune had been forgotten over the years.

The simple words portrayed a time of innocence, virtue, and unquestioning trust, and I felt a pang of jealousy for something my generation had seldom experienced.

WE SING THY PRAISE, MINERVA
WITH EVERLASTING PRIDE.
OF THY STATELY HALLS AND CHAMBERS
WHERE KNOWLEDGE DOTH ABIDE.
AGAINST THE GENTLE HILLSIDE,

BENEATH THE WILLOW'S SHADE,
YOUR WINDING PATHWAYS LEAD US
IN A NOBLE CAVALCADE.
BESIDE THE SWIFT SALUDA,
THAT DAILY SINGS YOUR NAME,
IN FRIENDSHIP AND IN WISDOM,
MINERVA, WE ACCLAIM!

The "swift Saluda" was where my great-grandmother's sister drowned, probably about a year after this verse was written. Annie Rose—and so like a rose according to family stories—sweet and pretty, just beginning to bloom.

And soon after that, a classroom building burned at the academy taking the brave young professor with it.

Minerva's alma mater didn't seem so guileless anymore.

Local legend claimed the town of Angel Heights took its name from the stone outcropping that was supposed to resemble an angel on the hill behind the village. It seemed to me if there really was an angel in Angel Heights it was time for her to flap down from her heavenly hill and "wing it" with the rest of us.

Chapter Two

I DIDN'T EXPECT TO MEET HER SO SOON—THE angel, I mean. Naturally, I didn't realize she was an angel right away, although she had the presence of one, with that church-window radiance and hair like old gold.

11

After leaving the academy later that afternoon, I collected the key to the home place from my grandmother and stopped there to drop off some of my things. The family would be gathering at my cousin Gatlin's to make plans for Otto's funeral, and I didn't want to haul around my entire winter wardrobe, plus other essentials I'd brought from home—or what used to be home. The house Jarvis and I had built sold less than a month after I put it on the market, and our furniture was now in storage. Now I carried the memory of it like a hot coal somewhere below my heart.

"So, you've come. Good! It's cool out here." The woman called out to me from a porch rocker as I approached my grandmother's old home, and it startled me so I almost dropped the box of books I was carrying. The huge old magnolia in the front yard shaded the porch, and I could barely make out the vague silhouette of someone waiting there. The house had been empty for several months, and I didn't expect anyone to greet me. She stood briefly at the top of the steps in the fading rays of the afternoon sun, and for just a few seconds her hair looked . . .Well, it *shimmered*! She might have posed for paintings in the art history textbook I'd had in college, and though her face seemed motherly, it was hard to judge her age. But if this woman was older than forty, I'd like to know what kind of face cream she used.

She hurried to meet me, wading through curled brown leaves that plastered the flagstone walk, and in one graceful movement, she scooped up a heavy dictionary, a looseleaf cookbook compiled by my mother, and my well-worn copy of *To Kill a Mockingbird* that had skidded to the ground. "Please, let me help," the woman offered, and I accepted. Her voluminous skirt of sunset

12

colors rustled when she walked, and a shawl that seemed to be knitted of iridescent silk floated after her. A flash of pink-painted toenails peeked from gold sandals with just the tiniest hint of a heel.

"Augusta Goodnight," the stranger said, introducing herself once the car was unloaded. She seemed to have made at least five trips to my two and wasn't the least bit winded. When she smiled, the calmness in her eyes washed over me, and for the first time since I'd found Cousin Otto I felt the tension ease.

"I thought you might like some of my apple spice muffins for your breakfast," she said, presenting me with a basket covered with a yellow flowered cloth.

She must be a neighbor, of course, and the muffins were a welcoming gesture. Or maybe she'd heard about Cousin Otto and gotten a head start on the funeral baking. But how could that be? It had been scarcely two hours since my grim discovery in the ladies' room.

I hesitated on the front steps with the basket in my hands and wondered if I should invite my neighbor inside. My grandmother—or someone—had remembered to turn on the heat, but the old house still had that stuffy, closed-up smell.

The woman smelled of summer and of the strawberry jam Mom used to make. When I looked into her eyes I thought of the lake at Camp Occoneechee, where I'd learned to swim as a child, whose waters made me feel part fish and all new.

"I'd ask you in," I began, "but Gatlin's expecting us soon for supper. I suppose you've heard about Otto?"

Augusta nodded, and for a moment the shadow of a frown clouded her eyes. "I'm so very sorry about that, Minda," she said, almost as if she blamed herself.

"I'll be staying at Gatlin's until after the funeral," I

13

told her, "and I'm sure these muffins will be welcome there—especially with two hungry children. Gatlin says she can't seem to fill them up." I smiled. "I guess you know how that is."

Or not, I thought when she didn't answer. In spite of the age-old wisdom in her face, there was a look of almost child like innocence about Augusta Goodnight.

"Gatlin has her hands full," I babbled on, "with all the relatives crowding in—including me. And, of course, Otto's death is especially upsetting for Mildred and Vesta."

Now my visitor fingered the lustrous stones of amber and jade that circled her elegant neck and swung almost to her waist. "This is a difficult time for you, too, Minda, and I'm here to help where I can. I hope you'll remember that."

"Why . . . thank you," I said. Who *was* this person? Was she from one of those denominations that barge into your home and try to convert you to their religion? She hadn't mentioned a church—not yet, anyway—and thank goodness for that! I hadn't been too chummy with God since my mother died of cancer while I was still in high school.

Don't be so suspicious, Minda Hobbs, I told myself. She's probably just a helpful neighbor, although I thought I knew everyone on Vesta's street. "I'll be here until summer, at least," I told her, "so I expect I'll be seeing you again."

Augusta Goodnight spoke softly. "You can count on that," she said, and then added something about unfinished business in Angel Heights.

I turned to put the basket of muffins in the car, and when I looked back, she was gone.

14

Everyone says my cousin Gatlin looks more like my mother, Beth, than I do, and sometimes when I see her after having been away for a while, it ties my heart in a knot. It did today. Gatlin is petite, with auburn hair that curls about her face like Mom's did, huge, pansy-soft brown eyes, and freckles enough to share.

At five nine, I'm taller than most women, and I have hair like Dad's: straw-straight and yellow as butter. In snapshots of me as a toddler, my hair looked almost white. A towhead, Vesta called me. When my mother took me shopping, people sometimes made a fuss over my light hair, but I would have traded with Gatlin any day.

My cousin was five when I was born, and I followed her around like an inept gumshoe. She didn't seem to mind. And when I came to live with Vesta after Mom died, she became my best friend. She still is.

Now she met me at the door with her usual warm greeting, a hug and a kiss on both cheeks, although she had to stand on tiptoe to reach me; then she swept me into her wonderful, harum-scarum lifestyle. My young cousin clutched my sleeve, and the family's black lab, Napoleon, clamored to be petted.

Elizabeth (Lizzie), named for my mother, is ten and almost as tall as Gatlin already. "Minda! Come in the kitchen, I'm making spaghetti sauce," she said, grasping me by the arm. "I'm so glad you're here! Isn't it awful about Cud'in Otto? Mama says he probably drank himself to death." This last was supposed to be a whisper, but it was loud enough to elicit a loud "Shh!" and a warning look from my grandmother across the room.

I went over and kissed Vesta's cheek, which she offered, I thought, somewhat reluctantly. She seemed to

15

be doing okay when I left her in Gatlin's capable hands at Minerva Academy, but she looked pale under her golfing tan, and I thought her hand trembled a bit. My grandmother had recently turned eighty, but she liked to joke that she looked only seventy-nine. Usually she seemed at least ten years younger, but not today. "Tell me what I can do to help," I said, trying to resist Lizzie's urgent tugs. "What about Faye?" At least I could keep an eye on Gatlin's youngest while Lizzie helped her mother in the kitchen.

My grandmother fluttered her fingers. "Farmed out with neighbors. You might look in on Mildred, though. Hank's given her a sedative, and she's resting in Lizzie's room."

Hank Smith and his wife were old friends of Vesta's, and although he'd retired from his medical practice, Vesta and her friends still called on him in emergencies.

"Speaking of neighbors," I said, "I met one at the old house today. Augusta Goodnight—sort of strange, but nice. Sent muffins that smell wonderful." I'd almost forgotten the basket I left by the door when I came inside. "Must be new in town; did she buy the Bradshaw place?"

"Augusta Goodnight? Never heard of her." Vesta closed her eyes and leaned back in the worn lounge chair that was usually occupied by Gatlin's husband, David. "The Historical Society bought that house back in the summer. Plan to have teas there, wedding receptions, things like that." She made a face. "Told 'em they'd better get ready to spend some money. Irene Bradshaw hasn't done a blessed thing to that house since she moved in fifty years ago!"

"Maybe she's visiting or something," I said.

But Vesta nixed that, too. No one she knew was

expecting company, she told me. Even though my grandmother had moved from Phinizy Street, she still kept tabs on her old neighborhood.

I tiptoed back to Lizzie's room to find Mildred Parsons lying straight as a pencil and not much bigger among an array of teddy bears on Lizzie's pink Barbie spread. I couldn't remember when her hair had been anything but gray, but Gatlin said she used to be sort of a strawberry blond. Now, pink scalp showed through strands the color of dirty string. Her eyelids twitched slightly, but she seemed to be asleep. I listened to be sure she was breathing normally. Finding one corpse a day is more than enough for me!

Mildred is only a few years older than Vesta, but the years haven't treated her well. According to my grandmother, Mildred was in her early fifties when she came to keep house for Vesta's mother, Lucy, and moved in with the family. That was when she took Otto under her wing. A good thing, I guess, since his mother more or less abandoned him, and everybody says his father didn't have much time for him, either.

Otto's daddy was Vesta's brother, my great-uncle Edward, who still lived at home at the time. Mom said Otto's father traveled a lot in his work, and his mother had become so unhappy living with her husband's relatives in Angel Heights, she went back to her people somewhere out West. That left Mildred to raise Otto, who was about eight or nine years old.

When my great-grandmother, Lucy, died a few years later, my grandparents, Vesta and Charles Maxwell, "inherited" Mildred along with the family home. By then, my mother and Gatlin's were married with families of their own, and Mildred stayed on to do light housework and cook whatever Otto took a notion to eat.

17

"If Mildred hadn't babied him so much, Cousin Otto wouldn't be such a loser," Gatlin once confided, and maybe she had a point, but I didn't think anybody was prepared for our relative dying like he did.

"Just like Elvis," Gatlin said later. "They say he died on the toilet, too."

The two of us were relaxing at last with a glass of merlot and the last of the ham biscuits a neighbor had brought earlier. Vesta had persuaded Mildred to go home with her, and everyone else was tucked away for the night—including Otto, who had been carted away by the coroner before being turned over to Houn' Dawg Wilson (so named because of his mournful expression), who ran the Easyrest Funeral Parlor. "Customary procedure," we were assured, "in event of an unexpected death." And Cousin Otto, we learned, had probably been dead for almost twenty-four hours when I found him.

"Reckon what in the world made Otto pick the ladies' room—of all places—to die in," Gatlin said, reaching for the last ham biscuit.

"Too sick or too drunk to care, I guess," I said. "Maybe he never knew where he was, but what was he doing there last night? The only thing they found, other than his wallet and the usual stuff, was a dirty, wadded up handkerchief. Probably took it out to wipe his face before he took sick and died. The coroner says this must've happened before midnight. Looks like Mildred would've missed him if he didn't come home."

"Movies 'n' Munchies," my cousin said.

"What?"

"Movies 'n' Munchies. The Methodists sponsor a movie night for seniors the first Friday in the month. As far as I know, Mildred's never missed one. They have

18

sandwiches and potato chips, and somebody brings dessert. This week I think they featured Van Johnson in one of those old war movies. Afterwards, Mildred went home and went to bed. When she woke up this morning, I guess she thought Otto had already left for the academy."

"What in the world will she do now?" I wondered. "Papa's Armchair will have to be sold, and I can't imagine her staying on there."

"She could live with Vesta, I suppose, but her place is small, and you know they don't get along so well. Besides, Vesta likes her space."

I didn't think Mildred had ever forgiven my grandmother for moving into that condo and leaving Otto and her behind. It was like breaking up a family.

"There's plenty of room at the Nut House," I said. "Mildred lived there for a good part of her life; she should feel right at home, and it won't cost a cent."

The small living room was cluttered with cups and saucers, empty glasses, and crumpled paper napkins left by earlier callers, including Gertrude Whitmire and her brother Hugh, who still seemed to be in shock. I started to collect the dishes, stacking them on a bent Coca-Cola tray I recognized as Vesta's. "Hey, that'll wait," my cousin protested. "They'll still be there in the morning—I promise."

And so would I, I thought, and I'd rather not be faced with them, but I didn't say so. Gatlin looked tired and seemed to have something on her mind. I knew she was upset over Otto's death, as we all were, but I suspected something more. "Just don't ask me to do windows," I said, in my best proper-Mildred voice. "You know how my sciatica acts up when I overdo."

If I expected a smile from my cousin, I was

19

disappointed. "Sorry, I shouldn't have said that. Especially now." I set down the tray and sat on the arm of Gatlin's chair. "You're worried about Mildred, I know. Do you think Otto's provided for her? Maybe the sale of the bookshop . . ."

"That's just it." Gatlin kicked off her shoes and curled up in the chair. "Papa's Armchair belongs to Vesta—always has. Otto had part interest, but Vesta's the one who got him started; she's the one who put up money for the building."

"But surely Vesta will see that Mildred's taken care of," I said. "And I expect Otto's share of the shop will go to her."

Gatlin shrugged. "If there's anything left to share. Otto wasn't much of a businessman, I'm afraid." My cousin glanced at the closed door of the bedroom she shared with David and lowered her voice to a whisper. "Minda, I'm thinking . . ."

"What?" I leaned forward. "What are you thinking?"

"I'm thinking I'd like to buy Otto's share. I still have the few thousand Dad left me, and I don't earn squat filling in as an office temp. It might be rough going at first, but I'm sure I can make something of it."

"Have you spoken to Vesta about it?" I asked.

"Not yet, but she knows I've been thinking about making a change. I like to be here for the children as much as I can, but it's getting next to impossible to live off a high school coach's salary." Gatlin frowned. "We've always had food on the table, but Minda, we have two kids to educate, and David's already working part time at the recreation center. There just aren't enough hours in the day!"

I smiled as a loud snore came the master bedroom. David had crashed earlier after serving as greeter for the

20

evening to friends who dropped by. The night before, his team had lost their last game of the year to their arch rivals in the next town, and his somber mood suited the occasion. The Angels, Gatlin confided, hadn't had many occasions to celebrate this season.

But I wasn't completely carried away with the idea of the bookshop, and I guess it showed on my face.

"What's wrong? Hey, don't let the noise scare you, Minda. That's really not a bull elephant in there, it's just my husband sleeping on his back!"

I laughed, glad to see a spark of her usual good humor. "It's just that—well—I'm not sure how much money a used bookshop will bring in."

"Right. But there's an empty store next door, and if I can get it, it would be a great place for a coffee shop— soup and sandwiches—things like that. You must've noticed there aren't many places to eat here in Angel Heights, and I could combine the two." My cousin stretched her dainty feet and yawned. "In fact, I had already mentioned it to Otto, and he seemed to think it was a good idea. Said he'd look into it, but you know how Otto is—was. I don't know if he ever did."

I added our empty wineglasses to the tray. "Not a bad idea. You can count on me for your first customer."

My cousin had that same sly look on her face I remembered from the time she gave me a push and sent me solo on my first bike. "Actually I had something else in mind."

I knew it! "I don't want to hear it," I told her.

"Assuming this all works out, I'll need help in the bookshop while I'm getting things brewing next door. I was hoping you'd remember all those times I let you sit between Harold Sturgis and me when he took me to the movies, and be grateful enough to help out." Gatlin

21

hung her head and rolled her eyes heavenward.

"You *begged* me to sit between you! You didn't even like Harold Sturgis!" I reminded her.

She shrugged. "But I liked going to the movies, and he always bought us popcorn, remember?"

"Poor Harold. It took him forever to catch on. But I can't help you, Gatlin. I'm supposed to start teaching after Christmas."

"Bah! That's almost two months away. And you might like this better. Besides, what else are you going to do with your time?"

She was right, of course. Gatlin's almost always right, and in her case, I don't even mind. Later, I stretched out on the pull-out sofa in their small upstairs guest room and hardly noticed the huge boulder I've accused them of hiding under the mattress. I dreamed I was standing on a stool at my mother's kitchen table while she measured strawberries and sugar into a big pot on the stove. And now and then she would smile at me and pop a sweet berry into my mouth. When her hand brushed my face, I felt the warmth of her touch like lifeblood flowing into me. And then I noticed the woman standing behind her. It was the same woman who had been at the old home place earlier. Augusta Goodnight, and for some reason I didn't question her presence there.

When I woke the next morning, it occurred to me I hadn't thought about Jarvis for at least eight hours. It had rained briefly during the night, but now the sky was clearing and I could see a patch of blue big enough to make a pair of Dutchman's britches—which my grandmother claims means fair weather ahead. A sweet gum leaf the color of cranberries sashayed past my window, and something with a sweet spicy smell drifted up from the kitchen. I was with the people who loved

22

me most, people I loved, and I felt the cold hurt inside me begin to dissolve just a little.

And then I remembered Otto. Poor Otto. Even with all his problems, he had a life worth living. What a shame he'd put an early end to it by pickling his liver!

But when the phone rang a few minutes later, we learned that although my cousin's drinking was self-destructive, it had nothing to do with the way he died.

Otto Alexander had been murdered.

Chapter Three

"SUFFOCATED," MY GRANDMOTHER VESTA SAID. "The coroner said Otto was suffocated, probably with the plastic bag they found in the bathroom trash."

Since it was Sunday, Gatlin and I had left her two daughters with their dad and hurried to our grandmother's after hearing the coroner's appalling announcement. Now we huddled in Vesta's high-rise living room and tried to make sense out of this turn of events.

"It would have prints on it, wouldn't it?" I asked.

"Ordinarily, but if this is what they used, apparently whoever did it wore gloves." Vesta lowered her voice as she spoke, and glanced at Mildred Parsons, who sat at one end of the sofa, feet primly together, a vinyl-bound scrapbook on her lap.

"You don't have to whisper around me, Vesta," Mildred said in a louder-than-usual voice. "I suspected Otto's death was no accident. He had stopped drinking, you know. He promised. Drank mostly orange juice—

always kept some around." She drew herself up as well as anyone can who is only a little over five feet tall. "I can assure you that Otto hasn't had any alcohol in almost three months."

I didn't look at Gatlin, but I knew if she wasn't rolling her eyes, she was thinking about it.

"I know some people didn't like Otto," Mildred went on, "didn't understand him. But that was no reason to—" Her lip trembled, and impatiently, she shook off my grandmother's hand. "Otto had a brilliant mind, and I don't think any of you appreciated that. He could've done anything—might have. He didn't deserve to die!"

"Of course not." Gatlin moved closer to sit beside Mildred. "I can't imagine why anyone would do such a horrible thing. Somebody must have broken into the academy intending to burglarize it and found Otto there alone."

"I don't know what they planned to steal," Vesta said. "There's nothing of any value."

Mildred shook her head. "No, I think somebody meant to kill him, and they did it when they knew I'd be away from home. Everyone knows that's Movies 'n' Munchies night."

"But who?" I asked. "And why?"

Mildred shoved her bifocals aside and blotted her eyes with a yellowed lace handkerchief. "I don't know," she said, slamming her small fist onto the album she held in her lap. "But I mean to find out if it's the last thing I do."

"Mildred!" My grandmother set her coffee cup on her new glass-topped cocktail table, and dark liquid sloshed into the saucer. "We're all shocked and saddened about what happened to Otto, but I think we'd best let the police handle things like that."

24

"Oh, butt out, Vesta," Mildred Parsons said. And tucking her scrapbook under her arm, she marched into the adjoining bedroom and shut the door.

Vesta looked like she'd swallowed something cold that hurt going down, and I thought she'd keel over right then and there, but my grandmother surprised me. "Mildred's not herself," she explained, shaking her head. "After all, Otto is all she had."

In a way, I guess she was right. And the four of us were all that remained to mourn Otto Alexander. My cousin's mother had died while he was still a young man, and his father, Edward, a few years later.

Gatlin's own mom, who had taken a job in California after her husband's death, was saving her vacation days to come for Christmas.

"I'm afraid Mildred's gone round the bend," Gatlin whispered to me after the funeral the next day. In spite of Otto's lack of close friends, the Methodist Church had been packed, and the Lucy Alexander Circle (named for my great-grandmother, and the one to which Vesta belonged) had outdone themselves preparing our dinner. Again we gathered at Gatlin's, and a trio of the ladies lingered to wash up the dishes and put away the remainder of the meal while friends consoled the two older women in the living room.

My cousin and I were clearing the dining room table when Gertrude Whitmire bustled in. "You girls let me take care of that," she said, snatching a cake-smeared plate from my hand.

"You seem to be holding up well, Arminda. A shame you had to see that. I had no idea Otto was—"

"I'm all right," I said. "I hope you've been able to get some rest."

25

Gertrude looked tired around the eyes, and the tension showed in her face. She and her brother had arrived earlier with a sliced ham and paper plates, but Hugh didn't have much to say, and he left soon after.

"I'll rest when they find out who did this," she said. "Do you have any idea what Otto was doing there that night? Saturday was his usual day in the library."

"I can't imagine. Maybe he wanted to catch up on something."

"Here, let me get a tray for this," I said, noticing Gertrude's hand trembling. Gatlin, I saw, was quickly removing everything breakable from the table.

"Wordy Gerty's kinda shook up," my cousin said later.

Although a cold November wind stripped brown leaves from the water oak in Gatlin's yard, the two of us escaped the crowded house and sat for a few minutes on the back steps watching the children's rope swing sway eerily in the dusk.

"Wouldn't you be? I'd be terrified to go back in that place again!" I pulled up the collar of my coat and wished for warmer shoes. "You don't really think Mildred means it about finding the murderer, do you?"

"Don't ask me. I've never seen her this way. Okay, it's a given Otto was murdered, but I can't believe it was planned." Gatlin warmed her hands around a mug of hot spiced punch and let the steam waft into her face.

"Then what do you think happened?" I paused to pet Napoleon, who had been chasing a squirrel through the leaves.

"He either stumbled upon a would-be burglary or irritated somebody to the point they couldn't take it any longer. Otto could be unbearable at times, always looking down his nose at people, and he had that

26

annoying laugh."

"Gatlin, people don't get murdered because of an annoying laugh," I said. "And if it wasn't planned, why did the plastic bag have no prints?"

She shrugged and offered me a sip of her drink. "We don't know if that was what he actually used."

"You say *he*. Do you think it was a man?" I slipped the dog a bite of cheese I'd sneaked out for him.

Gatlin pretended not to notice. "No idea, but I'd place my bet on a woman. Cousin Otto was an awful chauvinist. I don't see how Mildred put up with him!"

"Mildred made him that way," I said. "Her world revolved around Otto. I can't imagine what she'll do now."

I was about to find out.

"So there you are!" Vesta opened the back door and streaked the dark steps with yellow light. "I wish you'd come in here and talk some sense into Mildred. She insists on going back to those rooms behind the bookstore tonight!"

After a period of weepy withdrawal, Mildred Parsons seemed to have undergone some kind of metamorphosis from a shy and shadowy background figure to an outspoken woman of purpose. It remained for the rest of us to try to figure out what that purpose was.

Gatlin went first. "Mildred, if you don't want to go back to Vesta's, you can stay with us until you decide what to do."

"I've already decided what to do. I'm going home and get to the bottom of this." Mildred tucked her worn black purse under her arm and looked around for her coat and her funny old hat with the pink feather.

"Did you take the tranquilizer Hank gave you?" Vesta asked. "You still have them, don't you?"

"I think the rest of you need a tranquilizer a lot more than I do." Mildred snapped open her purse, fished out an almost full bottle, and rattled the pills in my grandmother's face. "Here, you take them."

Vesta flopped, puppetlike, into a chair and let her long arms dangle. Tall, angular, and ever active, she had always been the strong one in our family. Now the spunk seemed to be seeping from her, and I didn't like it. "The doctor didn't prescribe the tranquilizers for me, Mildred, but right now I think I could use a few!"

"What you could use is some sleep," I said, putting my arms around her. "You go on home now and get some rest. Gatlin and I will take care of Mildred."

I whispered the latter, but Mildred overheard me. "I'll take care of myself if you'll just get me back to my own place," she said.

And I did.

One of the ladies from the Lucy Alexander Circle promised to see my grandmother safely home, and I left Gatlin to look after Faye, her youngest, who was coming down with a cold.

I was sorry for Mildred; I knew how she felt, but I wanted to shake her for heaping misery on top of anguish. Didn't she know Vesta was grieving, too? Didn't she care? And then I remembered how I had reacted when Jarvis died. I had turned from friends, rejected family, and steeped myself in bitterness until I reached the point where even I couldn't stand to be around me.

"Mildred, I know what it's like to lose someone you love," I said as we drove through the dimly lit streets of downtown Angel Heights. "Believe me, I know how lost and helpless you feel. I hope you'll let us help you." My words sounded oddly familiar, as if I were quoting

28

someone else. The woman, of course! The one with painted toenails and shimmering hair. She had said almost the same thing to me.

Mildred spoke with a tinge of her former shyness, and I could barely see her face in the darkness. "I'm sorry about your husband, Minda. That was an awful thing! And your sweet mother—I loved her, you know. Next to Otto, she was my favorite." She paused. "And I'm glad to see you and your grandmother are trying to work things out."

She turned away from me as we drove past Phinizy Street, where she had lived a good part of her life, and I had to make an effort to hear her. "I know I'm making things difficult, and I regret that, really. But if I have to become a hateful old woman to see things through, then so be it!"

"I'm sure the police are just as eager as you are to find out who killed Otto," I said, slowing as we neared the center of town. "The chief told Gatlin they were checking on everyone with a criminal record who might be in the area, and I know they dusted for prints."

"Well, I could tell them they're wasting their time! Gertrude Whitmire told me herself she found the front door unlocked when she arrived at the academy Saturday morning, and there was no sign of a forced entry."

"Hugh was there that morning. He probably unlocked it," I said.

"No, no! Hugh didn't get there until later. Gertrude assumed Otto was working in the library upstairs, so she didn't think much about it. Whoever killed Otto was already in the building that night, or else he let them in."

Mildred seemed convinced she was right and I was too tired and it was too late to argue. Instead of parking in the narrow alley behind Papa's Armchair, I found a space in front of the shop and waited while Mildred groped for her key. The windows of the small store were dark, and the place gave me the creeps—especially after what had happened to Otto. "I wish you'd stay with me at the home place, at least for tonight," I said as I helped her out of the car. "Don't you think it would be better to come back in the daylight? I really don't like leaving you here."

But Mildred didn't answer. I might as well have been talking to the wooden sign creaking over our heads. She fumbled for a minute with the lock, and I pushed open the heavy door with peeling green paint, then quickly stepped inside and switched on the light.

Mildred stood blinking in the fluorescent glare. "Someone's been here," she said.

"What do you mean?" I looked around. Everything seemed in order to me.

She frowned and looked about her. "I'm not sure, but something's not right." Mildred disappeared between rows of shelves that towered above her, and I trailed after, afraid to let her out of my sight. What if someone waited there? I watched while she nudged a book into place, shifted another to a different shelf. Insignificant things. What did they matter?

"I knew it! Here, look." Mildred stood in the doorway of the tiny back office. "Somebody's been in this desk."

Papers were scattered on the desktop, and a drawer had been opened a couple of inches, but other than that, it appeared undisturbed. "Otto might've left it that way," I said, smothering a yawn.

"But this isn't Otto's desk. He keeps his files and computer in our living quarters in the back. This is the desk I use for household accounts and to write up the minutes of the UMW, things like that.

"United Methodist Women. I'm secretary," she explained, seeing my blank expression. "And just look at that mess! I would never leave a desk like this."

I thought it looked neat compared to mine. "Maybe you'd better check to see if anything's missing," I said.

Mildred ruffled through her papers and peered into the desk drawers. "Everything appears to be here. There's nothing here of interest anyway—at least to anyone but me. And they've moved my jar of pencils, too."

Under ordinary circumstances, I might've laughed, but I knew she'd never forgive me. "Your pencils?"

"Yes." She kicked at something beneath the desk. "See, they even dropped a couple on the floor. I always keep that jar on the left side of the desk because I'm left-handed. Somebody must have been looking for something in there and put it back on the wrong side."

"Looking for what?" I asked.

"When we know that, maybe we'll know who killed Otto," she said.

"I think we should call the police," I said after we had searched her small apartment behind the store. It consisted of only two bedrooms and bath, a small kitchen and eating area, and a narrow sitting room with just enough space for a sofa, two side chairs, and a television. I could tell that Mildred had tried to make it homelike with crocheted doilies on the chair backs and a potted yellow chrysanthemum on the end table.

"What for?" she said. "So they can tell me I'm imagining things? Obviously whoever was here has already found what they were looking for. I doubt if they'll be back. At any rate, I'll worry about it in the morning. Right now I'm going to bed."

31

"What do you mean they've found what they were looking for? Is anything missing? Tell me what it is, and we'll report it to the police."

"I'm not sure; I'll have to look again tomorrow when I'm not so tired." She gave my arm a dismissing pat. "You run on home now, Minda, and get some sleep. I'll talk to you tomorrow."

No amount of cajoling could convince this stubborn woman to come home with me, so I made her promise to call at the first sign of an intruder, waited until I was sure she'd double-bolted her doors, and then headed for the familiar house on Phinizy Street.

Jarvis would be surprised to see me turning in before midnight. *Oh God! I forgot he was dead! Again!* The familiar hot, stinging sadness oozed through me like lemon juice in a cut. My husband used to tease me about being a night owl because I could read until the small hours and forget what time it was. Not tonight. Parking behind the family home, it was all I could do to drag myself from the car and up the steps to the back porch. A dim light came from somewhere inside. I didn't remember leaving it on, but was glad I had. If Gatlin's small house hadn't been so crowded and she didn't have a sick child to contend with, I would have stayed there one more night. I wasn't looking forward to coming here alone.

After Mom died and my dad remarried and moved to Atlanta with his new wife, I had spent the remainder of my high school years with Vesta in this house. During that time, Otto had clerked for a while at City Hall, tried his hand at selling insurance, and enrolled in a division of the university to study for his master's degree in world history. He never received it. The Nut House was home to me until I married Jarvis, and we had hosted

32

our wedding reception on the front lawn.

But I wasn't going to think of that. Tonight I would crawl gratefully into the cherry sleigh bed that had been my mother's in my old room with the yellow striped wallpaper. And tomorrow I would get started with the rest of my life.

If only Cousin Otto didn't have to go and get himself murdered! And what if the person who searched the bookshop came here? What if he was now?

Arminda Hobbs, you're getting as nutty as Mildred! Nobody was in that bookshop, and nobody is going to be here. Now get upstairs, turn off your mind, and go to bed!

Yeah, right. But Otto's still dead,

Other than the tiny light, the house was dark. It was big. And I was alone in it—I thought.

I switched on every light in the house and looked neither to the right nor the left as I took the stairs two at a time. If somebody was waiting there, I didn't want to see them.

But it was hard to miss the bright-haired lady in the upstairs hall.

Chapter Four

IT WAS THE SAME WOMAN WHO HAD GREETED me from the front porch the day Otto was killed, and she seemed to be admiring the paintings lining the upstairs hall. When she turned toward me I saw that she held a mug of something that smelled like coffee. And cinnamon. The rich aroma wafted to greet me, and I stood stock-still about four steps from the top and clutched the railing like a lifeline.

Could this be the person who had been poking about in Otto's bookshop? The one who had killed him? She didn't seem dangerous, and the muffins she'd brought had been absolutely heavenly, still . . . what on earth was she doing here at this hour? I took a step backwards.

"I thought you'd never get here! You must be exhausted." Mug in hand, my visitor leaned over the railing and smiled at me, her long necklace swinging. It winked at me in turquoise and violet, and I found myself watching the colors blend and change. "I expect you could use some of my apricot tea." Smiling, she moved toward me. "It'll warm you, help you sleep."

I'll bet, I thought. Cousin Otto wouldn't be suffering from insomnia, either. I knew I should run, get out of this house as fast as I could and bellow for help at the top of my lungs, but I didn't. I stood on the stairs and waited for her to come closer with her good-neighbor smile and summer-kitchen smell. "What do you want?" I said finally. I should have been afraid, but she seemed harmless, and what could she do to me? Whack me over the head with her coffee mug? Or maybe she was "just a little addled," as my mother used to say, and had somehow wandered into the wrong house. "Do you live around here? If you know your address, I'll help you get home," I offered. I hadn't heard of anyone missing who was—well—not quite right in the head, yet I had to admit her attire was *different*. I glanced again at the bright pink toenails in glittering gold sandals, the colorful swirling skirt. Was she making a fashion statement, or what? My guess was *what*.

"I am home," she said, covering my hand with her own. "Don't you remember? We met earlier. I'm

Augusta Goodnight."

"I know," I said. "You told me, but I believe you're in the wrong house. This is my grandmother's place. Vesta Maxwell. Maybe you know her."

"It's been a while since I was here last." She spoke with a faraway look in her eyes. "So much has changed."

I didn't see how she could have been away so long she didn't know my eighty-year-old grandmother who had lived here all her life, but that wasn't my main concern at the moment. How was I going to get this woman out of my house? "Is there someone I could call?" I asked, moving at last downstairs toward the telephone in the kitchen.

"I really don't think that's necessary. First I believe we should talk. I'll put the kettle on, shall I?" She whirled past me in a froth of brilliance, filled the kettle at the sink, and set it on the stove. "I'm so glad this is gas. I never got used to those electric things. You do take tea, don't you?"

I nodded numbly. I would just pretend to drink while I tried to think what to do. Or maybe I would wake up and find this was all a dream.

But dreams don't smell. The apricot tea smelled faintly of ginger, and when she put a slice of something dark and moist in front of me, I found myself shoveling it into my mouth as if I'd had nothing to eat all day.

"Date nut bread," she said. "Made it this afternoon. Would you like another slice?"

"Yes, please." I noticed Augusta was putting away her share, too, so it must be okay to eat it. This woman might be crazy, but she sure knew how to cook! The tea was sweet and warm, and I could feel myself relaxing. She sat across the table and looked at me over her cup,

35

and again I thought of those carefree summer days at Camp Occoneechee. I could almost hear the laughter of children as they splashed in the cooling waters of the lake. "Who *are* you?" I said.

"I'm your guardian angel, Minda."

"Right," I said.

"I'm here for a while to help you if you'll let me. You've been through trying times, I know, but we'll work through this together."

"You're a little late," I said.

She refilled our cups with steaming tea and dribbled honey into hers. "What do you mean?"

"Where were you when the only man I've ever loved was struck and killed by lightning? Must've been your day off."

She nodded sadly. "If only we could prevent things like that from happening! Henrietta was most distressed about that."

"Henrietta?"

"Your guardian angel. Well—until recently. With so many babies being born, we've had to accelerate our apprentice program, and Henrietta was chosen to assist in their training." Augusta Goodnight smiled. "It's an honor to be selected, and Henrietta was pleased, naturally, but she regretted having to leave you— especially now."

Well, goody for Henrietta! I thought. "If you can't keep people safe, then what good are you?" I asked, turning the fragile cup in my saucer. Augusta had used the good stuff, I noticed, instead of the sturdy, everyday ceramic ware Vesta had left behind. I ran a finger along the edge of the round oak table, took in the apple green walls with the sunflower border. Was I actually in my grandmother's kitchen having a conversation with some weirdo who claimed to be my guardian angel? I deserved to live in a nut house!

"Before I leave, I hope you'll find that out," the woman said. "Henrietta personally requested I take her place while she fulfills her other duties, and I don't plan to disappoint her. Or you."

Augusta whisked the dishes to the sink, and in seconds they were clean, dry, and put away. "We can't change things, Arminda. We can only counsel and lend support. But by our influence, we seek to guide you as best we can—if you'll let us."

Again she sat across from me and ran the lovely stones of her necklace through her fingers, and from the expression on her face, I could tell she considered me a first-class challenge. "It was a sad and shocking thing to lose your Jarvis at so young an age, and of course you still miss your mother, but I believe there's a purpose for you back here in Angel Heights—and one for me, as well."

I didn't remember telling this woman my husband's name, but she might have heard it from someone else. "Are you telling me that Jarvis died so I'd have to come back to Angel Heights?" My tranquil mood seemed to have worn off.

"Certainly not! But you have to be somewhere, and right now, I think this is a good place to start. Your family needs you, Minda, and I believe you need them. Things here aren't as they should be."

"No kidding. I suppose you're referring to Cousin Otto's unfortunate demise."

"I'm afraid it began long before that," she said.

"How? When?" My eyelids were getting heavy, and I thought longingly of the bed waiting upstairs.

"That's what I hope to find out," she said quietly.

"You don't know? I thought angels knew everything." I yawned.

"I'm afraid you're confusing us with The One In Charge," Augusta said.

One second she was sitting across from me, and the next, she stood behind my chair, her hand resting lightly on my shoulder. "Come now, you'll feel better after a good night's rest."

I don't even remember going upstairs, but I turned at my bedroom door to find her sitting on the top step, her long skirt cascading about her. "I suppose you don't know who killed Cousin Otto?" I said.

She glanced at me over her shoulder. "Go to sleep. We'll think about that tomorrow."

Which meant she didn't, and that was just as well. If who ever murdered Otto turned out to be somebody I knew, I didn't want to hear about it tonight. "Surely you aren't going to sit out there until morning?" I said.

"You can rest assured I will be close by," she said, and smiled. "It's in my job description."

A temporary angel was better than no angel at all, I thought as I snuggled under my great-grandmother Lucy's wedding-ring quilt.

She was still there. I knew it the next morning as soon as I sniffed that crispy brown pancake smell and hurried downstairs to find Augusta setting the table with the rose-flowered Haviland. How could I have been so gullible to accept this woman's wild tale? There had to be some logical explanation for her being here! The night before, I had been too exhausted to challenge her. Not today. I filled glasses with orange juice while she poured warm strawberry syrup into a small pitcher shaped like a lily. I remembered the lily from childhood.

It had always been a favorite of mine, and Vesta said she meant for me to have it some day. The china had been in our family for years, but my grandmother rarely used it.

I waited until after breakfast to burrow into the subject of Augusta's identity. "I don't mind your staying here," I began, "but I do need to know more about you. Are you going to tell me who you really are?" A brisk wind sent golden leaves skidding across the backyard where I once played in my sandbox. Every room in this house was familiar to me. The table where I sat was solid and real. I was not living a fantasy, and I wanted some answers.

Augusta studied a chipped nail and frowned. "I believe I told you that already, Minda."

"Uh-huh. You're an angel. But you're here only until what's-her-name completes her current heavenly assignment."

"Henrietta. That's exactly right." She rummaged in a huge tapestry bag until she produced a nail file; then she set to work on the offending digit.

"I don't believe you," I said. Ignoring me, the woman concentrated on examining her nails. "What happened to Otto's angel?" I asked. "Did he have a substitute, too?"

"Arminda, that's an unkind remark and unworthy of you. I must say I'm disappointed."

She looked so sad I almost apologized, and I then thought better of it. Why should I say I'm sorry to someone so obviously full of it?

"I don't know the details of Otto's death, but according to Curtis, your cousin was a bit headstrong, didn't always heed warnings."

"And Curtis would be—?"

"Your cousin's guardian angel, of course. Except in extreme cases, we angels can't stop bullets, lift drowning victims from the water, or prevent planes from crashing."

"I guess Jarvis wasn't an extreme case."

"The lightning bolt was an act of nature, Minda. There was very little warning, but from what Henrietta tells me, your husband did have a chance to act."

"Then why didn't he get out of the way?"

She began to clear the table without giving me an answer, and exasperated, I rose to help her. "Well?" I said, putting my dishes in the sink.

Augusta sighed. "Because the lightning would have hit you."

"Oh, please! Are you telling me Jarvis took a lightning bolt to save my life?"

"He was reacting to instinct, Minda. At that moment, he had no idea what would happen."

I thought back to that cloudless day in June when Jarvis and I had spread our blanket under a huge sycamore in a park near our new home. We had eaten our picnic lunch, and were resting side by side with only our fingers touching. At peace with the world and satisfied with life in general, I gave my husband's hand a squeeze and was thinking of finishing off the last of the chocolate chip cookies when I looked into the branches above me. Not one leaf moved.

Suddenly Jarvis gave the blanket a jerk and sent me rolling down a gentle incline and into a privet hedge. "Hey!" I yelled, instantly plotting my revenge. My husband liked to tease, and life with him was never boring. And that was when the lightning struck.

I had put the blanket incident out of my mind, had never told anyone about it. The memory hurt too much.

Now I watched Augusta Goodnight fill the sink with rainbow bubbles. "And how did Jarvis do that?" I asked, trying to keep my voice light.

She studied me for a moment that seemed to stretch forever. "I think you know the answer to that, Arminda. He rolled you off the blanket."

The heaviness I'd held inside for the last few months found release all at once, and my emotions took control. I don't know how long I cried, but when it was over I felt Augusta's cool touch on my cheek and saw that she'd pressed a dainty, lace-edged hankie into my hand. "Do you think Jarvis rolled me off that blanket to save my life?" I asked, sipping the water Augusta offered. "Did he *know* what he was doing?"

She smiled and reached for a dish towel. "Not consciously. I believe he did it as a joke, but he was also obeying his intuition. Something deep inside him must have signaled danger."

"You mean his angel warned him?"

"I think so. Yes. And in that wink of an instant, he chose to protect you."

"I wish he hadn't. I'd rather have gone with him." I wanted to cry again, but there were no tears left, and besides, my handkerchief was sopped.

"Don't you ever think that, Arminda Grace Hobbs! Any time you find yourself thinking your life has no value, just remember why you're here. Besides, I could use a little help down here right now, and you're nominated."

I shrugged. "Okay, fine. Throw me that sponge, and I'll wipe off the countertops."

"And I don't mean with the dishes!" Humming some tune I'd never heard, she twirled about and then tossed me the sponge with one hand while fanning herself with my grandmother's dainty saucer—to air-dry it, I suppose.

Suddenly I felt about ten pounds lighter and found myself smiling at Augusta's antics. "If Vesta saw you waving her mother's Haviland about, you'd need your own angel," I said.

Augusta set the saucer in the cupboard with the others. "It wasn't her mother's, it was her grandmother's," she said. "She used it every day. I remember it well."

"You knew my grandmother's *grandmother*? And when was that?"

But Augusta didn't answer, and somehow I knew she wasn't going to. Augusta Goodnight had been to Angel Heights, South Carolina, before, and I had a feeling I wasn't her only mission.

Chapter Five

"*D*ON'T YOU GET SICK AND TIRED sometimes of hearing about Great-grandma Lucy?" Gatlin asked. "I mean, was anything the woman couldn't do? It's beginning to give me a complex."

"Yeah, I know. The Martha Stewart of Angel Heights. Vesta says she didn't even use a butter mold like everybody else back then, but etched a little design on top."

Gatlin had come over early that afternoon to help me get settled, she said, and the two of us now waded through the obstacle course in the attic in search of an old library table Augusta insisted was there. My grandmother had taken her antique mahogany table with its two extra leaves to her new condominium, leaving the dining room at the Nut House bare.

"It looks so empty in here," Augusta had said earlier, twirling on tiptoe in the center of the large paneled room. "And that table in the kitchen can't seat more than six." She waltzed from the bay window overlooking the muscadine arbor to the built-in cupboard in the corner. "There's just so much space, and I'm sure that old table's still in the attic."

I didn't ask her how she knew. I wasn't sure I even wanted to know. "A table for six is more than I'll need, Augusta. I'm not planning any big dinner parties."

But I could see she wasn't going to leave me alone until I explored my grandmother's cold, dusty attic to see if the table was there.

"It's made of oak if I remember right," Augusta said. "A heavy old thing, but a perfect place to grade papers if you plan to teach next year, and there's room for a sewing machine at one end."

"How heavy?" I asked. "And the last time I used a sewing machine was in home economics class in high school." I had made a C-minus on my baby doll pajamas.

"You're not the only one here, Minda," Augusta reminded me, tucking a strand of her autumn-glow hair back in place. Today she wore her glorious tresses in a bright braid twined around her head, and her dress floated about her, looking as if it might have been hand-screened by Monet himself. "We'll look for it after lunch. I'll help you."

It really didn't surprise me that Gatlin couldn't see her. The day had turned blustery and cold, and my cousin

43

blew in the back door, shivering in a gust of frigid wind. Augusta had just taken a loaf of pumpkin bread from the oven, and the whole house smelled of cinnamon and nutmeg. My cousin and I ate it warm with some of Augusta's apricot tea. "What good timing!" Gatlin said, scooping up her last bite. "You've been hiding your talents, Minda. This bread is fantastic! What's that extra little flavor? Tastes like orange."

"Don't ask me," I said. "I didn't make it."

She looked around and then frowned. "Then who did? Not Irene Bradshaw. She can't boil an egg!"

"My guardian angel," I told her. "Augusta Goodnight. She's standing right over there." I nodded toward Augusta, who obliged me with a graceful little curtsy.

Gatlin glanced in the angel's direction, then shook her head, and smiled. "How convenient. Send her to my house when she's done, okay?"

"Find your own angel," I said. "There's supposed to be an old library table in the attic. Want to help me look for it?"

"Oh, I was so hoping you'd ask," Gatlin said, making a face. "I'll have to hurry, though. I've left Faye with a sitter while I run some errands, and Lizzie's due home from school in about an hour."

I sneezed at the dust in the attic, shoved aside a rocking chair with no bottom, and stumbled over a porcelain chamber pot. Did my grandparents never throw anything away? "Is Faye better today? I hated leaving you last night with all that clutter, but there was no holding Mildred back!"

"It's just a cold, but I'm keeping her in for a while, and the Circle ladies took care of washing up. Wish they'd come back every night!" Gatlin examined a washstand with a broken leg and moved aside an ugly

44

iron floor lamp. "Boy, does Mildred ever have her drawers in a wad! I've never seen her like this. How was she when you left her?"

"A lot calmer than I was," I admitted. "But she thinks somebody has been in the bookshop, says they moved her pencils."

"Moved her pencils?" Gatlin laughed and then cursed when she bumped her ankle on an andiron.

I explained as best I could. "Mildred said she could tell somebody had been prying around, and there were papers scattered about. Seems to think something's missing, too—wouldn't tell me what it was.

"What will you do about Mildred if you can work out something about the bookshop?" I asked. "I worry about her living alone."

"She can stay as long as she wants," my cousin said. "If Otto didn't leave her his share, we'll just have to see she's taken care of. He might not have thought to, Minda. Who would've imagined Mildred would outlive him?"

Once we were downstairs, I reminded myself, I would telephone Mildred Parsons and invite her to dinner in case Vesta hadn't asked her already. And I mentally chided myself for not phoning earlier.

"Here it is! Or at least I think this is what we're looking for," Gatlin called from the far side of the room.

We had to lift two rolled-up rugs and a suitcase full of rocks (I later discovered they were filled with an old set of encyclopedias) to get to it, and the legs on the thing were as big as tree trunks, but the table looked to be in fairly good condition. It was bulky and solid and weighed a ton. Gatlin and I together could barely lift it off the floor, much less maneuver it downstairs.

"Maybe if we take the drawer out . . . ," my cousin

said. I didn't think that would help, but we tugged at it anyway, and of course the drawer was stuck. When it finally squeaked free, the two of us almost tumbled into a box containing enough picture frames to fill a museum. Except for a small paperbound booklet of Shakespeare's sonnets, the drawer was empty. And the table was still too heavy to move.

"Might as well put the drawer back," Gatlin said. "I'll ask David to get some of the boys on his team to get this down for you tomorrow."

I was helping her to slide the bulky drawer into place when I saw the paper inside. "Wait a minute! Something must've fallen behind and become wedged underneath." I snatched out a folded rectangle, yellowed with time, and carefully smoothed it out. A brittle corner broke off in my hand.

"Don't expect a passionate love letter," Gatlin advised me. "From all I've heard, our ancestors were too straitlaced and proper."

"Except for your parents," I reminded her. "Are you forgetting I know how you got your name?" My cousin's mom and dad had conceived her on their honeymoon in Gatlinburg, Tennessee.

"You tell and you're dead meat!" she warned me. "I just let everybody think I was named for a gun."

The paper wasn't a love letter, but it proved to be almost as interesting. "Looks like the minutes of some kind of meeting," I said, holding the paper to the light. *The Mystic Six.* Must've been a secret club or something. Isn't that cute? I guess I never thought of people doing things like that back then."

"I don't know why not. We did—or I did anyway. The Gardener twins, Patsy Hardy and me. We called ourselves *the Fearless Four,* and met underneath

46

Vesta's back porch. You used to follow us around and try to learn the password!"

"The password," I said, with my best attempt at a smirk, "was 'frog farts.' "

"Was it really? How disgusting! No wonder I'd forgotten." Gatlin looked over my shoulder. "I guess this bunch was too refined for that."

"No frog farts here," I said. "Just minutes." The proceedings of the meeting had been recorded in a delicate script in fading brown ink.

> The meeting of the Mystic Six was called to order by Number One. Number Two led the group in the Club Pledge and collected dues of five cents from each member. Number Three entertained with a lovely solo, "Beautiful Dreamer." This was followed by a business meeting, during which a report was given by Number Four on the subject of Honesty. Plans were made for our next meeting at the home of Number Two. Number Five then served delicious refreshments of sandwiches, lemonade, and nondescripts. Number Six read the minutes of the last meeting, and Number One dismissed the group in the usual manner.
>
> *Respectfully submitted,*
> *Number Six*

At the bottom of the page, someone (Number Six?) had sketched a tiny six-petaled flower with a star in its center. It was identical to the ones I had seen bordering my great grandmother's needlework at Minerva Academy and to the pin I'd found on the bathroom floor.

The pin! What had I done with the pin?

"I'll bet anything Lucy was the one who sang 'the lovely solo,' "Gatlin said. "That would have been right up her alley, and this looks old enough to have dated back that far."

I put the paper inside a copy of somebody's old botany textbook and took it downstairs. So far I hadn't told anyone about finding the pin. I wasn't ready to share it. Not yet.

"Wonder if they went around calling each other by num ber?" I said. "And did you notice the insignia at the bottom? It's the same thing I saw at the academy."

"I've seen it somewhere, too. Seems like it was on a quilt or something. Vesta would know. Or Mildred."

But Mildred would have to wait. As soon as my cousin left that afternoon, I scrambled through the soiled clothing I'd brought back from Gatlin's, and there it was in the pocket of my jeans—smaller than a dime and as dainty as the ladies in the Mystic Six had surely been.

How could a long-ago society of young women be related to my cousin's recent murder?

I tucked the trinket away and decided to keep it a secret for now. If Otto had been killed for that pin, I didn't want to be next.

Mildred didn't seem to understand what I was talking about when I phoned that afternoon. "What kind of flower?" she wanted to know. "And you say it had a star in it?"

"Gatlin thinks she's seen a quilt with that pattern, and I thought you might remember it," I said. After all, she was the person who had cleaned all the nooks and crannies at the Nut House for the last thirty years or so. If anyone would know where something was, Mildred would.

"I'm sorry, Minda, but I don't remember seeing anything like that," she said. And maybe it was because of all that had happened in the last few days, but I had a feeling she wasn't telling the truth.

I found my grandmother in an agitated state when I dropped by her place later for supper. "I'll never eat all this funeral food," she'd said when she invited me. Not an appetizing thought, but I went anyway.

"What's wrong?" I said when I saw her setting the table for four. I knew only two of us would be eating.

"I believe they're going to have to change the name of this town to Devil Heights," Vesta said. "Gatlin called a few minutes ago to tell me somebody tried to run down Gertrude Whitmire while she was out walking this morning."

"Is Mrs. Whitmire all right?"

"I think so. I phoned to see how she was, and she said she was pretty well scratched up—scraped her knees and got a few bruises when she tried to jump out of the way. I'm afraid it messed up her ankle, too. Had an ice pack on it when I called."

"Where did it happen?" I asked.

"You know where she lives, way out in the middle of nowhere, and the house sits back from the road. I've been telling Gertrude she needs to move closer to town.

"Anyway, she'd started on her daily walk—does three or four miles every morning—and just as she came out of her driveway, she says a car careened around that curve there and headed straight for her!"

"She must've been terrified! How did she get out of the way?"

"Gertrude said she thought the idiot would see her

49

and swerve, and when she finally realized it wasn't going to, she sort of rolled backwards into the ditch."

I tried not to think of that.

"And listen to this, Arminda," my grandmother added. "While Gertrude was climbing out of the ditch, *she saw the same car turning around to make another pass!*"

"I'd probably drop dead from fright," I said.

Vesta put the extra place settings away. "No, you wouldn't, and neither did Gert. She knew if she tried to escape down the driveway, the car would follow and run her down, so she cut across the woods to a neighbor's. Only trouble is, the closest neighbor lives about a half mile away and is deaf as a post." Vesta shook her head. "Ben Thrasher. His daughter's been trying to get him to wear a hearing aid for years."

"Can she identify the car?" I said.

"Gertrude said it was sort of a tan color. Maybe a Toyota or a Honda—or it could've been a Saturn."

"That really narrows it down," I said.

There were times back in high school when I wished Gert would come down with acute laryngitis, but I never considered turning the poor woman into road kill. "Why would anybody want to do that?" I said. " . . . Unless they think she knows something about Otto's murder?"

"Don't see how she could," my grandmother said, "but it's another reason for Gertrude to move closer to town."

"Isn't there a Mr. Whitmire?"

"Oh, Arminda, he's been gone for years."

"Oh," I said. "I didn't know." Gertrude Whitmire and I had something in common.

"Have you heard from Mildred?" Vesta asked.

I nodded. "I asked her to join us for supper, but she

said Edna Smith was bringing vegetable soup and corn muffins."

Vesta frowned. "Still has her nose out of joint, but I suppose she's all right for the time being. I don't know why Hank Smith isn't as big as a barn with all the baking Edna does. Why Sylvie must've gained ten pounds since she's been back," she added, speaking of the couple's daughter.

Born late in her parents' marriage, Sylvia Smith was a cou ple of years younger than Gatlin but had been educated at some prestigious boarding school, so I never really got to know her. "I thought she was living in London," I said. "Doesn't Sylvie work in a museum over there?"

Vesta nodded. "Did. And seemed to be doing very well, according to Hank. She was in line for a big promotion when Edna had that knee replacement surgery last summer and Sylvie came home to see about her parents. Don't know why she never went back." My grandmother made a noise that sounded like something between a grunt and a snort. "I said something to Edna about it once, but she made it clear she didn't want to discuss it. Edna can get a little stiff-necked at times, but they've always been good friends to us, and it's kind of her to keep an eye on Mildred."

We sat at Vesta's heirloom dining tablc eating leftovcr chicken pie from the night before, and looked out on her tiny balcony, where a dead fern waved in the wind. "Mildred gave it to me when I moved in here," my grandmother said. "I told her I'd forget to water it, but she wouldn't listen.

"And since we're speaking of Mildred," she continued, "I went by the bookshop this morning to see how she was doing, but she wouldn't let me in. Said she

51

was taking inventory, of all things. I was going to see if she wanted to go somewhere for lunch. Thought it might do her good to get out, but she wasn't having any part of it. Acting the martyr, if you ask me."

I hadn't asked, but I agreed. "She thinks somebody was prowling around the shop while she was away. Said she was going to check and see if anything's missing."

"What would anyone want? Nothing there but old books, and most of them aren't worth more than a quarter . . . Here, please have some of this salad. The Circle committee brought enough for a battalion, and I'll never get rid of it all."

The salad was green and wiggly, but I took some, anyway. "And why would anybody want to kill Otto?" I reminded her. "Nothing about this makes sense! I don't guess you've heard any more from the police?"

My grandmother helped herself to one of Mary Ruth Godwin's yeast rolls and passed them along to me. "If they know anything, they haven't shared it with the rest of us. Gertrude Whitmire says she doesn't know if she'll ever work up the nerve to set foot in that place again." She buttered her roll and sighed. "Well, enough of that. Tell me, how are things at the Nut House?"

If you only knew! I thought. But I told Vesta about the library table with the club minutes in it. "Must have been some sort of secret girls' thing," I said. "Had something that looked like an emblem at the bottom—a flower with a star in the center. The same thing's on that alma mater your mama stitched that hangs at the academy, and Gatlin said she thought she'd seen something like it on a quilt."

"Dear heaven! I haven't seen that thing in ages. They took time about keeping that quilt, you know."

"Who did?"

"Why, the girls who made it. The Mystic Six. My mother was one. It was some kind of silly secret thing they organized at the academy. The quilt was supposed to tell a story about the school. I always thought it was kind of sad with that young professor dying in the fire and all."

I smiled. "The Mystic Six. Wonder what that was all about?"

"Who knows. But they were quite serious about it, I believe. Even had a pin."

I declined more salad. "Really?"

"I guess it was kind of like a sorority pin," Vesta said. "Mama had one, although I never saw her wearing it, but it looked like that design you saw in those old minutes, and it had her initials on the back. I keep it in my jewelry box."

Elvis was singing somewhere upstairs when I got home that night, and I found Augusta in the room at the end of the hall with the record player that had belonged to my mother. She was shuffling to the music of *Jailhouse Rock* and the expression on her face could only be described as blissful. Mom's collection of 45s were fanned out on the table behind her.

Augusta opened her eyes when she heard me and pulled me into the dance. "I haven't heard anything this good since Glen Miller did that thing about the little brown jar," she said, swinging me out and around.

"That's *jug*," I said. I was beginning to get a little dizzy.

"Oh. Well, anyway, I'm sorry I missed that era."

"What era?" I asked.

"The fifties. What do you call this—boogie woogie?"

"Rock and roll," I said. "So, where *were* you in the

53

fifties?"

"Heaven, of course. I'm only a temp, Arminda. Between assignments I'm in charge of strawberry fields up there."

"Really? They actually grow strawberries?"

"Well, of course. Or it wouldn't be Heaven, now, would it?"

The music ended and I was glad for a break, but Augusta found another record to her liking—this time something called *"Heartbreak Hotel."*

"You're going to have to teach me the steps," she said, listening to the beat.

I laughed as she tapped her feet in time. "I think *you'll* have to teach *me.*"

I was having such a good time dancing, I almost forgot to check the initials on the back of the pin I'd found. If my grandmother had Lucy's pin, then whose pin did I find on the bathroom floor?

I turned the gold disk under the light. The initials *A.W.* were inscribed on the back. *Annie Westbrook.* So Lucy's younger sister had not been wearing her pin when she drowned in the Saluda. But what was Otto doing with it?

I showed the minutes to Augusta, pointing out the emblem at the bottom.

"The same design is on the alma mater my great-grandmother stitched," I said, "and Gatlin says she's seen it on a quilt."

Augusta studied the brittle paper with something close to a frown. "Where did you find this?"

In that old library table in the attic. You wanted it moved into the dining room, remember?"

"Of course." Augusta gave the yellowed paper back to me.

54

I paused. "And there's a pin, too. I think it belonged to Annie Rose, the girl who died . . . and Augusta, it was in the bathroom at the academy right next to where we found Otto." *There, it was out!*

"Where in the bathroom?"

"Right there in the stall next to where Otto died. It was wedged in a corner."

"I'd keep these in a safe place if I were you. I have a feeling they might tell us something important."

And I had a feeling Augusta Goodnight had meant for me to find those old minutes in the attic, and that something that happened years ago might have led to my cousin Otto's murder.

Chapter Six

ATLIN'S HUSBAND, DAVE, DROPPED BY A LITTLE later that night with four husky Angels, members of the high school football team, and with much banging and grunting they maneuvered the unwieldy library table down from the attic and into the dining room. Afterward I made the mistake of treating the boys to pizza at their favorite hangout, the Heavenly Grill, although Dave tried to warn me against it. It was a darn good thing I'd eaten earlier, as I had barely enough money to pay the bill and was grateful when Dave offered to take care of the tip.

I knew from Gatlin that her family was just managing to squeak by on Dave's coaching salary and the spasmodic returns from their part-time jobs. Unfortunately things were not booming in Angel Heights, South Carolina, and I hoped my cousin's plans for a lunchroom-bookshop would bring an end to their hand-to-mouth lifestyle.

The next morning I heard hammering coming from the old Bradshaw house next door and went out to take a look. A couple of trucks were parked in the driveway, and renovations, it seemed, had begun.

It felt strange not having the Bradshaws close by. Irene and her husband, Frank, had lived next door to the Nut House for as long as I could remember, but, according to Vesta, they recently moved in with their daughter's family when the place got too much to keep up.

Not that Irene bothered to do much "keeping up," if what my grandmother said was true. According to Vesta, labeling our old neighbor a poor housekeeper would be putting it kindly. Irene Bradshaw spent her time playing bridge, reading, or doing whatever else she pleased. Today she pleased to pick up pecans in our backyard.

Swathed in a gray knitted sweater that must have been Frank's and with a red beret pulled over her ears, she wore ancient galoshes and looked like a bag lady with a plastic bag dangling from her hand. Irene straightened when she saw me and gave me sort of a half-wave as she dropped nuts into her sack.

"Minda? That is you, isn't it? Glasses get all misted over in this cold air." Irene paused to wipe her spectacles on her sleeve. "Hope you don't mind me picking up some of these nuts . . . just lying there, you know, and Bonnie said if I could find enough, she'd make us a pecan pie.

"We're living with Bonnie now, Frank and myself— have a cute little apartment in the back." Irene giggled. "Almost like being newlyweds again, except without all that sex!"

I didn't want to go there at all. "Vesta says you sold your home to the Historical Society," I said. "It won't seem the same without you two next door."

"Next door . . . yes. Vesta and Charles were such good neighbors, and your great-grandmother Lucy, too, bless her heart. Always there when we needed them, and so generous to share these pecans—got to where I didn't even ask." Irene stooped to scoop up a handful of nuts, and I combed the grass for more, adding them to her bag, then stepped quickly out of reach. Irene was an arm-grabber, an overenthusiastic greeter. She didn't mean any harm, of course, but Vesta swears she's had bruises.

"You know you're always welcome to them," I said. "There's more than we can use." I noticed that Irene wore leather gloves, but I didn't, and my hands were bare and red from the cold. I shoved them deep into my jacket pockets. "I wish I remembered Great-grandmother Lucy," I said. "Everyone seemed to think so highly of her."

"Highly, yes. Grand lady. She and my mother were friends, you know. Went to school together."

"At the academy?" Was Irene's mother one of the Mystic Six?

"The academy. Yes. And what a dreadful thing to happen to poor Otto! I haven't slept well since—let me tell you! And just as he was beginning to relax and enjoy himself a little, too. Otto was always so serious; I don't believe he even knew how to play." Irene glanced around for more pecans and, finding none, weighed the bag in her hand and tied a knot in the top. "I thought maybe the old love bug had finally bitten him," she said.

If the idea hadn't been so ridiculous and Otto hadn't

been so dead, I would've laughed right then and there. I looked at Irene to see if she was joking, but she appeared to be serious. "What do you mean, *love bug*?" I asked. If Otto had ever had a romance, I'd never heard about it. I couldn't imagine who would have him. "Was Otto seeing somebody special? Vesta hasn't mentioned anything about it, and Mildred's never said a word."

"A word . . . no, she wouldn't. I suppose Mildred hoped it would go away if she just ignored it long enough." Irene Bradshaw smiled as we walked together over the frosty ground, brown leaves scattering in our wake. "Didn't look like it was going away to me."

"But who? Was he seeing someone from around here?"

Her look told me I was probably the only person in Angel Heights who didn't know about Otto's love life. "I suppose you wouldn't have heard, being away and all. Otto was seeing Sylvie Smith, Arminda."

"Are you sure? I mean, did you actually see them together?"

"Together? Certainly. Several times. Back in the summer they'd often picnic by the river. There's a nice little recreation spot there now with tables and walking trails, and you can rent canoes. My grandchildren like to go there. And once in a while we'd run into them at the picture show." Irene reached for my arm, but I pretended to dig in my pockets for a tissue. She dropped her voice, although it was obvious we were alone. "That's why Sylvie didn't go back to England, you know. Didn't want to leave Otto."

She must have noticed my stunned expression, because Irene seemed to be searching for something to say. "Well, I'm sure Vesta's happy to have you back for a while, Minda. And I do believe you're getting to look

58

more like your great-grandmother Lucy every time I see you. Something about your eyes and the set of your chin."

"Thank you," I said, although from looking at her pictures, I always thought Lucy had sad eyes. Maybe mine were sad, too. "You said your mother and Lucy were friends. For some reason I didn't think you were raised in Angel Heights," I said as we neared the house.

"My mother moved away when she married. She was Pauline Watts before then," Irene told me over coffee and some of Augusta's honey-wheat loaf. "I was raised in North Carolina, but I used to visit cousins here in Angel Heights, and this is where I met Frank. It's been home to me most of my life."

"Vesta said her mother belonged to a group of girls that called themselves the Mystic Six," I said, pooling jam onto my bread. "I think they had a pin and held meetings—the works. Do you remember hearing anything about that?"

Irene shook her head and smiled. "No, but it sounds like something Mama would've done. She and a few of her old friends used to pass a quilt back and forth. I do remember that."

"Do you know what happened to it?" I swallowed my coffee so quickly it burned my throat.

"Happened to it? No, but I'd like to. It seemed important to Mama—something about the academy." Irene studied my face over her cup. "Why?"

"Just curious, I guess. You'll have to admit it was kind of unusual. When women made a quilt back then it was meant for a specific person, usually a bride, but they took time about keeping theirs. There must have been a reason."

"I can't imagine. Don't know why I never asked."

59

Our old neighbor sipped her coffee and frowned. "And you say they had meetings?"

"Wait. I'll show you." I retrieved the brittle paper from the bottom of my dresser drawer and placed it in front of her, watching her face as she read.

"Nondescripts. I remember Mama talking about nondescripts," she said, smiling. "She never could make them, though."

"Do you know who did?"

Irene shook her head. "Somebody my mother knew. One of her friends, I guess. Sounded like a pain to make . . . this bread is wonderful, Minda. Bonnie has one of those bread machines, but hers isn't nearly this good."

I was glad she didn't ask for the recipe.

"What about that little star-flower thing at the bottom?" I asked. "Have you seen that before?"

"Star-flower? Of course. It was on the quilt—the one my mother and her schoolmates used to share."

"Why didn't you tell me Otto had a girlfriend?" I asked Vesta when she dropped by later that morning. Her condo was chilly, she said, and she needed an extra blanket or two, but I think she really wanted to see if I'd settled in okay and had enough to eat.

"Oh, it wasn't anything serious. I think both of them were lonely, that's all." My grandmother peered into a kitchen cabinet and found it stocked; then she disappeared into the pantry. "Don't tell me you made all those strawberry preserves," she said, holding a jar to the light.

"Okay, I won't. And please take some. They're absolutely divine." I could see Augusta hovering in the background, and smiled when she rolled her eyes.

"Irene Bradshaw thinks otherwise," I said, referring

to Otto's relationship with Sylvia Smith.

"Irene Bradshaw? When did you run into her?" Vesta wiped the jar of preserves with a dishcloth and put it into her purse.

"This morning. She was out back picking up pecans. Told me Otto was the reason Sylvie didn't go back to London."

"You know how Irene exaggerates! I'm sure Mildred would've mentioned it, and Edna Smith—Sylvie's own mother—never said a word," Vesta spoke with that "final say-so" tone in her voice. "I saw the two of them together on occasion, but I'm sure it was nothing more than a friendly relationship. Why, I don't even remember Sylvie being at the funeral."

Vesta stood in the doorway to the dining room. "My gracious, I'd almost forgotten this old table! We used to do our homework on it." She ran her fingers over the scarred oak surface. "If only this old thing could talk."

And maybe it did, I thought. "Irene told me her mother and yours were friends," I said. "Went to the academy together; I think she might've been a member of that club they had. Irene remembers the quilt they made. Said her mother would keep it for a year or so, then pass it along to somebody else."

"Of course—Aunt Pauline. Irene's mother used to bring us chocolate drops when she came to visit. Naturally she was a favorite of ours—not really an aunt, but we called her that. She and Mama were always close. I believe she died a few years before Mama did."

Vesta frowned. "Whatever happened to that quilt, I wonder? Guess it stayed with whoever had it last. Of course all those 'girls' are gone now. No telling who ended up with it. Funny, I don't remember my mother ever really using that quilt."

"Do you remember who they were?"

"My goodness, Minda, that was a long time ago! Frankly, I never paid much attention to it."

"What about the nondescripts?" I asked. "Do you know who made them? They were mentioned in the minutes of their meeting as being served as part of the refreshments."

"Hmm . . . I think Mama served something like that once or twice, but pies were her specialty. I remember a sliced sweet potato pie with whiskey in it that would make your head spin!" My grandmother laughed and gave my shoulders a squeeze. "A lot of good food was eaten in this room, Minda."

Now she sniffed and inhaled deeply as we moved into the living room. "Ahh . . . I thought I smelled wood smoke! How ambitious of you, Minda! You've a fire going in the fireplace already! After your granddad died, I just didn't have the heart or the energy to take the trouble to build one, but I do love the smell, and this is certainly the day for it. Do we need to order more wood? Must be getting low."

"I'll check and see," I said, having no idea. Augusta had a bright blaze going when I came downstairs that morning. "Don't worry; I'll take care of it. You do have time for a cup of hot tea, don't you? I have some ginger-apricot you just have to try!"

She glanced at her watch. "Why not? I don't have to be anywhere until noon. The renovation committee of the Historical Society is meeting for lunch to discuss our plans for the Bradshaw place. Something tells me we'll need more than tea to tackle that one!"

The living room furniture my grandmother had left behind was worn but comfortable. Vesta sat nursing her tea in the club chair that had been her husband's, now slipcovered in a faded blue floral print, and I pulled the squishy leather ottoman closer to the fire. I heard a drawer open and shut in the kitchen and the clatter of a pan on the stove and knew Augusta had begun to prepare her savory peanut-pumpkin soup. It was a favorite of George Washington Carver's, she'd told me.

"In fact, he gave me the recipe. And everyone seems to be *nuts* about it!" And Augusta had smiled at her own awful joke.

But Vesta chatted on, pausing now and then to *um and ah* over her tea and never heard a thing.

It wasn't until she had left for her meeting that I realized my grandmother hadn't taken the extra blankets she claimed she needed.

"I seem to have developed a sudden appetite for pizza," Augusta said after my grandmother left.

It sounded good to me. "I'll pick one up. Care to go along?"

She folded her huge, gaudy apron over a chair. "I believe I will."

"I thought angels liked fancy things like ambrosia," I said. (Augusta, thank goodness, seemed to favor barbecue and pizza.) "There are restaurants in Columbia and Charlotte that offer more elegant fare."

But Augusta was already halfway to the car. "I've never been concerned about keeping up with the . . . what are those people's names?"

"Joneses," I said, and headed for the Heavenly Grill.

I got a pepperoni with extra cheese and two orders of lemon ice-box pie to go, and pulled into the driveway at the Nut House, looking forward to eating it.

"There's a man at the back of the house," Augusta said. "Wonder what he's doing there."

A man in a brown overcoat was peering into the

63

kitchen window. I wasn't sure, but it looked as though he might have been trying to open it.

I slammed the car door to get his attention. Hugh Talbot!

He hurried down the back steps to meet me. His legs were short, I noticed, and he puffed as he walked. "Arminda! I was afraid you weren't at home."

Balancing the pie on top of the pizza box, I made my way inside.

"Mr. Talbot! I didn't expect you." What was I supposed to say? "Won't you join me for pizza?"

Please say no!

I saw Augusta in mock prayer behind him and knew she was asking the same thing.

"No, no, thank you. I just wanted to see how you were after the strain of the last few days. I'm sure it must have been difficult for you."

"It hasn't been easy, but I believe we'll see things through. I don't suppose you've had any word from the police?"

He shook his head. "They're checking everybody who has a record, but nothing was stolen, so it doesn't look like a robbery."

"And how is Mrs. Whitmire?"

"Hobblin' and grumblin'." He smiled. "She'll be all right."

"Are you sure you can't stay?" I asked as he turned to leave, but he said he had stopped by for only a minute.

But why the back door instead of the front, I wondered. And I hadn't seen a sign of a car.

What was Hugh Talbot after?

"I wish we knew the rest of the Mystic Six," I said after we'd finished off the pizza and pie.

Augusta was smashing cooked pumpkin through a sieve with a big wooden spoon, but she paused in her cooking to take a small notepad from her huge tapestry handbag. "At least we now know three of them," she said, with a quick flourish of her pen. "Lucy, Annie Rose, and Irene's mother, Pauline."

"But what about the others?"

Even as I waited for her answer, I knew there wasn't going to be one. "You know something, don't you? You were *there*! If you know about the Mystic Six, why don't you tell me?"

The angel gathered her sparkling necklace into a handful of stars and turned to face me, the wooden spoon dripping jack-o'-lantern orange. "There are things you don't understand, Arminda. Things I don't even know myself. Pauline Watts practically lived here—a dark-haired girl with dimples—always reading novels . . . But don't ask me about the others, because I just don't know."

Chapter Seven

"MINDA?" I COULD TELL BY MY COUSIN'S voice something was wrong.

"Gatlin? What is it? Vesta hasn't had a wreck, has she?" I pictured the dangerous intersection near Calhoun Street, where I knew our grandmother was meeting for lunch. Vesta drove like she was racing the devil and had the speeding tickets to prove it. If she hadn't taught the local police chief in Sunday school, she'd be under the jail by now.

"No, no, nothing like that. It's Mildred. She's not answering her phone, and I'm kinda concerned is all.

You know how she's been since Otto—"

"Maybe she's not there." I looked at the kitchen clock; it was almost two in the afternoon. "Even Mildred has to eat. She probably went to the store."

"Minda, she could've walked to the next county and been back by now! I've been calling all morning."

"I'll meet you there," I told her. A nasty little tongue of fear flickered inside me, but I wasn't having any part of that. "I'm sure she's okay," I said. "But how do we get in? I don't have a key."

"I do," Gatlin said. "Actually, it's Vesta's. She left it with me that night Mildred insisted on going back there. Said I might need it sometime."

"Mildred may be in trouble. I hope her angel's on duty," I told Augusta as I grabbed my coat. "She does have one, doesn't she?"

Augusta was washing the kitchen windows with something that smelled like new grass and looked like spring water. She didn't turn around. "Of course she does, Arminda, but I don't have my directory handy just now."

"Huh!" I said. Sometimes I couldn't tell if Augusta was joking, but I wouldn't be surprised if she really did carry an angel directory in that great big bag of hers.

The front of Papa's Armchair looked dark and deserted, and a blind was drawn in the doorway, so I parked behind Gatlin's ten-year-old red Pontiac at the back entrance to the rooms Mildred and Otto had called home. Gatlin already had her key in the lock by the time I got out of my car.

"I've rung the bell three times and knocked until my knuckles are raw," my cousin said. "I'm going in."

"Maybe we ought to call somebody first," I said. "What if something's happened? You don't know what

66

we'll find in there."

But it was too late. Gatlin swung the door wide and stepped boldly inside the dark, narrow hallway with me crowding her footsteps, only to be met by a pink apparition.

I'd like to say I imagined it, but I'm almost sure I screamed. The apparition made a funny growling noise, snatched a lamp off the hall table, and shook it at us.

"Look out, it's got a lamp!" I yelled just as the pink figure and the lamp hit the floor together.

"Minda, for heaven's sake, it's Mildred!" Gatlin ran to hover over the dazed-looking woman who sat, still muttering, in the hallway while I rescued the lamp.

"What's going on?" Mildred spoke in a hoarse, hesitating whisper. "I don't understand . . . and . . . oh, my head hurts so . . ."

Mildred Parsons was not a heavy person, but even with our support she walked like an adolescent in her first pair of heels, and it took the two of us several minutes to help her to a chair. If I hadn't known about Mildred's strict Methodist principles, I'd have suspected she'd been into the booze.

I whispered to Gatlin over Mildred's head. "Maybe we'd better get her in bed."

"No, no!" Mildred croaked weakly. "Just let me sit a minute—and water—a glass of water . . ."

"Easy now . . . sip it slowly." In the tiny living room Gatlin held the glass to Mildred's lips while I shoved a footstool under her feet and covered her with a throw. The throw had a smirky-looking cat on it and read IF YOU CAN'T SAY ANYTHING NICE ABOUT PEOPLE, COME AND SIT NEXT TO ME. This woman I had known all my life was surprising me at every turn.

Gatlin and I watched anxiously as she drank most of

67

the water, leaned her head back, and closed her eyes for minutes that seemed longer than an off-key wedding solo. I was about to grab her wrist for a pulse when Mildred opened her eyes and announced that somebody had "slipped her a Mickey."

"A what?" Gatlin grinned and jabbed me with her elbow. "You've been watching too many of those old movies, Mildred. You must've eaten something that disagreed with you, or picked up a virus somewhere."

"Don't tell me what I picked up! I reckon I know what I picked up—I picked up a drink with some kind of dope in it!" Mildred sat a little straighter and then winced with the effort. "What time is it? I feel like I've been asleep a thousand years."

"It's close to three in the afternoon, and whatever you picked up, you need to see a doctor," I told her. "How long have you been sick?"

"Since I got home last night. Hardly made it to bed before my head started swimming. Sick as a dog and up half the night." She rubbed her eyes and pulled the coverlet closer about her.

"Got home from where?" Gatlin wanted to know.

"UMW. Wouldn't have gone, but we're in the middle of planning for the Christmas Bazaar, and I'm in charge of the quilt raffle this year."

"Did you eat anything there?" I asked, touching her forehead to check for fever. It felt clammy.

"A couple of pieces of Scotch shortbread and coffee. We met at Janice Palmer's, and she always serves that." Mildred put a trembling hand to her mouth. "Don't think I'll be wanting any more for a while."

"Who else was there? Maybe somebody else got sick," I said, although I couldn't imagine those refreshments causing an upset as severe as Mildred's.

"The usual—except for Gertrude Whitmire. She hardly ever comes. And Edna Smith. Vesta, too, but she came in late, so I'm not sure if she ate anything."

"What about supper? Did you have anything to eat before the meeting?" Gatlin reached for the phone as she spoke.

Mildred made a face. "Just some of Edna's vegetable soup and corn bread. But it couldn't have been that."

I wedged a pillow behind her. "Why not?"

"Because she had some with me. Said she didn't like to think of me eating alone." Mildred reached out for Gatlin. "Look now, who're you calling?"

"The Better Health Clinic. Somebody should take a look at you, Mildred. You might have food poisoning."

"I'm eighty-three years old. I don't have time to spend the rest of my days in their waiting room, thank you. Besides, what could they do? If this was going to kill me, I'd already be dead—and believe me, there were times last night I wanted to be!" Mildred reluctantly accepted the cold cloth I applied to her forehead. "I told you—somebody slipped something into my coffee—something to knock me out."

"They could check your stomach contents," Gatlin reasoned. "See if there's anything toxic—"

"What stomach contents?" Mildred looked a little green and turned away.

"Or the soup. We'll have them analyze what's left of the soup," I suggested.

"Too late. We ate it all, and I'm afraid I rinsed out the jar." Mildred attempted a smile. "Edna does make good soup . . . You might call, though, and see if she's all right. Wouldn't hurt to see about Vesta, too."

"She was fine when she came by this morning," I told them. "But I'll try to track her down."

Willene Christenbury, who had hosted the luncheon for the Historical Society's renovation committee, told me my grandmother had left about thirty minutes before for a fitting at Phoebe's Alterations. "Said she was going to have that long black coat cut down to jacket size," Willene said. The coat was at least twenty years old, and I could tell by Willene's tone of voice that she wondered why Vesta would bother. I could have told her why. Vesta Maxwell got her penny's worth out of every thread she wore. My grandmother had never forgotten the Great Depression.

"She didn't seem sick or anything, did she?" I asked. "Mildred seems to have come down with something, and we aren't sure if it's a virus or something she ate."

Willene laughed. "I didn't see her turning down a second piece of lemon chess pie. Seemed fine when she left here."

Edna Smith sounded hearty enough, as well. "I can't imagine what it could be," she said when I phoned her about Mildred. "I ate the same things she did, and we only had light refreshments at UMW. Sounds like she's picked up a nasty germ somewhere. Tell you what— Hank left early this morning to go hunting, but I'm looking for him any minute. Soon as he gets back, I'll send him over to take a look."

"He isn't going to find anything," Mildred said when I told her. "Whatever stuff was in me is gone now."

Gatlin brought ginger ale and soda crackers and persuaded Mildred to take some liquid. "What makes you think somebody put something in your drink, Mildred? It could be a virus, you know."

"Then why am I the only one who got sick? And it made me feel like a zombie, like I'd been given some kind of drug. Remember when I had that gall bladder

70

operation? It was like that. Felt just like I did when I came to—only worse!"

"But why?" I smiled. "You don't have a stash of priceless gems somewhere, do you? What would they want?"

She bit into a cracker. "There are things that might be worth more than that to certain people."

"Like what?" Gatlin asked. But Mildred wasn't talking.

"I have to pick up Faye from a birthday party, and Lizzie will come home from Scouts at any minute," Gatlin said, glancing at her watch. I nodded in reply to her questioning look. Now that we were reasonably sure Mildred wasn't going to bow out on us, I felt capable enough to stay until Hank Smith could get there.

The ginger ale and crackers seemed to have revived her some, for now Mildred began to fuss about her appearance. "I want to wash my face, brush my teeth . . . and for heaven's sake, let me change out of this gown." She clasped a small, age-speckled hand to her bony chest as if to cover it. "Why, Hank Smith could see everything I've got!"

It was a family joke that Mildred pinned handkerchiefs to the underside of her clothing so that no one would suspect she had a crease in that area. I could have told her she might save herself the trouble.

Gatlin stood, arms folded, in front of her. "Consider it done," she said, but I could tell by her voice something was up. It was. "But first," my cousin continued, "you'll have to answer a question—just one!" She held up a warning finger to Mildred's silent protest. "And you have to promise to tell the truth."

"For goodness' sake, have you no shame? Bullying an old woman, and as sick as I am, too! . . . Oh, go on, then. What is it you want?" Apparently Mildred could see she was on the losing end of this one.

"Why didn't you tell us Otto had a girlfriend?" Gatlin asked.

"There was nothing to that." Mildred should never play poker. It was clear she was holding something back.

"That's not what I heard," I told her. "And what would it matter if he did? Otto was a grown man. He had a right to some kind of love life."

"Maybe so, but there are those who might not agree with you."

"Mildred, we know he was seeing Sylvie Smith. Why are you being so mysterious?" Gatlin looked around for her bag as a prelude to leaving.

"I got the idea her parents disapproved," she said. "Our Otto wasn't good enough for their precious Sylvia."

"What makes you think that?" Gatlin asked.

"You mean other than the fact that Edna told me she thought Sylvie was making a big mistake to put off going back to London?" Mildred looked almost as upset as she did that time I actually dried my hands on her freshly ironed guest towel.

"That doesn't mean she disapproved of Otto." Gatlin kissed our patient on the cheek and started out the door. "You behave now, and do as Minda says or I'll come back and bite you. I'll be home soon if you need me."

The last was directed to me, but I hoped I wouldn't have to take advantage of it.

"Was Otto still seeing Sylvie when he died?" I asked as I brushed Mildred's thinning hair. She seemed stronger now, but I was afraid she might be too weak to walk down the hall to the bathroom, so we had done the best we could with a washrag and a basin of water.

"Hard to say, since he never brought her here." Mildred fastened the top button of her clean flannel gown, gave it a final pat, and held out her arms for her robe. "He had something on his mind, though. I kinda thought it might've had something to do with that woman, but Otto didn't talk to me about things like that."

"Maybe they had a quarrel or something," I said. "Her mother would know, wouldn't she? Did Edna ever mention it?"

"She was probably the cause of it." Mildred made a face. "Now, don't get me wrong . . . I've always liked Edna Smith. She's been a good friend to me, but I know for a fact Otto wasn't welcome in their home, and I can't help but hold that against her."

I laid the hairbrush aside. "How do you know?"

"Oh, just things he let slip—like once Sylvie had wanted to try her hand at cooking, have him over for dinner, but Edna decided to have the kitchen painted. And another time I think they had houseguests—relatives from out of town—and Otto said he felt like an intruder."

It sounded to me like Otto needed to lighten up, but it was a little late for that. "I don't remember seeing Sylvie at the funeral," I said.

"That's because she wasn't there. Doesn't that make you curious, Arminda? Even if they weren't on the best of terms when he died, you'd think she'd at least pay her respects."

"Maybe she was too broken up, couldn't handle it."

Her look told me what she thought of that. "If I live to see another day, I intend to find that out. And how do we know Sylvia Smith didn't have something to do with the way Otto died? I wouldn't be surprised!"

"Mildred! You can't be serious. She and Otto might have come to a parting of the ways, but it didn't have to be terminal." Whatever bug had taken hold of Mildred had surely scrambled her brain, I thought. Before I could ask how she meant to go about investigating, the doorbell rang, and I hurried to admit Hank Smith, Sylvie's father.

"She seems some better," I whispered as we stood in the hallway, "but don't be surprised at what she might say. Mildred seems convinced somebody drugged her coffee at the UMW last night."

Hank Smith shook his head and smiled. "I don't suppose she gave you a reason?"

"Says they were after something," I said. "And she did sleep through most of the day. Whatever she had just about wiped her out, especially after losing Otto the way we did."

He gave my shoulder a sympathetic pat. "Given Mildred's age and emotional status, an illness of this sort might sometimes bring about delusions."

But I wasn't having delusions a few minutes later when, to give Mildred a little privacy with our family doctor, I unlocked the connecting door to the bookshop and found the room looking like somebody had picked it up and shaken it.

Chapter Eight

"*L*OOKS LIKE A STAMPEDE OF ELEPHANTS came through here," the young policeman said, running a hand through unruly brown hair. He reminded me of Paddington Bear with his bright yellow slicker and rounded tummy. I later learned his name was Rusty Echols and he was Chief McBride's nephew. Nepotism has never been a problem in Angel Heights. They just ignore it.

The lock to the front door had been forced, the chief told us later—although, according to him, a five-year-old could've done it. And as for fingerprints, the shop was covered in those of every book-lover in town.

On discovering the break-in, my first instinct had been to gather the books that littered the floor like scattered building blocks and put them back where they belonged before Mildred could see them. Thank goodness my few common-sense brain cells banded together to remind me this was not a good thing. Not only would I be destroying evidence, but I also had no idea where anything went. We didn't even tell Mildred what had happened until after Hank Smith shipped her off to County General for an overnight stay—just in case, he said.

"I told you somebody slipped me a Mickey," she reminded us later from her hospital bed. "Wanted me out of the way so they could search Papa's Armchair."

"Search for what, Mildred?" my grandmother asked. "If you'll tell us what you think they're looking for, we'll put it in a safe place."

75

"Don't you worry, it is in a safe place. I've taken care of that." In her white hospital bed, Mildred looked like a washed-out rag doll in need of stuffing. Beside her, Vesta, although close in age, seemed almost robust except for the worry in her eyes and the weariness in her face.

Vesta stood, drawing herself up to her full five feet ten inches, and gave Mildred a heaping taste of her frustration and displeasure. "Mildred Parsons, need I remind you how Otto died? And he was probably killed for a reason—by somebody right here in this town. Do you think they would hesitate to do the same to you?"

Mildred looked back defiantly—or as defiantly as she could in her position. "But they didn't. Else I'd be dead now, wouldn't I? Well, I'm not, I'm and that young doctor who was in here earlier said I could go home tomorrow." ✓

"Home to where?" I said. "You certainly don't expect to go back to those rooms behind the store."

"And why not? It's a lot safer there than at the UMW!" Mildred sat up to sip water, then lay down with a sigh. "I like where I live. It's close to everything, and the bookshop's right there with nothing but a door between us. I can just walk right in."

"Obviously so can anyone else," Vesta reminded her. "You're coming home with me."

"Or me," I offered. "After all, there's plenty of room, and I'm the only one there." *Well . . . almost.*

"I've been thinking it might be a good time to go and see Lydia," Mildred said. "She's moved into her own place now, and she's been after me to visit since she left here."

Lydia Bowen and Mildred had been like salt and pepper since Mildred first came to Angel Heights, and

76

when Mildred wasn't taking care of Otto and the rest of us—and Lydia wasn't clerking at the Dresses Divine Boutique—you seldom saw one without the other. Vesta had once confided to me that she didn't know how the local Methodists knew to put one foot in front of the other until Mildred and Lydia showed them how. But soon after Lydia's husband died, a year or so ago, her older sister fell ill, and she moved back to Columbia to be near her.

"That's a wonderful idea," Vesta said with obvious relief in her voice. I wasn't sure if it was because Mildred would be in less danger or that she wouldn't be staying with her. "I know how you've missed her, and Lydia must be lonely . . . I'll phone her tonight, and one of us can drive you over in a few days when you're stronger."

"That's kind of you, Vesta, but I can take care of it myself—only it'll have to wait until tomorrow. Right now I need to sleep." Mildred gathered the sheet to her chin and closed her eyes.

I volunteered to stay the night. Since we weren't sure what Mildred had ingested, Dr. Hank, as well as the rest of us, was concerned about a possible delayed reaction. But our patient slept the whole time except for when she was awakened periodically by nurses. Gatlin dropped by for a couple of hours after she got her family settled for the night, and in a nearby waiting room we hunkered on green plastic chairs and whispered, trying to distance ourselves from other vigil keepers who slept restlessly or thumbed through magazines. November wind blew gusts of rain across the lamplit parking lot below, where rows of wet vehicles shone in a one-color world.

"Looks like Mildred might not have been so paranoid after all," Gatlin admitted, moving a stack of dog-eared newspapers to make room for me beside her. "But where on earth did she get it?"

"She said she had only coffee and cereal for breakfast yesterday," I said, "then nothing until Edna Smith brought her supper. If Edna meant to poison her, you'd think she'd be more discreet."

"Minda, you don't suppose she did it to herself? Otto was Mildred's life. Maybe she didn't feel like going on without him."

"I don't think so—at least I hope not. She's mad as hell, though. I can't see her even considering dying until she finds out who killed Otto and then yanks out his nose hairs one by one before throwing him to the alligators."

A man lying on the one sofa made an issue of turning over and resettling his raincoat about his shoulders, so I lowered my voice. "Or *her* nose hairs. Mildred seems to think Sylvie might have become disenchanted with our Otto."

"Do tell," my cousin said.

I knew better than to meet her eyes. "Give me a break, Gatlin. Don't make me start to laugh . . . They'll throw us out of here."

"Sorry. It was just the idea of anyone being enchanted with Otto in the first place." She shifted in her chair and sighed. "So, was Sylvie at the UMW thing last night?"

"Mildred didn't mention her, and anyway, why would Sylvie want to tear apart the bookshop? What could she be looking for?"

"I can't imagine, unless Otto had a rare volume that's worth a lot of money and told Sylvie about it. She collects things like that, I hear."

"The Smiths aren't hurting for money," I said. "Sylvia could probably afford to buy it for herself."

"Depends." My cousin yawned. "Vesta says they're having what's left of the shortbread analyzed just to be sure. Poor Janice Palmer! She'll have to find some new recipes now."

"They ate all the soup and corn bread, and Hank says he finished off the rest," I said.

"How convenient," Gatlin said.

"Oh, get real! We've known them forever. Dr. Hank sewed up my knee when I fell off my bike and set my arm that time the rope swing broke."

"And nursed me through a nasty flu and about a million throat infections. I know. I don't even like to think it, but somebody wanted Mildred out of the way last night, and they didn't care how they went about it."

"If what Mildred says is true, they didn't find what they were looking for. But she claims it's somewhere safe."

Gatlin frowned. "And what and where would that be?"

I shrugged. "Beats me. She's not telling."

We looked in on Mildred to see if she was breathing, and I tucked the covers around her; then Gatlin walked with me to the snack machine, where I bought my supper—a pack of crackers and a cup of disgusting coffee. "By the way, Irene Bradshaw says her mother was one of the Mystic Six," I told her. "She says she remembers the quilt they made but doesn't know where it is."

"Aunt Pauline. I think I remember her. Does Irene know who the other four were?" Gatlin bought a candy bar and pressed it into my hand. "Dessert," she said.

I thanked her and stuck it in my purse. "The other three," I said. "Annie Rose was a member, too." But I didn't tell her how I knew, or that my guardian angel

79

had pointed it out to me. The psychiatric ward was right around the corner.

Mildred seemed much better the next morning, so after I helped her with breakfast and brought the morning paper, I left her in the charge of the nurse with the soap-and-water brigade. The doctor who had admitted her was due to make his rounds before noon, at which time we expected him to discharge her, and Vesta planned to shanghai Mildred to her place for a couple of days, until she felt like traveling.

Augusta seemed not to have noticed I'd been gone, as she didn't look up when I let myself in by the kitchen door that morning. She sat at the table with a mug of steaming coffee and a stack of cookbooks in front of her, and now and again she'd murmur and smile, then make a note in her ever-present scribble pad.

"Coffee's still hot," she said without turning around. "And I expect you could use some breakfast, too. That hospital food hasn't improved a lot since Florence Nightingale walked the corridors with a lamp. You haven't eaten, have you?"

"No, but right now I'd rather sleep," I said, and did. I didn't even bother to ask how she knew where I'd been.

I woke to the aroma of something that hollered *Eat me!*, and I could guess by the smell that whatever it was had more calories than I wanted to know about. Augusta was at it again. Surely there's no dieting in Heaven, I thought. If there were, it wouldn't be Heaven.

A fan of thin, fragile pastries under a snow of confectioner's sugar on Vesta's rose crystal platter beckoned from the center of the old library table. I broke off a crisp, golden finger of one and let it dissolve in nutty sweetness on my tongue.

"Are we having a party?" I asked, reaching for another.

Augusta stood by the window making a great to-do with a whispering of leaves and the graceful dancelike arcing of her arms. When she stepped aside I saw that she had turned my great-grandmother's big wooden bread bowl into an autumn work of art. Ears of dried corn, winter squash, cotton bolls, and nuts rested in a jaunty nest of red and gold from sweet gum, hickory, and maple. Now she studied it for a minute, shifted it about half an inch on the window seat, and turned her attention to me. "Sleep well? I hope you're rested."

I nodded, licking sugar from my fingers. "Mmm . . . what is this?"

"Some recipe I found in one of your old family cookbooks. Like it? It really was quite a nuisance to make." Augusta smiled at me like a child with a secret and swept into the next room to settle by the fireside, her skirt spread in a celestial circle around her. Today she wore a simple gown that seemed to have been woven into a swirl of cosmic colors in plum, rose, and the green of an ancient forest.

"Okay, what is it?" I asked, going along with her game.

"Nondescripts." She looked up at me from her seat on the ottoman, and a tawny gold strand of hair fell across her face. For some reason, it made me smile.

"Whose was it? Where did you find it?"

"In one of those recipe books. It was from some kind of woman's club, I think. *Daisy Delights*, it was called. I believe Daisy was the name of the club."

"But *whose recipe*?" Angel or not, I was ready to shake her.

"The recipe was contributed by a Mrs. Carlton

81

Dennis. Does that strike a gong?"

I giggled. Couldn't help it. "Strike a gong? Do you mean 'ring a bell'? Nope, I don't even hear the faintest ding. When was that thing published?"

Although she tried to hide it, I could tell Augusta was annoyed at my reaction—or *vexed*, as my grandmother would say. A dainty little flush spread across her perfect cheeks. "I don't know, but I'll look," she said, and disappeared into the kitchen, returning seconds later with a small blue paperbound book that was little more than a pamphlet. It was speckled with age and possibly with food. Augusta glanced at the flyleaf. "1912," she said.

"This Mrs. Dennis could have been the mother of one of the Mystic Six," I said. "I don't know anybody with that name here, but I'll bet Vesta would."

Augusta spoke softly. "Then why don't we give her a call?"

I'd had almost nothing to eat since the day before, so I put my grandmother on hold while I inhaled two bowls of Augusta's pumpkin-peanut soup with several pieces of her honey-wheat bread. The nondescripts, I found, made an elegant dessert.

"It's not a thing in the world but egg yolks and flour with a little vanilla," Augusta said, "but you have to roll them thin enough to see through. It was hard to lift them from the frying pan without breaking them."

"Maybe you can teach me to make them," I said, but Augusta didn't answer—which usually meant she didn't want to.

I waited until midafternoon to phone Vesta—I wanted to get a report on Mildred, too. "Do you remember a family here named Dennis?" I asked when she finally answered the phone. She sounded breathless, as if she'd

82

run up a flight of steps. "What's the matter? Your elevator not working?"

"I was in the shower, Arminda. Now, who's this you want to know about?"

"Oh. Want me to call you back?" I pictured her towel-wrapped and scowling, dripping water on her lush burgundy carpet.

"No, it's all right. I grabbed a robe. Dennis who?"

"A family named Dennis. We—I found that recipe for nondescripts in an old cookbook, and it was submitted by a Mrs. Carlton Dennis."

"The name sounds familiar. I know I've heard it somewhere. When was this?"

"1912. It was published by a club your grandmother belonged to. Sort of like a garden club I guess—called themselves the Daisies. I thought maybe her daughter might be one of the Mystic Six."

My grandmother laughed. "The Daisies. Met faithfully once a month. I don't think they ever gardened . . . but I don't remember a Mrs. Dennis belonging."

"Maybe they moved I was hoping you might know if they had a daughter." It was hard to keep the disappointment from my voice.

"I'm sorry, Minda. Is there some special reason you want to know?"

"Well . . . no. Just curious," I lied.

"Wish I could help you, honey, but I do well to remember my social security number."

It wasn't until I'd hung up the phone that I realized I hadn't thought to ask about Mildred, but I decided it might be wise to give Vesta time to get dressed before I called again.

She saved me the trouble. "Minda, I've thought of

where I saw that name," my grandmother said when she phoned me a few minutes later. "It was in the cemetery. The Dennises have the plot down from ours. I've walked past it for most of my life, going to the hydrant for water."

"The Carlton Dennises? Are other family members buried there?"

"I don't know. Don't think so. I just remember the name on the stone. You've seen it, Arminda. It's a big old thing with lilies carved on it. Mama used to say she thought it was ostentatious."

"Good," I said.

"What?"

"I mean, thanks for the information. How's Mildred?"

Vesta groaned. "Well, I'd really like to tell you how she is, but Mildred's flown the coop."

I tried to picture that. "What do you mean? Where is she?"

"Called from the hospital this morning to tell me her friend Lydia was driving down to get her and she'd see us in a couple of weeks."

"I can't blame her for wanting to put Angel Heights behind her for a while," I said. "Maybe this visit will be good for her."

"It's just as well, I suppose," my grandmother said. "They phoned a few minutes ago to tell me they're ready to settle Otto's estate, and I don't have a good feeling about it."

Chapter Nine

J'D HAD ENOUGH OF CEMETERIES. AFTER JARVIS died I visited his grave site several times a week, but the experience did nothing to comfort me. If anything, the sight of the shiny new marker against raw, red earth made me hurt even more. Before leaving for Angel Heights, I had left a pot of bright yellow chrysanthemums and said good-bye. Jarvis was in the laughter we'd shared, the love we had for each other. He wasn't there.

My mother lay in this cemetery, and for that reason I hadn't been back here in years, but I knew where she was buried as if I'd made it a daily ritual. Now it was time to go there for real. A magnolia shaded her headstone—a simple slab of granite engraved with her name and the dates of her birth and death. There was a place for my father beside her, but I didn't think he'd be using it, since there wasn't room there for his second wife. Mom had died of a brain tumor, sudden and final. We hardly had time to say the things we wanted to say, do the things we needed to do to ease her going. I was only fourteen, and she was my lifeline. Her death left frayed ends.

But today Augusta walked with me, and I brought the last of the lingering roses from the bushes under the dining room window. Pink and yellow, they weren't nearly so vibrant as my mother had been, but they would have to do. After a couple of days of rain, the weather had turned warmer and I shed my sweater as we walked the mile or so through residential streets and up the curving road to the town cemetery on the hill. The sky was so blue it almost hurt my eyes, and here and there leaves still clung to trees like colorful confetti. The angel-like rock formation on the hill above us seemed to smile her blessing. It was the kind of day that made me glad to be alive, and I felt a slight pang of guilt as I walked past those who weren't here to enjoy it.

Augusta left me alone to spend some time by my mother's grave, and I cleared it of fallen magnolia leaves, arranged the roses in a jar, and said some things to her that were in my heart. I was getting ready to leave when I heard a car approaching on the gravel road nearby and saw Sylvie Smith get out with a large white potted mum. She seemed to be heading for Otto's grave in the adjoining lot, and not wanting to intrude on a private moment, I stepped behind the magnolia. I heard the rustle and crunch as she waded through the mound of now-dead flowers on his grave to make room for her chrysanthemums. And then I heard something else.

"I'm sorry, Otto. I hope you can forgive me. I didn't know what else to do."

I stood for frozen minutes with my face pressed against the tree, my hands digging into its sooty black bark, until I heard the car start up and she was gone.

Augusta, of course, was nowhere in sight. I found her on the far side of the hill, arranging a spray of autumn leaves on a lonely looking grave set apart from the rest. The person buried there had died in the early part of the twentieth century. "Family must have moved away and left her," she explained. "She's not here to care, I know, but it doesn't hurt to brighten the spot a bit."

I told her about Sylvie Smith. "What do you think she meant? She asked Otto for his forgiveness, Augusta. Do you suppose she killed him?"

"Was she grieving? Remorseful? How did she act?"

"She didn't stay long, and I couldn't see her without giving myself away, but she sounded sad. Kind of quiet. I wonder what she's sorry for."

Augusta didn't answer, but I could tell by her tiny hint of a frown she thought it worth considering.

The Dennis family plot was right where Vesta had said it would be, and easy to recognize because of the huge lily-festooned stone. Augusta gingerly stepped over the low rock wall to read the inscription. "*Louise Ryan Dennis* and *Carlton Clark Dennis* . . . Why, they died only a few days apart: February eleventh and February fifteenth, 1918." She paused with her hand on the stone as if giving it a blessing. "The flu epidemic, of course! So many soldiers died—others, too. It was merciless, spreading through towns, cities, sometimes taking whole families."

"Are there other markers?" I looked about for a daughter or daughters who might have met the same fate.

"None named Dennis, but there seems to be another family in the same plot. Relatives, perhaps." Augusta knelt by a small stone in the corner almost hidden by a holly tree. Carstairs . . . Susan D. Carstairs. Husband's buried here, too. Name's Robert."

The Carstairses had died in the 1930s, but over to the side we found a third and more recent gravestone from that family dated 1978. Dennis R. Carstairs seemed to have been the last of the clan. "I wonder if there are relatives still in Angel Heights who might know about the Dennis family," I said, pulling up a pine seedling that had sprung up in the middle of the last Carstairs grave. "Maybe a wife or children." But I didn't have

87

much hope, as the plot didn't look as if anyone tended to it on a regular basis other than the infrequent mowing.

I made a mental note of the latest occupant's name and looked around for Augusta, thinking she might have returned to our family plot to pay her respects to Lucy and her parents, whom she claimed to have known, but I didn't find her there. Farther down the hill through a hedge of crape myrtle, now bare, I caught a glimpse of her seaweed gown, her upswept hair that rivaled the autumn leaves spiraling past. She stood looking up at a trim, willowy marble angel that towered above her. The angel's wings were folded, as were her hands, as if in prayer, and she seemed to be standing on tiptoe as she looked out over the graveyard with a stony, benevolent gaze and a Madonna-like smile. As I watched from behind the Potts family mausoleum (or the Potts Apartments, as Vesta calls it), Augusta rose up on her toes, brought her rounded arms into a reverent gesture, and sucked in her stomach, keeping an eye on the statue the whole time. I managed to stay quiet until she smiled, mimicking, I suppose the marble angel's expression. She looked like her lips were glued together. Then she threw out an arm for balance, tottered, and grabbed an overhanging dogwood limb to keep from falling over altogether.

"Very well, let's see you do it, Arminda Grace Hobbs!" she said when she saw me laughing. "No one can stand on their toes like that. It isn't natural." She stood back to examine the stone angel. "And no one looks like that, either; her waist is too small, and her wings are crooked."

Augusta laughed as I hopped on a pillar at the end of a wall and attempted to duplicate her stance.

"This reminds me of a game children used to play," she said, pulling me out of a bed of ivy.

"Follow the Leader? They still play it."

"Then, shall we?" With that she skimmed over a low wall, hopped on one foot around a cedar tree, and spun around three times singing her favorite song, which I had learned was "Coming In on a Wing and a Prayer."

Feeling ten years old, I followed, giggling. "That's not fair! I don't know the words," I told her.

"Then sing one you do know!" Augusta swung into an oak tree, sat on a limb, and balanced an acorn on her nose.

Bellowing out a rendition of "Jingle Bells"—(it was all I could think of)—I did the same. By the time we skipped, ran, and sang our way back to the cemetery gates I was dizzy and exhausted. I had also forgotten for a few happy minutes the somber reasons for our visit.

The phone was ringing when we reached home. "Where in the world have you been? I've been trying to reach you," my grandmother demanded to know.

"I was up on cemetery hill checking out that lot where the Dennises are buried. (I decided not to tell her about Sylvie Smith.) There's nobody else in the plot except for some people named Carstairs. Do you know if any of them still live here?"

"There's Jewel Carstairs—no, wait a minute—she married the Knox boy and moved to Alabama, but I think her brother still lives here . . . Why are you so out of breath? You been running?"

"Just trying to keep in shape. Her brother—is he related to the Dennises?"

"Gordon Carstairs? Remotely, I think. What's all this hullabaloo about the Dennises, Arminda? My goodness, they've been dead since before I was born."

"She made nondescripts. I think their daughter might have been a member of the Mystic Six."

Silence. "And what if she was? She's dead, too—unless she's found the fountain of youth. If you're thinking of tracing down that old quilt, you've got your work cut out for you. Give it up, Minda. That thing's long gone."

"It's not the quilt. It's the women who made it. I need to know who they were, what happened to them."

She didn't ask why. I was glad I didn't have to explain that my angel and I thought they had something to do with Cousin Otto's death.

"I called to tell you they're reading Otto's will tomorrow, and I can't get in touch with Mildred." My grandmother sounded put out. I don't know what she expected me to do about it.

"Are you sure you have the right number?" I said.

"It's Lydia's voice on the answering machine, all right. I've left two messages."

"Maybe they went on a leaf tour or something—you know, one of those all-day trips. She'll probably call you back tonight. What time are they reading the will?"

"That's just it. It's at ten in the morning, and if I don't get in touch with her soon, she won't get back in time."

"Frankly, I'm surprised Otto left a will," I said. "I didn't think he was that organized."

"I think Butler Pike shamed him into it," Vesta said. "Had his law office where the bookshop is before he built that place downtown. He was the one who sold us the building."

I knew my grandmother and I were thinking the same thing, but she was the one who finally spoke it. "I do hope he remembered Mildred," she said. "I honestly dread for tomorrow to come."

But it did come, and fortunately for us—and for her—Mildred never showed. Otto had left his share of Papa's Armchair to Gatlin.

"It took only ten minutes," Vesta said when she and Gatlin stopped by the Nut House afterward. Otto's share of the shop was all he had to leave."

Gatlin was still flabbergasted. She looked from Vesta to me and tried to speak, but nothing came out—a first for my cousin.

"I—well, I guess—" Gatlin shrugged. "Don't you think Otto left it to me because he didn't think you or Mildred would outlive him?" she asked Vesta. She was wide-eyed and pale, and her voice actually trembled when she spoke.

"That's exactly what I think," Vesta said, putting an arm around her, "and I can't think of anyone I'd rather it go to. I just don't know how to explain it to Mildred."

"Do we have to?" My cousin regained a flush of color. "I mean I know we'll have to tell her he left me his share of the shop, but can't we say he made provisions for her to live there? She seems to want to stay, and I can't see any harm in it."

"What about money?" I said. "She has to live on something."

My grandmother spoke in her "don't question me" voice. "That's taken care of. You don't have to worry about that."

Gatlin and I exchanged glances. I knew Mildred had a modest income along with her Social Security, but I never knew until now who supplied it.

My cousin followed me to the kitchen to help make sandwiches for lunch. "All this time Mildred's thought Otto was putting money into her account! Do you think she ever suspected it was Vesta?"

"I don't think she really wanted to know," I said, slathering bread with pimento cheese. "I just wish she'd call and let us know where she is. It's not like her, and I can tell Vesta's worried."

"If we don't hear from her by tomorrow, let's drive over and see what's up," Gatlin said. "It's Sunday, so Dave can look after the kids." She lifted the cover from a bowl of fruit salad I'd put on the table and sniffed. "Where on earth did you get these heavenly strawberries? . . . And what's this? Fresh peaches in November?"

Where on earth, indeed? I glanced at Augusta and smiled.

Chapter Ten

"HOPE YOU DON'T MIND IF FAYE COMES along," Gatlin whispered the next morning as we started for Columbia. "I usually end up dragging her everywhere with Lizzie, but we seldom have a chance to do things together." She grinned. "And I think she likes you even better than Tigger!"

I smiled at the five-year-old cuddling a stuffed tiger in the backseat. "That's because I'm a pushover at the candy store." My young cousin and I had much in common besides our blond hair. We both loved chocolate, silly jokes, and storybooks.

Faye started with the jokes right away. "What did the hat say to the hat rack, Minda?"

I pretended I didn't know.

She giggled. "You stay here. I'm going on ahead!"

"When is a door not a door? When it's a jar!" she

answered before I could reply.

Thirty miles and fourteen knock-knock jokes later, I climbed in the back to read the latest selection of library books she'd brought along. Faye arranged them in order of preference and made room for me beside her, shifting her oversize stuffed Tigger to the corner of the seat. It wasn't until she progressed to her "busy" book and a new pack of crayons that I had a chance to tell Gatlin about Sylvia Smith.

Content with her treasures, Faye seemed not to notice when, after a bathroom stop, I abandoned her for the front seat. "Remember Otto's special friend?" I said to Gatlin in what I hoped was an undertone.

She glanced at me and mouthed the woman's name.

"Right. She was at the cemetery Friday putting flowers on his grave."

"Better late than never," Gatlin said. "She never made it to the funeral. Didn't even sign the register."

I looked back at Faye, who was carefully connecting the dots. "Asked him for forgiveness. Said she was sorry," I murmured.

"Sorry for what?" Gatlin turned off the expressway onto Columbia's Two Notch Road.

"Beats me," I said, and told her how I'd come to overhear Sylvie Smith's one-sided conversation.

"She's an odd one, all right. Are you sure she didn't see you?"

I wasn't, but I didn't want to think about it. "I found where the nondescript lady's buried."

" 'Scuse me? . . . Faye, don't be peeling the paper from those new crayons!"

(How did she know?)

"Guess I forgot to tell you there's a recipe for nondescripts in one of our great-great-grandmother's

93

old cookbooks, and it was contributed by a Mrs. Carlton Dennis. The recipes were compiled by a group of ladies at about the time Lucy was still a child."

Gatlin slowed for a traffic light. "Can you read that street sign? It's not Sandhill Avenue, is it?" I told her it wasn't.

"So," she continued, "you think this woman might have been Number . . . Which one served the refreshments?"

"Five, I think. It's the only lead we have. The Dennises are buried in that lot below ours. The one with the big lily stone."

"Ugh!" Gatlin made a face. "What about the daughter?"

"The only others were some people named Carstairs. Her name was Susan, and I guess she could've been a daughter. There was a Dennis Carstairs buried there, too."

"Carstairs. The man who used to sub some when I was in high school was named Carstairs. Worked at the newspaper for a while, I think."

"Gordon Carstairs?" I said.

"That's the one. Don't you remember him? Filled in some for Mrs. Whitmire."

I shook my head. "I wasn't that lucky. Gerty never missed a day. Is he still around?"

"As far as I know. Lives out on Old Mill Road in that little log cabin with the big oak tree out front. Kind of a quaint-looking place."

I remembered the house and always thought it looked like an illustration from a fairy tale. I was about to ask my cousin if she'd go with me to see him when we pulled up in front of Lydia Bowen's. It looked deserted.

"See if there's a light inside," Gatlin said. "Doesn't

94

look like anybody's home."

"Maybe they're in the back. I'll check." I left the others in the car and rang the bell of the small brick bungalow. The house was like many of its neighbors, built probably in the 1930s, on a wide, tree-shaded street. Except for a few brown oak leaves that had drifted onto her porch, Lydia's place seemed neat and cared for. Pansies bloomed in a hanging basket, and the nandina bushes by the front steps were filled with clusters of bright red berries. I looked through the living room window to see a cozy arrangement of slipcovered chairs grouped about a table piled with books. One book lay open facedown, as if the reader meant to return shortly. But nobody came to the door, and I couldn't see a light inside.

I turned to Gatlin and shrugged. "Where could they be?"

"If you're looking for Mrs. Bowen, she's gone somewhere with a group from her church." I turned to see a man who looked to be in his thirties approaching from the yard next door with a huge gray cat on a leash. The cat growled at me and didn't look at all happy.

"Do you know if anyone was with her?" I asked, explaining our errand. "We haven't heard from Mildred since she left home, and we're a little concerned. She hasn't been well."

The man, who said his name was Albert Reinhardt, didn't know about Mildred, but was collecting Lydia Bowen's mail and newspapers until she returned. "Left a couple of days ago and said she'd be back by the middle of next week," he said, scooping up the cat, who was hell-bent on digging up Lydia's chrysanthemums. "Some kind of church retreat, I think . . . Stop that right now, Herman!" He deposited the squirming, hissing feline on the ground, and I thanked him and jumped into the car before Herman decided to go for me.

"What now?" Gatlin wanted to know.

"I guess we wait. Lydia's gone on some sort of Methodist retreat, and it looks like Mildred went with her."

"Sounds like just her kind of thing, but you'd think she'd at least let us know." Gatlin frowned as she eased back onto the street. "After all, she's eighty-three and just out of the hospital. What if she gets sick?"

"I'm sure Lydia would get in touch with us. Don't know what else we can do. But maybe—"

"I'm hungry!" Faye announced from the backseat. "Tigger wants some ice cream."

"Tell Tigger he can have some ice cream after he eats his lunch," her mother told her, grinning at me. "What do you think His Highness would like?"

Faye made a big issue of whispering to the stuffed animal and cocked her head as if listening to his reply. "Hot dogs," she said. "And fries."

"Doesn't Tigger ever get tired of hot dogs?" Gatlin asked, searching for a fast-food place.

Her daughter considered this. "Well, sometimes he likes pizza."

I don't know what it is about riding in a car that makes me hungry, but just then I would've been glad to settle for either.

Content after having eaten her fill of junk food, Faye fell asleep in the backseat clutching the bedraggled Tigger, giving Gatlin and me a chance to discuss more openly what might have happened to Great-grandmother Lucy's round-robin quilt.

"You seem to be more interested in that quilt than Vesta ever was," Gatlin said. "Mind telling me why you

96

think it's so important?"

"Because it was made by the Mystic Six," I said. "I think they made it for a reason, and if we can locate the quilt, we might be able to find out what that reason was and learn who the other three members were."

"Most quilts were made for a reason, silly—to keep people warm. What's so different about this one?"

"For one thing, they passed it around, and from what Vesta says, it sounds like it told some kind of story." And I have a heavenly hunch it might tell us something about Otto's murder, I wanted to add. "Don't tell me you aren't curious."

"Yeah, I'm curious. I'm curious to know what's going on with you, Arminda Grace Hobbs."

"Whatdaya mean?" I looked out the window as we drove through the little town of Chester, South Carolina, where streets were Sunday silent except for a squall of little boys skateboarding along the sidewalks, followed by a big brown dog. "Don't you love that old house?" I said, admiring a large Victorian set back from the street. "Must cost a fortune to paint, though."

"You're different," my cousin persisted, ignoring my tactic. "Can't put my finger on it, but it's like you know something I don't."

"There's a first time for everything," I said, making a face. "Do you think it'll be too late to pay a visit to Gordon Carstairs when we get home?"

Gatlin had promised to help Lizzie with a homework project, so she dropped me off at home and I gave Gordon Carstairs a call.

"By all means, do come by," he said. "I've been working all day and would welcome the respite."

I almost expected to be greeted by Goldilocks when I

97

knocked on the door of the rustic cabin, but I was met by one of the bears instead—or that was the appearance he gave. Gordon Carstairs was a stocky, heavyset man with a head full of iron-gray curls and a beard to match. Bifocals slid halfway down his large nose, and an unlit cigar protruded from a corner of his mouth. It jiggled as he spoke. "Trying to quit—rotten habit," he said, removing the gnawed brown stub. "You must be Vesta's granddaughter—you have the Maxwell look, all right. Come on in and excuse all this hodgepodge. If I ever get through with this project, maybe I'll be able to clear a path through " He winked. "But I doubt it."

Mr. Carstairs had told me when I called earlier that he was working on a history of the county, and from the look of things, he must have started with Adam and Eve. "Here, have a seat," he said, removing a sheaf of papers from an orange plaid sofa, and for the first time I noticed the sleeping dog at my feet. "Scoot over now, Colonel," he said, scratching the animal between the ears. "Make a little room for our guest.

"Looks just like an officer I served under back in my army days," he explained with an affectionate glance at his pet. "We've been together a long time, haven't we, old friend?"

The dog, who looked to be a mixture of hound and German shepherd, replied with a yawn and a thump of his tail before resuming his nap. I didn't blame him. The room was close and much too warm, with a wood fire blazing in the big stone fireplace, but the heat didn't appear to bother my two companions.

I declined my host's offer of coffee but was glad to let him relieve me of my coat. If Gordon Carstairs knew enough about Angel Heights to compile a history of the area, he was the very one I wanted to talk with, and if I had to melt into a puddle to accomplish this, then so be it.

I thanked him for seeing me on such short notice and told him about finding the nondescript recipe in the Daisy Delights cookbook. Gordon Carstairs nodded his head and smiled. "There were a number of clubs like that for the ladies here in Angel Heights. Daisy was just one of them. Another organization called themselves the Teaset, I believe, and then there were the Pathfinders—a more adventurous bunch—who went on hikes and such."

"I wonder if you've heard of a group called the Mystic Six? My great-grandmother belonged, and I think one of your relatives might have been a member."

"Oh? And who might that be?"

"I'm not sure if this is the right person or not, and I'm hoping you can help me." I told him about finding the minutes of the meeting and noting the refreshments they served. "There were six of them, and Vesta tells me they even had a pin—a daisylike flower with a star in the middle—the same design that's on the alma mater Lucy stitched that's on the wall at the academy."

"Well, of course! I've noticed that many times—read it, too, but I guess I never thought much about the emblem." Gordon Carstairs frowned. "And I've seen it somewhere else, too . . . Wish I could remember where."

"Maybe your mother had a pin like that?" She would have been about the right age if I guessed right.

But he shook his head. "My mother was from Virginia—lived there until she married, but my father was born and raised here."

I tried to remember the names on the stones in the cemetery. "Was Dennis Carstairs your father?"

He laughed. "Good heavens, no! Dennis was my first

99

cousin, although he was about ten years older than I was. His papa, Robert Carstairs, was my uncle . . . Now wait a minute! You must be talking about my cousin Flora. I seem to remember her wearing a pin like that, and she would've been about the right age, too. I think she left here soon after her parents died."

"Do you know what happened to her?" I asked. "Her mother was the one who contributed that recipe for nondescripts."

"Can't remember her coming here much, but her boy Chester was about my age, and he used to visit a lot. Stayed with Aunt Susan and Uncle Robert. Dennis—he was their son—didn't have much to do with him because he was so much older, so the two of us—Chester and I—we palled around together. Crazy about baseball, Chester was. I've often wondered if he might've made it in the big leagues . . . " Gordon reached down to rub Colonel's tummy.

"Might have?"

"Chester was killed in the war—World War Two, and his young wife died of polio soon after. Cousin Flora and her husband raised their little girl; Peggy, her name was. They used to send me pictures."

"Oh," I said. I was running out of fingers to keep track. "Your cousin Flora—where did she live?"

Mr. Carstairs frowned. "Some little town in Georgia; I haven't been there in ages." He rose to put another log on the fire, and I wondered if I could remove any more clothing and still keep within the bounds of decency. I slid the scarf from around my neck and stuffed it into my pocket.

"We weren't really related, you know," he continued, wiping his hands on green corduroy pants that looked as if they'd been used for that purpose before. "Her

100

daddy's sister, Susan Dennis, married my uncle Robert, but she was always like family to me. When Chester's daughter Peggy married, I went to the wedding there."

Where? Where? I wanted to plead; instead, I looked at him expectantly. The house smelled of dog and wood smoke, and something else—old grease, I think. I picked up a magazine and flipped through it, letting its pages fan my face.

He must have gotten my message. "Place where they lived had this statue of a big red apple right in the center of town . . . had a girl's name . . . Amelia? No. Cornelia! The family lived in Cornelia."

"Do you think she still lives there?"

"Did the last I knew. Sends me a Christmas card every year." He looked about and kind of groaned. "I'm sure I have that address here somewhere." Gordon went to a big rolltop desk in the corner, pulled out a cardboard box, and then shuffled through its contents. "Here it is: Peggy and Harold O'Connor. Still live on Garden Avenue—been there long as I can remember."

My host scribbled the information on a scrap of paper and gave it to me as I gathered my wraps and headed for the door. "May I ask why you're so intent on learning about these six women? After all, they all died years ago. What's the fascination?"

I started to lie and tell him I was working on a family history, but he was too intelligent for that. "I'm digging for old secrets," I said, and I could see he understood.

It was dark when I stepped outside, and the cold zapped me in the face. It felt great. I was on my way down the steps when Gordon Carstairs called to me from the doorway. "I remember now where I've seen that flower-star design you described to me. It was on Cousin Flora's tombstone."

101

Chapter Eleven

*I*RENE BRADSHAW STUCK HER HEAD IN THE door of Papa's Armchair and squinted over her glasses. "Well, Gatlin, I hear you've become an heiress. What do you think you'll do with this place?"

"If we can ever get this inventory straightened out, I guess we'll stumble along from there." Gatlin filled another carton with age-stained volumes. "I don't know why Otto bothered with all this stuff. Nobody reads them, and they just take up space. There's not enough room in here to swing a cat."

"Swing a cat. Right." Irene stepped inside and closed the door behind her, pulling off her red beret. "Small, yes, but cozy, don't you think?"

"A little too cozy for me. Vesta and I are thinking of opening a tearoom—some place where people can get lunch—in that building next door if we can get Dr. Hank to let go of it." My cousin climbed a ladder and began handing books down to me. "And Minda's going to help us, aren't you, Minda?"

I gave her my "we'll see" expression, which she ignored.

"Of course, Vesta's not interested in making sandwiches and ladling up soup; she'll only be a silent partner," Gatlin continued, setting aside a book with a peeling binding, which she apparently meant to keep.

I couldn't imagine our grandmother being silent about anything, but I couldn't see her pocketing tips and wiping off tables, either.

"Vesta? No, that wouldn't be her cup of tea at all," Irene said, running her finger along the stacks.

I edged out of the way in case she got in an arm-grabbing mood.

"I guess I'd forgotten she and Otto were in this together." Irene pulled out a volume with a torn cover and turned it over in her hands without seeming to be aware of it. "But is there room next door for a restaurant? Looks like a tight squeeze to me."

"Not if we knock out that wall." Gatlin gestured behind her. "Make this all one big room."

Still Irene shook her head. "Hank would never sell that building. Why, where would he store his records?"

"Vesta says he made copies of his active patients' files when he sold the practice," Gatlin told her. "The rest of them are so out of date, most of the patients have either died or moved away."

Irene set the book aside. "Moved I don't know. Have you discussed this with him yet?"

"I think Otto mentioned it, but no, I haven't had much of a chance to do anything since Otto died. Can't see why he'd object, though. It's not like he really needs the space."

Gatlin turned away from our visitor and lifted an eyebrow at me. Irene Bradshaw wasn't usually this nosy. Why was she so curious about my cousin's plans for the shop?

"I'm afraid you'd be in for a lot of expense." Irene moved toward the door and then stopped, smashing her beret into a wad. "Don't know when that old place has ever had any work done on it. Must've been built almost a hundred years ago, and there's no telling what condition the roof's in."

"What in the world was that all about?" I asked after the door closed behind her.

Gatlin made a face and shrugged. "Who knows? After what happened to Otto, nothing in this town surprises me anymore."

"Maybe she's interested in something here, a rare book or something. Do you think Irene might be the person who ransacked the shop after sending Mildred to the Land of Nod?" The sample of Janice Palmer's shortbread the lab had tested turned out fine, but there were traces of a strong sedative in the coffee Mildred had ingested, and since no one else was affected, it seemed obvious the drug must've been added to her serving only.

"How could she? Irene wasn't even there that night. And how would she know which cup was Mildred's?"

"I wish I knew," I said. "I don't suppose you've heard from Mildred?"

"No, but they aren't due back until sometime in the middle of the week, are they? And I'm sure Vesta would let us know if she called." Gatlin pushed bright hair from her forehead and sat on a box of books to rest. "Did you find out anything from Gordon Carstairs yesterday?"

I grinned. "I was hoping you'd ask. Number Five lived in Cornelia, Georgia—at least I think that's who she was—and she had that flower-star thing engraved on her tombstone."

"Get outta here!" My cousin swatted me with a dust rag. "Why would she do a thing like that?"

"She's not talking, but I'm hoping her descendants will. Mr. Carstairs gave me her granddaughter's address, and I'm going to try to get down there tomorrow. Wanna keep me company?"

She shook her head. "No time. That's an all-day trip, Minda, and there's too much I need to do here." Gatlin stood and leaned against the shelf where I sorted books in stacks of those that I thought could be worth keeping, those that probably wouldn't, and the few that might be valued at more than $5.98.

"I wish I knew what I was doing," I said, studying over a history book published in 1924, before adding it to the "keep" pile. I hoped my cousin knew more about the book business than I did.

"It's something to do with what happened to Otto, isn't it?" Gatlin persisted. "That group of women, the quilt they made, and that blasted pin they wore. Why won't you tell me what it is?"

"Because I don't know myself," I said. I didn't add that I was afraid if I shared my secret about the tiny gold pin, I might put my cousin and her family in danger.

"Just be careful, then," she said. "That's a long way to drive alone."

I wouldn't be driving to Georgia alone, but that's another thing I didn't tell her.

Augusta and I left early the next morning with Gordon Carstairs's directions to the O'Connors' house, a thermos of coffee, and a basket of Augusta's strawberry muffins. The muffins were still hot as we passed the town limits of Angel Heights, and I ate two of them before we'd gotten ten miles down the road. Augusta, I noticed, put away a good supply herself.

A couple of hours later when we stopped for a midmorning break, I gave in to temptation and had another and was surprised to find them still warm. There also appeared to be as many of them as there were when we started.

"How do you do that?" I asked my heavenly passenger, but Augusta only smiled. She had shed the voluminous wrap she'd started out in that looked to me like the lining of clouds when the sun shines through

105

them and had finally stopped asking if my car heater was broken. I didn't know angels could be cold-natured, but Augusta said it all went back to her being at Valley Forge that freezing winter with Washington's army.

Now she sat fingering her wonderful necklace that seemed to have changed from sunrise pink to a kind of maple-leaf gold and back again. "I assume this woman's expecting us," she said. "Seems an awfully long way to drive and then find her gone."

"You assume wrong," I told her. Sometimes Augusta can be a bit of a know-it-all. "I didn't call on purpose; it might scare her off. You'll have to admit it would be sort of strange having somebody you never heard of asking questions about your grandmother. And even if she's not there, we can go to the cemetery. I'm curious about that emblem, Augusta. Gordon Carstairs says it was on Flora Dennis's stone."

"That is curious. I hope the granddaughter will be able to tell us something about Flora," Augusta said. "What did you say her name was?"

"Peggy. Peggy O'Connor. And she should know if anyone would. Gordon Carstairs says Flora and her husband raised her after her parents died."

Clusters of autumn leaves still clung in places, and their orange and gold was reflected in the water as we passed Lake Hartwell at the Georgia state line. The bright collage stirred a memory. This was my husband's favorite season. Jarvis and I always went hiking in the fall and had gone camping in this area several times. I swallowed a would-be moan. At the same time, Augusta touched me lightly on the arm, and when I looked into her eyes I saw that she was hurting with me. I didn't want her to hurt any more. I didn't want me to hurt any more, and when Augusta smiled, I smiled back. It

106

helped.

"I wish you could remember who the other two Mystic members were," I said as we neared the turnoff for Cornelia. "If this doesn't work out, I don't know where else to look."

"It's not that I can't remember them, Minda; I never knew who they were. I'm as much in the dusk about this as you are. Rome wasn't built in a week, you know."

I let the dusk thing go. "You mean a day?" I said.

"That, either." Augusta dug into her bottomless bag, unfolded a soft-looking fabric in a sunny yellow print, and began to sew.

"You're not going to have time to get started on that before we get there," I told her. "What is it, anyway?"

"Pajamas. Snug, aren't they?" Augusta held up a tiny pair with feet already finished that looked like it might fit a six-month-old. "I dislike it when my feet get cold," she said. "This is for the little boy in that house right next to the water tower. Father lost his job."

"Where? In Angel Heights?"

She nodded. "The pajamas will grow as he grows. Should last awhile."

"How do you plan to deliver them?" I asked.

"There's more than one kind of angel, Arminda." Augusta Goodnight carefully folded the small garment and laid it on the seat beside her. I knew who the other "angel" would be.

Peggy O'Connor was baby-sitting her grandbaby when I called from a convenience store just outside of town and seemed understandably confused as to why I would want to see her.

I told her who I was and that my family, like hers, was from Angel Heights. She didn't seem impressed.

107

"I'm researching some family history and ran across some minutes from a meeting of a group of young women calling themselves the Mystic Six," I explained. "I think your grandmother, Flora, might have been one of them."

Peggy O'Connor's only comment was a soothing shush to the baby wailing in the background.

"I should've called ahead, I know, but we—I—was passing through and hoped you might be able to spare a little time," I babbled. "If it's not convenient now, maybe sometime later this afternoon?"

"Right now I'm trying to get Cassandra down for her nap, and I just don't know . . . "

"Oh, I hope I didn't wake her!" Naturally this woman wasn't going to invite me over. She didn't know me from Adam's house cat. I might be a child-snatcher or even somebody trying to sell magazines or cosmetics. "Your cousin Gordon suggested I get in touch with you," I said. "You see, my great-grandmother was Lucy Alexander. She was a Westbrook before she married, and Vesta—that's my grandmother—said she used to talk about somebody named Flora." A lie. Augusta, standing beside me, lifted an eyebrow. "I think they were close friends growing up."

"Cassandra usually sleeps until around two-thirty . . . I suppose it would be all right if you dropped by after then, but I really don't know how I can help you." The woman spoke as if she had to wrench out each word with pliers.

I gratefully accepted the crumbs. "That would be fine, thank you. I'll see you then." I got off the phone before she could change her mind.

Augusta's thermos of coffee seemed as bottomless as her handbag, but both of us had lost our taste for strawberry muffins, so I picked up sandwiches from a fast-food restaurant, and we picnicked under a big sycamore tree in the town cemetery. A light rain began to fall as we packed away our paper wrappers and scattered crumbs for the birds, and neither of us had any idea where Flora Dennis was buried. Gordon Carstairs had told me that her husband's name was Douglas Briggs, so at least we had something to go on.

Rain was coming down harder by the time I dug out an umbrella from the clutter in my backseat and waved down a caretaker at the bottom of the hill. The Briggs plot, he told me, was against the far wall on the other end of the cemetery. "You might want to take your car," he suggested, wondering, I suppose, why anybody would be wandering around a graveyard on a day like this. I sort of wondered myself.

We found Flora's son Chester and his wife, Julia, buried in the small plot along with the older Briggses. Augusta hesitated at each stone—to say a prayer, I supposed, for the ones who rested there—but she stopped short when she came to the place where Flora lay, then knelt, and ran her fingers over the star-flower emblem there.

"How sad," she whispered. "How very sad."

"What do you mean? Because of the design?"

"That poor child!" Augusta stood looking down at the stone as if she could make the engraving disappear. "To think she still carried this after all those years!"

"Still carried what? What does this have to do with Annie's pin and the Mystic Six?" I could understand loyalty to a group of friends, but this was taking things a bit too far!

Augusta was silent as we walked back to the car. I flapped water from the umbrella, tossed it onto the floor in the back, and slid in beside her. "This all has something to do with Otto's murder, doesn't it?" I asked.

"I had hoped not, but yes, I'm afraid it might."

"Do you think whoever killed him dropped the pin I found, or could it have been Otto himself?"

"Either is possible, I suppose." Augusta unleashed hair that would put the harvest moon to shame and let it fan out to dry behind her. "Arminda, where did you put that pin?"

"In the box where I keep all my other junk—I mean jewelry. It's in my sweater drawer along with those old minutes from the meeting."

"Then I suggest you put it somewhere safe and promise you won't tell anyone you have it. It might have caused one death already. We don't want it bringing about another."

Chapter Twelve

PEGGY O'CONNOR MUST HAVE BEEN WAITING by the window, because she opened the door before I could ring the bell. Her home on Garden Avenue was a comfortable-looking Georgian set back from the road. A new beige Honda Accord sat in the driveway. Blue pansies nodded from a large urn by the front steps, and a baby's plastic swing hung from the limb of an oak in the yard.

"Cassandra's still sleeping," she whispered. "I was afraid the doorbell might wake her."

If, as her cousin Gordon had said, Peggy Briggs O'Connor was born at about the time her father was killed during World War II, she would have to be in her late fifties. She didn't look it. The woman who invited me in was trim, blond, and smooth-skinned in a green tweed skirt and matching sweater set. The latter appeared to be cashmere, and I wondered if she had changed after getting the baby down for her nap. It seemed much too expensive to chance being anointed with spit-up.

The room I was ushered into was formal but lived in. A child's playthings were scattered about the room, and a gas fire burned on the hearth. My hostess hesitated before sitting. "Can I get you something? Coffee or hot tea? The weather's taken a nasty turn."

I'm sure I must have looked as if I could use some, and I could. I accepted, grateful for the offer. The tea, when it came, was orange spice, accompanied by a couple of homemade gingersnaps, and I was pleased when Peggy joined me. I wondered if she ever made nondescripts.

"There was a recipe in one of my great-grandmother's old cookbooks for a pastry called nondescripts," I said, jumping in with both feet. "It was contributed, I think, by your great-grandmother."

When Peggy smiled, I noticed for the first time the tiny lines around her mouth and eyes. "Goodness, I'd almost forgotten about those! Gram used to make them for her circle meetings once in a while, and I remember how those ladies gobbled them up. I rarely got more than a taste, but I've never had anything like them." She took a dainty sip of tea and broke off a bite of the fairy-size cookie. "All that sugar and cholesterol—it's a wonder they didn't kill us! And Gram said they were a horror to make."

I told her I had heard the same. "Mrs. O'Connor, I

111

think I mentioned an organization my great-grandmother belonged to, and your grandmother, too, I believe. Did she ever say anything about a group called the Mystic Six?"

"Not that I recall." She looked down to smooth an invisible wrinkle in her skirt. I couldn't see her face. "Would you like more tea?"

"No, thank you. I was hoping you might help me learn who the other members were," I said.

"But this was long before you were even born. My grandmother's been gone almost twenty years now. Why, surely none of them could still be alive!" She lifted her cup as if to drink, but there was nothing left in it.

"I thought she might have mentioned it, or even saved some letters. These women made a quilt together—passed it around for years. Vesta, my grandmother, says she never knew what became of it."

"I'm afraid I wouldn't know, either. Gram never spoke of belonging to a group like that. I don't remember her ever going back to Angel Heights. She had no brothers or sisters, and her parents both died in that terrible flu epidemic."

"I just assumed she kept in touch," I said. "Your cousin Gordon told me he and your dad were close friends, that he visited there often."

Peggy O'Connor straightened a brocaded sofa pillow. "My father was killed right after I was born. I never saw him."

"I'm sorry." I could tell she was getting impatient for me to leave, so I gathered my purse and coat to give her the notion my parting was imminent. But I wasn't out the door yet.

"There was a pin, you know. The girls in the Mystic

112

Six wore a small gold pin: a flower with a star in the center."

She started toward the door, then turned to face me, and I had the distinct feeling she had just thrown down a gauntlet. Peggy O'Connor spoke in that calm, controlled voice some teachers use five minutes before the last bell. "That's interesting, but it has nothing to do with my grandmother or with me."

"Then why would that same emblem be engraved on her stone? I just came from the cemetery, Mrs. O'Connor. I saw it there."

She reared back and bristled like a skinny green porcupine. "I can't imagine what you mean by that. That engraving on my grandmother's stone is merely a design, nothing more. It has nothing to do with that group of academy girls you speak of or with Angel Heights."

I felt her hand on my shoulder and knew she was about a sniff away from shoving me out the door.

"Now, if you'll excuse me," she said, "I must go and see to my granddaughter. I hear her waking from her nap."

"Boy, did she ever have her drawers in a wad!" I said to Augusta as we backed out of the driveway. "I'm beginning to have a sneaky little suspicion she was trying to get rid of me."

"Don't be vulgar, Arminda, but you're right. The woman was rude. And clearly not telling the truth."

It was cold in the car, and Augusta bundled herself into her downy wrap and turned up the heat. "I could use a cup of that tea," she added with a hint of a shiver.

"You were there?"

She nodded. "Oh, yes, but of course you didn't see

113

me. I didn't want to intrude."

"Then I suppose you noticed how upset she became when I mentioned the pin?"

"Indeed, I did. And that's not all I noticed," Augusta said. "Peggy O'Connor made a point of saying the engraving on her grandmother's stone had nothing to do with a group of girls from the academy."

"Right," I said. "She made that clear."

"Arminda, you never mentioned the academy . . . I believe there's a place up on the left where we can get some tea," my angel pointed out.

"Pluma," my grandmother said.

"Pluma what?" Augusta and I had just walked in after our unrewarding drive to Georgia and back when the phone started to ring, and I could tell from the demanding way it jangled that Vesta was on the other end.

"Pluma Griffin."

The name meant nothing to me, but she sounded as though she meant for me to respond in some way, and so I did. "Who's that?" I asked.

Deep sigh here. "You were asking about the other members of that group my mother belonged to, weren't you? Well, Pluma Griffin was one of them."

"I thought you said you couldn't remember."

"I'm eighty years old," Vesta said, sounding more like forty. "I'm supposed to forget things, Minda. And I probably wouldn't think of it now except that when I was helping Gatlin sort through some of Otto's mess this morning, I ran across an old book she'd given Mama. It was a volume of poetry—one of those maudlin, flowery things people used to weep over, and she'd written an inscription in the front."

"Do you know what happened to her?" I was so excited to hear the news, I almost forgot to be tired.

"Well, she died." Vesta paused, baiting me, I guess, and when I didn't answer, she continued. "Moved away from Angel Heights probably before I was born—worked in a library somewhere in Charlotte, I think. Anyway, when Pluma retired, she came back here to live with a niece."

"The niece—she still here? Do I know her?"

"Don't know how you could forget her," Vesta said. "Martha Kate Hawkins was Hank Smith's receptionist for as long as he practiced. Lives in one of those assisted living places out on Chatham's Pond Road."

"Do you think it's too late—?"

"Don't you dare go there before you come by here and get this book!" Vesta said. "I don't want the old thing, and yet I'd feel guilty throwing it away. Let's shove it off on Martha Kate."

Augusta had put on a Crock-Pot of chicken vegetable chowder before we left that morning, and it smelled almost as good as chocolate. Stomach complaining, I left her up to her elbows in biscuit dough and did as my grandmother commanded.

The slender volume of poetry titled *The Heart Sings a Blessing* was frayed at the edges and bound in a faded blue. On the flyleaf, Pluma Griffin had inscribed in now fading brown ink

> For Lucy, I won't forget!
> *Forever, Pluma*

"Forget what?" I wondered aloud.

If Vesta knew, she didn't answer, for just then her doorbell rang, and she went to admit Edna Smith, who

115

tumbled breathless and red-faced into the nearest chair.

"Scared of elevators," she explained to our unspoken question.

"Good grief, Edna, don't tell me you walked up four flights of stairs!" Vesta said, sending me a silent message to bring water.

"I didn't get this winded from sex—'scuse me, Minda," our visitor panted between gulps.

"You know I would've called first, Vesta," Edna said when she was able to breathe normally, "but this just came to me all of a sudden, and I can't talk to just anybody about it." She lowered her voice. "Didn't want to tell you over the phone."

"Do you want me to leave the room?" Oh Lordy, I really, *really* didn't want to hear intimate details of Edna and Hank Smith's love life—or lack of it.

"No, no. You'd better hear this, too, only keep it to yourself—both of you, please." Edna took another swallow of water and leaned forward. "Remember when Mildred got so sick the night of the UMW meeting?"

My grandmother looked like she could use some water, too. "Be hard to forget it," she said.

"I was sitting next to her when later on in the meeting she complained of feeling nauseated," Edna said. "I asked her if she wanted me to take her home, but she said no, she had something in her purse that was supposed to ease it. Looked like those stomach pills you buy over the counter—the ones for acid indigestion—but I can't swear that's what it was. Anyway, she washed one down with coffee."

"Dear God, Edna! Why didn't you tell us this sooner?"

"I guess I just forgot; it seemed like such a harmless thing. Just about everybody takes those things at one

116

time or another."

"Do you know where she got them?" I asked. "Maybe we can trace the pills back to the store where she bought them."

Edna drained her glass and set it aside. "That's just it. Mildred didn't buy the pills. She said Irene Bradshaw gave them to her."

My grandmother frowned. "Since when did Irene become a pharmacist?"

"It didn't seem unusual at the time," Edna said. "Mildred told me she'd mentioned to Irene about feeling kind of sick when she saw her in the grocery store that morning, said she marked it up to stress—you know, with Otto and all. Anyway, a little later Irene came by her place and dropped off those pills, said they did her a world of good. Mildred put them in her purse and forgot about them until her stomach started acting up at the meeting that night."

Vesta didn't say anything for a minute. "Mildred might still have them in her purse. Let's wait and see what they are when she gets back—might turn out to be something totally harmless. Meanwhile, you're right, Edna. I wouldn't mention this to anybody."

"Did Gatlin say anything about Irene's visit to the bookshop yesterday?" I asked Vesta after Edna left. "She had an awful case of the 'wannaknows' about what Gatlin planned to do with Papa's Armchair."

"I can't imagine why." My grandmother slipped off her narrow size-nine shoes and rubbed her feet. "Irene was a good customer, though. Maybe she's afraid Gatlin won't be able to find any more of those out-of-print mysteries she likes."

"I thought she was going to blow a gasket when Gatlin said we wanted to expand into Dr. Hank's place

117

next door. That building isn't worth anything, is it?"

"It's no historic landmark, if that's what you mean. And it's gut-ugly to boot. Besides, if Irene wants it, she can make Hank an offer as well as we can."

"Somehow I never thought of the Bradshaws as having money," I said.

"They don't, but their daughter, Bonnie, does—or Bonnie's husband does. She married into it. Robinson Sherwood came from money, and he's done all right with his legal practice. I like Robinson; he's an all right fellow, and I think he'll make a fine judge. He's just received an appointment, you know, and I hear he and Bonnie are adopting a baby."

It was so late by the time I left Vesta's, I decided to wait on my visit to Pluma Griffin's niece. And Gatlin agreed to go with me if I would help her clear a path at the bookshop the next day.

"What's Mildred going to think when she sees what we've done?" I said as the pile of books *to go* began to tower over the stack *to keep*.

"I don't know, but I wish she'd hurry back," Gatlin said. "I don't want to get rid of any of these books until Mildred's had a chance to look them over. She knows more about running this place than Otto ever did, and frankly, I'll be glad of her help. David's been great when it comes to actually moving things, but Mildred knows what people like to read."

The expression in Gatlin's eyes reminded me of the time she forgot her lines in the senior play back in high school. "I hope I'm not wading in over my head, Minda," she said.

"Hey, we're not going to let you drown," I said, sounding more confident than I felt. "Don't guess you've had any more visits from inquisitive Irene?" I was dying to tell Gatlin about the pills, but a promise was a promise.

"No, but Vesta and I made an offer to Hank Smith, and I'm almost sure he's going to sell us that building next door. I'd think most of those old records could be destroyed by now anyway. It's not like he needs the space."

I finished clearing a shelf and sneezed at the dust. "Vesta said she had no idea why Irene acted so peculiar about your buying that building," I said. "You'd think she'd be glad of a new place to eat."

"She's not the only one." My cousin flapped a dust rag at a spider web. "Hugh Talbot was in here yesterday hinting around about wanting to buy us out."

That didn't surprise me much. I told her about Hugh showing up at the house. "I think he was looking for something, and he obviously thinks we have it."

"I can't imagine what it could be," Gatlin said.

I could, but I wasn't ready to share it. "He said his sister seemed to be doing okay," I said.

Gatlin nodded. "Saw her in the drugstore yesterday. She had a bad bruise on her cheek and was wearing a bedroom slipper on one foot, but she told me she wasn't going to let that stop her.

"All that walking must've given her stamina," Gatlin said. "When we were in high school, Mrs. Whitmire would always get there early so she could get in her laps around the track. I couldn't keep up with her on a bet." She looked at her watch. "Which reminds me, I'd better start walking for home. It's almost time for my two to be getting back from choir practice.

"If Mildred shows up tomorrow, maybe we can finally clear a space in here and get rid of some of these old books."

But Vesta pulled into the driveway behind me as soon as I reached home, and one glance at my grandmother told me something was bad wrong.

"I just got off the phone with Lydia Bowen. Arminda, Mildred hasn't been with her at all! She says she hasn't heard from her in weeks and has no idea where she could be."

Chapter Thirteen

"IT'S JUST LIKE MILDRED TO PULL SOMETHING like this!" my grandmother said the next day. "She ought to know we'd be out of our heads with worry. It's just plain selfish, that's all!"

Vesta and I were on our way to the bookshop after checking with the hospital staff about Mildred's actions on the day she disappeared, and in spite of my grandmother's sputtering, I knew she was deep-down afraid of what might have happened to the woman who had become an important part of our family.

"The receptionist on duty said she remembers calling a taxi for her, and that an attendant wheeled Mildred out to the cab, but she didn't know where she meant to go," I said, trying to reconstruct what had happened.

"Shouldn't be difficult to find out," Vesta said. "There's only one taxi driver in Angel Heights, and that's Wilbur Dobbins. His mouth runs faster than that beat-up old cab he drives, but he'd know where she went if anybody would."

But Wilbur, parked in front of the town hall to eat his bologna and cheese sandwich, hadn't seen Mildred at all.

"Didn't call me," he said through a mouthful of pickle. "Must've been somebody else."

But who? The nurse on Mildred's floor had said Mildred had told her a friend was picking her up, but the receptionist was definite about seeing her get into a taxi. "She must have called a cab from somewhere else," I said. "Hope it's not Columbia—we'd never get through checking out all of those!"

"Too far away." Vesta shook her head. "Mildred would never spend that kind of money. Let's try Rock Hill; it's closer."

I used the phone at Papa's Armchair to make the calls while Vesta paced the length of the small room. Two of the four cab companies in Rock Hill had no record of making the trip to Angel Heights for a passenger on the day in question, I learned, but the other two promised to get back to us.

Gatlin had just left to pick up Faye from kindergarten when the dispatcher at the Get Up and Go Transportation Service phoned to tell us that a driver had called for an elderly passenger a week ago today and delivered her to the bus station there.

My grandmother rarely cried, but now she made no attempt to hide her tears. "She's been gone seven days, Minda—eight if you count today. Where on earth can she be?" She pulled a rumpled tissue from her pocketbook. "I've felt uneasy about this from the very beginning."

"Why don't we take a look at her apartment? See if she took anything with her. Might give us something to go on."

Vesta sighed, but followed me into the small rooms in back of the shop. "Might as well. Can't hurt to look."

"Find anything missing?" I asked when she'd had a

121

chance to look around.

"Her small suitcase is gone, and her coat, but she took that with her to the hospital." Vesta peered again into the tiny closet. "That silly hat's missing, too, and I don't see her lavender suit—the one she got on sale last year. I don't think all of her dresses are here, either."

"Looks like she planned to be gone for a while." I sat on the bed, relieved that at least Mildred had taken enough clothing, and watched my grandmother pulling out dresser drawers. "What are you looking for now?" I asked.

"That zebra. Scruffy old thing. Mildred gave it to Otto for Christmas when he was just a little tyke, and he dragged it around everywhere. She hangs on to it like it's some kind of icon. Now that Otto's dead, I wouldn't be surprised if she's taken to burning incense."

"Oh, I saw that zebra at the hospital," I told her. "It was in that little table beside the bed."

Vesta smiled. "Doesn't surprise me a bit. She hides things in it, you know."

"Hides things? In the stuffed animal?"

"Lord, yes! Of course she doesn't know I know. And it's so big I could get my foot in there. No telling what else she's got in that zebra. Mildred's sewn it up so many times, the poor animal must be molting."

"Vesta, maybe we should tell the police. At least they could help us look for her."

"I don't know, Minda. There's nothing wrong with Mildred's mind, and she'd never forgive me if we humiliated her by dragging her back, but I'm worried about those pills."

"The ones Irene gave her?"

"What if she takes more of them?" Vesta sat on the bed beside me and almost—but not quite—let herself sag. "Frankly, I don't know what to do."

"We can't very well drag her back if we don't know where she is," I said. "Why don't we ask at the bus station, see if anyone there remembers her? Somebody might be able to tell us where she went."

Gatlin insisted that our grandmother wait for David to accompany her on her bus station quest that afternoon, and their oldest, Lizzie, and I went along, too. Faye decided to stay and "help" her mother at the bookstore. Tigger liked it there, she said, because he could sit in the window and see what was going on. I'm sure it had nothing to do with the fact that the drugstore across the street sold hot dogs and ice cream.

Lizzie was working on her Toymaker badge for Girl Scouts, and during the ride to Rock Hill I tried my best to help her make a cornshuck doll, but the dried shucks became so shredded, we ended up with something that looked like confetti.

"What about a sock puppet?" I suggested. "Or maybe some kind of game?"

Lizzie turned up her freckled nose at the sock puppet, but the game, she thought, might be kind of fun. "We could make it sort of like *Clue*," she whispered, "except it would be Minerva Academy instead of that big old house, and the body would be Otto's!" My young cousin frowned. "Lessee . . . Sylvie Smith did it in the bathroom with a plastic bag . . . "

"Elizabeth Norwood! You're downright ghoulish!" I glanced at my grandmother in the front seat, but she appeared not to have heard. "You'd better not let Vesta hear you talking like that. And what makes you think Sylvia had anything to do with it?" (I really must've been the last one to hear about Otto's rumored

123

romance.)

She shrugged. "He dumped her, didn't he? Everybody at school knows that."

I remembered how much I thought I knew in the fifth grade and tempered my advice with a smile. "Still, it isn't in very good taste, is it? Especially with Otto being family and all. And we don't know for certain what happened between them. Why don't we think of some other game?"

Lizzie tossed her head and grinned. "Okay. How about Missing Mildred?"

I was glad when David pulled into the bus station a few minutes later. I stayed in the car with Lizzie while my grandmother and David went inside with a recent photograph of Mildred.

"They think Mildred's dead, don't they?" Lizzie said, watching them disappear into the building. "Maybe whoever killed Otto kidnapped her and is holding her for ransom in a cave somewhere."

"Why would they do that, Lizzie?" I asked.

"I don't know. Why would anybody want to kill Otto?" She linked her arm in mine, and we waited silently for her dad and Vesta to come back with a clue that might help us find Mildred.

But I could tell from their grim faces our trip to Rock Hill had been a waste of time. "The woman who sells tickets said she might've seen Mildred, but she couldn't be sure," Vesta told us. "And the man who works with her couldn't remember seeing her at all." My grandmother sank into the front seat with a moan, and that bothered me almost as much as Mildred's disappearance. Vesta Maxwell is not your everyday, run-of-the-mill moaner. In fact, she's not the moaning type at all.

"There's the police—," I began.

"I know, I know. I suppose we could take legal measures to find out if Mildred charged a bus ticket on a credit card or wrote a check for her fare," Vesta said.

"Of course, if she paid cash, we'd have no way of knowing," David said.

I wished he hadn't. It was a long, quiet drive back to Angel Heights.

We found Gatlin waiting with exciting news when we returned. Dr. Hank had finally agreed to sell the building next door. "Of course it's gonna take him a few days to get those old records out," she said. "I've talked with a couple of contractors about getting an estimate on the work that needs to be done."

"Let's hope the walls remain standing," Dave said, shaking his head. "Hank's old records might be the only thing holding them up."

"You'd think he'd be excited for me," Gatlin said later that night as we drove to see Pluma Griffin's niece in the assisted living center on Chatham's Pond Road. "I know it's a gamble taking a chance on this tearoom-bookshop idea, but there comes a time when you just have to hold your breath and jump in."

"David's just wary," I said. And with good reason, I thought, but for once I had sense enough to keep it to myself. "He'll come around when you get an opinion from the contractors."

My cousin didn't respond, but sat in the passenger seat with her arms folded and stared stonily ahead. "I left him to get Faye to bed and see to Lizzie's homework," she said a few miles down the road. "Still, I think he was glad to see me go."

"Probably," I said. "You're scary when you're mad."

"Boo!" Gatlin laughed. Finally relaxing, she noticed the loaf of date-nut bread I'd brought along that Augusta had wrapped in star-spattered cellophane. "You've been baking *again*? Looks good—what is it?"

"Date-nut bread." I shrugged. "All those pecans . . . I do live in a nut house."

"You belong in one," my cousin said. "And I don't believe for one minute you've become this domestic overnight. If I didn't know better, I'd think you were hiding a gourmet cook in the pantry." She closed her eyes and sniffed the rich, dark loaf. "She doesn't take orders, does she?"

"What makes you think it's a she?" I asked, and laughed. Gatlin laughed, too, but I could tell by her look she was kind of shocked that I'd even joke about having another man in my life. Frankly, I surprised myself.

I had found the loaf cooling on the kitchen table when I'd reached home earlier, but Augusta was nowhere around. Walking into a house without Augusta in it jolted me more than I was prepared to admit, and I sensed an urgency in her absence that gave me sort of an angelic kick in the pants.

Dusk had fallen early as it always does in mid-November, and although it was not yet five-thirty, backyard shadows enfolded the house and its surroundings in an indigo cape. I stepped out onto the back porch and called her name, and in the distance I heard her humming a song that would probably be familiar if Augusta could stay on key. She approached almost noiselessly in a swirl of autumn leaves, her purple, moon-splashed scarf billowing about her, long necklace glinting green and azure as she twirled. Arms out, head back, her small gold-sandaled feet moved

126

quickly, gracefully, in what surely must be some kind of heavenly dance. The song, I finally decided, was "Turkey in the Straw."

"I didn't know where you were," I said, my relief in seeing her obvious in my voice. "The bread smells great. Is that for supper?"

Her hair had come loose as she danced, and now Augusta caught the coppery mass in one fleeting motion and fastened it behind her head. "It's for Pluma's niece. You said you were going to see her."

It had been a tiring day. "Tomorrow," I said. "It'll keep until tomorrow."

Augusta paused at the foot of the steps and looked up at me. She didn't answer. She didn't have to.

"Are you telling me to hurry?" I said.

Augusta nodded. "Time and Mrs. Hopkins wait for no one."

"Huh?"

The angel smiled. "Mrs. Hopkins was a cow. So called because the family who owned her said she reminded them of a neighbor by that name. Mrs. Hopkins woke them, bellowing to be milked at five every morning, and that was an expression they used." Augusta moved past me into the house, and a crisp, earthy scent trailed after her. It smelled of apples and pumpkins and sun-dried grass. "That was in another time, of course. I wasn't with them long."

I followed her inside. "Don't leave me yet, Augusta. Please. I can't do this without you," I said.

"Don't worry," she said. "It's not time yet. I'll let you know when it is."

"Augusta, do you know what's happened to Mildred? Because if you do, I wish you'd tell me. Vesta's really worried, and so am I."

127

She shook her head. "I think Mildred's searching as we are. I can only hope, as you do, that no harm comes to her."

"But you think she's still alive?"

"Arminda, I don't know. We'll have to wait and see." My guardian angel opened the refrigerator and quickly closed it. "I'm afraid I didn't prepare anything for supper. Why don't we order pizza?"

Now, on the way to see Martha Kate Hawkins, pepperoni sat heavily in my stomach and Pluma Griffin's message to my great-grandmother weighed on my mind: *I won't forget!*

Augusta claimed never to have met her, but said the name sounded vaguely familiar. I guess if I'd been responsible for as many people as Augusta over the centuries, I'd forget a few names, too.

October House, the assisted living center where Martha Kate lived, was festive with pumpkins and fall foliage. A foursome quarreled at cards by the gas fire in the parlor, and somebody was playing "I Could Have Danced All Night" on the piano at the far end of the room. I had called ahead, so Mrs. Hawkins was waiting for us, and even managed a gracious thank you when we saddled her with Lucy's copy of *The Heart Sings a Blessing.*

"Well, my goodness," she said. "This does go back a long way, doesn't it?" She stuck it under her arm. "Do you think people really read stuff like this?"

I knew then if Pluma Griffin's kin knew anything to help us, she would give it to us straight.

She led us to a small sitting area where comfortable chairs were arranged around a marble-topped coffee table. "It's still not too late to get coffee—but not the real thing, I'm afraid. Would you like some?" Pluma Griffin's niece hesitated before joining us in the flame-stitched coral chairs. She wasn't very tall—probably not much over five two—but she was trim and straight. I remembered her as being pleasant but efficient when I visited Dr. Hank's office during my growing-up years.

I thanked her but declined—and got straight to the point. "We've become intrigued by a group of women our great-grandmother used to belong to," I began, ignoring the eye-rolling from Gatlin at my use of the pronoun *we*. "From what we've learned, there were six of them, and after finding this book, Vesta thinks your aunt Pluma may have been one of them."

Martha Kate Griffin took time to remove a dead leaf from the African violet on the table in front of us before she answered. "Why, yes, that would be the Mystic Six," she said, leaning back in her chair. "Did you know they passed a quilt among them? I always thought it had some kind of story behind it, but Aunt Pluma never said. She willed her pretty little pin to me. Look, I had it made into a ring." And our hostess held out a fragile finger bearing the encircled flower and star.

Chapter Fourteen

"DO YOU KNOW WHAT HAPPENED TO THE quilt?" Gatlin asked after admiring the woman's ring. "I remember seeing it once or twice when I was little, but I've forgotten what it looked like. Vesta said it had something to do with the academy."

"That seemed to be the theme of it, yes." Martha Kate

Griffin turned the dainty ring on her finger. "It fascinated me when I was a girl because it incorporated a burning building. Aunt Pluma said it represented the old classroom wing that was destroyed in a fire. Professor Holley died in it, they say."

"Seems a strange reason to make a quilt," I said, thinking Lucy and her friends must have been a morbid lot.

"People sometimes make quilts that tell a story," our hostess reminded us. "And in those days Minerva Academy was the focal point of just about everything that went on in Angel Heights. And not only did the fire deprive them of their center of culture, it also killed the very person who provided it." She paused to smile and flutter her fingers at two women walking past. "Fitzhugh Holley was sort of a celebrity in his own right, as well, from what I've heard. Wrote a little animal series for children. Something about a cat, I think. They were published, I believe, after he died."

"Callie Cat and Doggie Dan," Gatlin said. "I've seen copies at Holley Hall—under glass, of course."

Martha Kate nodded. "I believe they were on the quilt, too, and several figures—female figures, naturally, since the school was only for young women."

"Your aunt—did she have the quilt when she died?" I asked. "I'd really like to see it."

"I didn't find it among her things. It's a shame really, as it should be on display at the academy. In fact, I asked Gertrude Whitmire about it once, thinking perhaps the quilt had been donated to the museum there, but she didn't seem to be aware it existed."

I must have groaned, because Martha Kate turned to me in concern. "Is anything wrong, Arminda?"

"It's just that we were hoping you might be the one

130

who had it. I'm afraid we've come to the end of the trail, and no one seems to know where the quilt ended up," I told her.

"Oh, I do hope it hasn't been destroyed! Young people now don't seem to value the old family heirlooms as they should . . . " Martha Kate smiled at Gatlin and me. "Present company excepted, of course.

"Aunt Pluma must have been number six on your list—or were you unable to find descendants of the others?"

"We've tracked down all but one," I said and then noticed Gatlin's grin. "Sorry, didn't mean to make them sound like criminals or something, but it's taken a lot of detective work to get this far."

Pluma's niece leaned forward as if she meant to share a secret. "So, who have you spoken with so far?"

I counted on my fingers beginning with Lucy's daughter—my grandmother, Vesta. "And Irene Bradshaw—her mother was Pauline Watts, and then Flora Dennis's granddaughter, Peggy O'Connor. We— I—drove all the way to Cornelia, Georgia, to find her. Your aunt Pluma would make number four. My great-grandmother's sister, Annie Rose, belonged, too, but she drowned in the Saluda when she was only sixteen."

"There was something on the quilt about that, too, I believe." Martha Kate frowned. "A little strip of blue fabric representing a river, and a rose embroidered beside it. I remember Aunt Pluma telling me about your great-aunt. My goodness, she'd be your great-great-aunt, wouldn't she? Her death must have affected the others deeply."

Now she turned to Gatlin, who seemed to be at least making an effort to keep up with the conversation. "I'm sure you've asked your grandmother about all this?"

131

"Vesta couldn't tell us much," Gatlin said. "She said the women passed the quilt among them, but she couldn't remember what happened to it." My cousin looked at me and shrugged. "And from what Minda tells me, the others weren't much help, either."

"Then perhaps Mamie can tell you something," the older woman said. "The last I heard, her mind was sharper than my own."

"Mamie? Was she a friend of your aunt's?" Gatlin shifted her coat from one arm to the other and tried to cover a yawn. It had been a long day, and my cousin was ready to leave. So was I. Almost.

"Mamie Estes was the one you missed. She's number six." Martha Kate looked at both of us and smiled.

"Do you know if she left any descendants we might ask?" I said.

"Unless something's happened in the last couple of months, you can ask Mamie herself," Martha Kate said. "She lives in Charlotte with a daughter-in-law, and the last I heard was still reading a couple of books a week."

"But she has to be at least a hundred and ten!" Gatlin said, letting her wrap slip to the floor.

Martha Kate laughed. "She's no spring chicken, but at last count Mamie must've been about a hundred and two."

"And she was a member of the Mystic Six?" I had started to get up, but sat again. "But that was back in 1916 or '17. How could—?"

"Young people didn't attend what we call high school as many years as we do now. Mamie was probably around fifteen when all this happened. Certainly not much older." Our hostess rose. "I have her address and phone number if you'd like it, and I'd advise you to call first. At a hundred and two, it's best to plan ahead.

132

"And for goodness' sakes," she added as we were leaving, "don't let Mamie talk you into playing bridge! She cheats."

"No," Gatlin said as we hurried to the car.

"No what?"

"No, I can't go to Charlotte with you to track down this Mamie whoever. I'm expecting estimates from two contractors in the morning.

"What's this?" In the car, Gatlin drew out the tiny pajamas Augusta had made that had become wedged behind the passenger seat.

"Pajamas. They're for a baby," I said.

"Well, I can see that, Minda!" Gatlin held them to the light. "What beautiful craftsmanship! They look handmade. Where on earth did you find them?"

"A friend," I said. *And earth had nothing to do with it.* "I meant to drop them off yesterday. Family lives in that little house next to the water tower. The father lost his job."

"Do you know them?" Gatlin folded the pajamas on her lap.

"Not really. I just heard they could use some help," I said, wishing she'd drop the subject.

"So you're just going to knock on the door and give this woman those pajamas? That's a generous thing to do, Minda, but kind of a touchy situation, don't you think? How do you plan to handle it?"

I hadn't thought of that.

And Augusta Goodnight wasn't any help at all. "It was your idea," I said. "You could at least tell me what to say to her. I don't even know the family's name."

"Foster. The baby's mother is Maureen Foster."

133

"But what am I supposed to say?"

Augusta only smiled. "You'll think of something," she said.

The weather was brisk but not too cold when I started out the next morning, and since I needed the exercise after indulging in Augusta's culinary delights, I decided to ride my bike the three or more miles to the small cottage near the water tower. The bicycle had been a birthday present from Jarvis a few months before he died, and since that time I'd kept it in the family garage behind my grandmother's old home. I'd had to inflate the tires a bit, but other than that, it seemed in good shape, and I liked to think he rode along with me as I whizzed past familiar houses on Phinizy Street and on through the heart of town.

Angel Heights was like many villages that grew up willy-nilly around a crossroads over a period of two centuries, and it still hadn't decided where it wanted to go. I kind of liked it that way. Most of the houses (including ours) in the older part of town were built in the early 1900s and were as individual as their owners. A hideous brick Gothic with square pillars and heavy-lidded windows sat next to a sprawling yellow shingled house that had grown in every direction. Simple cottages nudged prestigious colonials, and scruffy, weed-choked yards thumbed noses at manicured lawns next door.

What was left of Minerva Academy, screened from the street by large oaks and surrounded by a shoulder-high stone wall, slept in the pale November sun, and a few blocks down the street the group of retired men Vesta referred to as the Old Farts Fraternity gathered for their usual breakfast of biscuits and gravy at the

Heavenly Grill. I waved at Dr. Hank (who should know better) as he crossed the street to join them and picked up speed outside of town. Tonight my muscles would holler for help, but I knew the exertion was what I needed—even the last curving pull to the top. Panting, I watched a couple of cars zoom past.

Augusta had agreed to go to Charlotte with me as soon as I completed my mission to the Fosters, and I was in a hurry to meet the last living member of the Mystic Six. You don't dally when keeping an appointment with somebody Mamie's age, and for the life of me I couldn't understand why Augusta was so hell-bent—oops, I mean heaven-bent—on my delivering her handcrafted baby gift first thing.

I could think of a lot of necessities the family might need more, I grumbled as I pulled up into the Fosters' lawn and propped my bike on its stand. Few houses populated the two-lane asphalt road leading past the tower, and only a couple of cars had passed me along the way, so I didn't bother to lock up my bike. Besides, all I wanted to do was drop off the pajamas and get on with it, and I still didn't have a clue how I'd explain my visit.

But Maureen Foster didn't seem to be at home when I knocked timidly on her door. Relieved, I placed the tissue-wrapped bundle just inside the screen door and turned to leave, eager to be on my way to Charlotte and Mamie Estes.

"Can I help you?"

A young woman stood in the half-open doorway.

"Uh-yes, I brought . . . " I stooped to pick up the package at my feet, waiting for divine inspiration. Nothing happened.

"Did Louise send you?" Maureen Foster—or I

135

supposed that's who she was—held out a hand for the pajamas. She was small and slender, with bright brown eyes, wore her sleek dark hair cut close, and carried a chubby baby low on her hip.

I gave her the pajamas. "Louise," I said. I felt like I was taking part in a spy-farce and *Louise* must be the password.

"Is this all of it?" The woman shifted the baby a little higher and frowned at the parcel I'd given her. "I hope you've brought more than this."

"Excuse me?" I didn't expect her to fall into a fit of ecstasy over a small pair of pajamas, but this woman wrote the book on rudeness!

"You didn't bring the quilting scraps from Louise? She said she'd send some over today." As she spoke, Maureen slowly unwrapped the bundle and let the paper fall to the floor. "Oh." The baby-size pajamas dangled from her hand. "Why, these are a work of art! Did you—?"

I shook my head. "A friend sent them. She—that is, we thought your little boy might like them."

I closed my eyes. *Might like them? Babies don't like pajamas! Babies like milk and being rocked, silly*! "I meant, we hoped he could wear them."

She held the door wider to let me inside. "You brought these for Tommy? They look like a perfect fit. Thank you!" She stepped aside to lead me into a small living room. "Please, sit down—that is, if you can find a space. Did you say your friend *made* these?"

I nodded, looking about me. Every surface was covered in quilts, or fabric on its way to becoming quilts. "She sews like an angel," I said. "And so do you, it seems."

Maureen placed Tommy in his bouncy seat, and,

removing a stack of what seemed to be Christmas pillow covers, sat on a small chair across from me. "Right now I'm behind in my orders," she said. "Louise Starr sells my things at her shop, Starr Bright, in Charlotte, and this close to the holidays, the demand gets ahead of the supply."

She smiled and offered tea, which I accepted. "Hope you like herbal," she explained. "I'm nursing. You must think I'm bonkers," Maureen said, pouring boiling water into a pot. "Louise sends me quilting scraps whenever she can get her hands on them, and I'm running low on red calico for a couple of crazy quilts I promised. I thought you were dropping them by for her." She smiled and stooped to offer a toy to Tommy. "I'm glad to get the pajamas. He's outgrown most of his others. Thanks."

I smiled back at Tommy, who gave me a toothless grin. "You're welcome."

I noticed how gracefully she accepted the gift—with no questions asked. Her baby needed the pajamas, and I supplied them. If only life could be as simple as that.

Later, over peppermint tea and introductions, Maureen told me her husband, whom she called R.T., had worked for a builder in California, but the cost of living was high there and the climate didn't agree with her, so they moved south to be closer to her family.

"That was soon after Tommy was born," she said. "But the company my husband went to work for here went out of business over a month ago, and he hasn't been able to find permanent work."

I told her I'd ask around and see if I could come up with any leads. "And I hope your quilting scraps arrive soon," I called as I was leaving.

"Now I know why I didn't hear you drive up,"

Maureen said, watching from the porch. "We'll have to bike together sometime. R.T. can baby-sit, and maybe you'll show me the good paths."

"I'd like that," I said, and rode away pleased that my stubborn angel had insisted I become acquainted with Maureen Foster. But I didn't think it was only because Tommy needed pajamas or I needed a biking buddy. Augusta Goodnight had something else up her heavenly sleeve.

According to Maureen's kitchen clock, it was a little after ten-thirty when I left. If I hurried, I could change, collect Augusta, and be in Charlotte in time for lunch. I remembered a barbecue restaurant on the south side that had a drive-in window and was known for its Brunswick stew. Augusta told me she'd sampled the stew in three of the states she'd visited lately, and was eager to see how North Carolina held up.

The idea appealed to me, as well, and I pedaled a little faster, then slowed as I came to the downhill curve.

"Jump!" urged a voice in my ear. Augusta's voice.

"What?" Was I hearing things? What had Maureen put in that peppermint tea?

"Jump, Arminda! *Now!*"

And I pitched off the bicycle and rolled onto the shoulder of the road just as I saw the rope snap taut less than a foot in front of me. Clawing at air, I grabbed the first solid thing I touched, which happened to be a pine sapling, and clung to it, trying not to look down at the ravine that yawned below.

Chapter Fifteen

I CLOSED MY EYES AND SMELLED PINE, FELT resin sticky in my hands.

"There's a root just above you to the right," Augusta said. "Grab it—hurry! Now put your left foot on that rock . . . Can you feel it? Good! No, don't look down!"

I reached for the root just as the sapling broke with a loud crack, and the pine tree gave way in my other hand. Fear sliced through me, cold and sharp, as if I'd been stabbed with an icicle.

My foot found the rock about the same time my heart found its rhythm again, and I slowly pulled myself up to lie dizzy and breathless on a mat of dead-looking vines. Kudzu, I hoped, but with my luck, they were probably poison ivy. Augusta stood above me and had the grace to look at least a little worried.

"Playing it a little close, aren't we?" I said, still gasping. I dug my toes into the rocky soil and did my best to burrow into the earth. Earth is good. Falling to it is not.

"I suppose it was feel and go there for a minute, but you're going to be just fine." *Now* she reached down to give me a hand up. "Let's don't make a mountain out of a gopher hole."

The part of me that wasn't still trembling was grateful to be alive. Both parts were confused. "I guess you mean *touch* and go." I crawled painfully to my knees and noticed for the first time the bloodstained tear in my pants. "As for the gopher hole—"

"Never mind that!" Augusta skirted my bike where it lay beside the road and propelled me to the other side. "Somebody wanted to kill you, Arminda. We have to get you to safety before they try something else!"

I looked back to see the rope, now slack, still attached to a tree on the side of the road where I'd fallen. Somebody had waited until I was almost upon it and then pulled it taut with a sudden jerk. If Augusta hadn't warned me, I would almost certainly have gone over the side and into the rocky ravine. Thankfully I patted my helmet. I hated to wear one, but this time it—and Augusta—had saved me from a severe injury or worse.

"Thank you, Augusta. Didn't mean to seem ungrateful. I'm just glad you came along." *However late*.

I felt her hand on my shoulder, still rushing me. "It's my job, Minda, but please remember I don't always know what's going to happen."

And I'm not sure, but I think she winked at me. "Sometimes, like you, I just have to wing it," Augusta said.

"Did you see who it was?" I asked, glancing over my shoulder at brown leaves scattering across an empty road.

She looked a little sheepish. "I'm afraid I lingered longer than I meant to at the Fosters'. Maureen's quilts are lovely, aren't they? I believe she does them all by hand."

"I didn't know you were there," I said.

"I felt I might be needed. Your cousin was murdered, Minda. This is not a game we're playing, and you're going to have to be more careful. You humans think you're invincible, and I can only do so much!"

Her cheeks were bright pink, and a silken strand of

140

hair fell over her forehead. Augusta shoved it out of the way and marched ahead of me. I had never seen her so annoyed.

When I heard a car coming, I darted into a clump of trees and underbrush, snagging my already-ruined clothing and scratching my cheek on briers, but I didn't recognize the car or the driver, and it passed without incident.

Maureen must have heard me limping up her drive, because she came outside to meet me. "Minda, my goodness, what happened? Is anything wrong?"

It was, and I told her.

"I need to use your telephone to call the police," I said. I hadn't thought to bring my cell phone along.

Maureen had cleaned my cuts and abrasions and brewed another pot of tea by the time the police arrived, and I was glad for the tea and the sympathy. Augusta is long on tea, but she's sometimes short on the other.

This time Chief McBride himself showed up, and I led him to where my bike had skidded into a signpost by the side of the road. "I jumped when I saw the rope across the road," I said, standing well back from the edge of the ravine, "and if I hadn't grabbed a root, I'd have gone right over."

He knelt to examine the broken sapling, the warped front wheel of my bike. "Now, where was this rope?" he asked.

"Just ahead, tied to that tree on the right."

But of course, it was no longer there. "It went all the way across the road and into those trees on the other side!" I looked all around the tree, tramped about the ground, and then checked out the ditch on the opposite side. "It was right here! Somebody must have come back and taken it while I was at Maureen's."

141

Chief McBride shook his head. "Something spooked you for sure. Heck, you're doggone lucky to walk away with scrapes and scratches!" He lifted what was left of my bike into the trunk of his cruiser and leaned against the side of the car. "Do you know of anybody who would want to harm you?"

"Not really," I said, "but my cousin Otto probably didn't know of anybody who wanted to harm him, either." My knee stung like crazy, my head ached, and I still felt a little dazed. "Somebody strung a rope across that road and it was less than a foot from my face." I pointed to the wooded area across from us. "It looks like there's some kind of trail back in there that would be wide enough for a car."

The chief shook his head and frowned; then he opened the passenger door and bowed me into the front seat. (I was glad I didn't have to sit caged in the rear!) He was still frowning when he spoke to his nephew over the radio. "Rusty, better get out here," he said. "Meet me at the water tower soon as you can. Something's been going on up here, and we need to check it out. And hurry. I've a young lady here who might want Doc Ivey to take a look at this bump on her head."

But the two men found nothing when they investigated what looked like the remains of an old logging road a short time later. "Ground's too hard and dry for car tracks," the chief said, "but it does look like somebody might have been in there recently. I found a limb broken off and the grass has been trampled. Did you notice any cars?"

I started to shake my head, and then remembered the two cars that had passed me earlier.

"Don't suppose you'd remember a license number?" he asked.

"No, but one of them was a beige Honda—an Accord, I think." *Just like the one that belonged to Flora Dennis's granddaughter, Peggy O'Connor!*

"Would many people know this was here?" I asked his nephew, who volunteered to drive me back to town.

"Oh, sure. Not many who wouldn't. I used to hike up here all the time with the Boy Scouts. Kids still play up here some." He grinned. "It's just far enough from town so your mama doesn't know what you're up to."

"Surely you don't think this might've been some kind of prank?"

His smile vanished. "No, I don't. Besides, this is a school day—but I'll check the attendance records just to be sure the absent ones are accounted for.

"Did anybody know you were riding up here today?"

"No, not that I know of. It was kind of a spur-of-the-moment thing," I said.

"Then somebody must have followed you. Any idea why?"

"I think it has something to do with Otto's death," I said. "I think he knew something."

He frowned at me as we waited for the light to change. "About what?"

"I'm not sure, but I'd like to find out." I came close then to telling him about finding the pin in the ladies' room at Minerva Academy, but Augusta had warned me not to mention it. To anybody, she said.

"Looks like somebody thinks you might know something, too," Rusty Echols said. "I wouldn't go on any more bike rides if I were you—at least until we find out what's going on."

At the chief's insistence, I let Rusty Echols drop me by the local clinic and was relieved to learn Chief McBride had called ahead and asked them to take me right away. The young doctor who saw me was the same one who had admitted Mildred the week before, and it surprised me when he asked how she was. Doctors see so many patients now, I can't imagine how they keep track of them all.

I was a little reluctant to tell him we didn't know where Mildred was. "She said she was going to visit a friend," I explained, "but we found out later her friend knew nothing about it. Now we're trying to learn where she went." I told him about the taxi driver delivering Mildred to the bus station in Rock Hill. "I'm afraid we've sort of run into a brick wall," I said.

He must have thought our family needed to be kept in a locked, padded room, but he didn't say anything except to tell me to look at a spot on the wall while he shined a light in my eyes. His eyes, I noticed, were kind of a grayish green.

Doc Ivey (whose first name was Harrison, I learned from his tag), said he thought Mildred was a sly one, and that I might have a mild concussion; then he tended my cuts with antiseptic and adhesive bandages.

"Do you have anybody to drive you home?" he asked.

I lied and said yes. The last thing I wanted was to have Vesta or Gatlin fussing over me. Wilbur Dobbins's taxi service would have to do.

"Go home then, and take it easy. No driving today. Will there be anyone with you tonight?"

I nodded. "My grandmother."

"Good. Have her wake you a couple of times during the night." He gave me a brief pat on the shoulder as he started to leave.

"And, Minda?" He hesitated at the door of the examining room.

"Yes?"

144

"How about giving me a call tomorrow? I'd like to know how you are . . . and your friend Mildred, too, of course."

Why in the world did I tell that doctor Vesta would be staying with me? I asked myself as Wilbur drove me home.

I knew the answer, although I didn't like to admit it, even to myself. I wanted Harrison Ivey to know I was single! And did he ask everyone to call him after a bump on the head? I'd like to think he didn't.

Wilbur was still chatting away when we pulled into the driveway. " . . . and I told your grandmama if she planted them rhododemdrams too close to the house, they'd block out all the sun . . . and sure enough, I'll bet it's dark as a dungeon in that front room! My wife's the same way—won't listen to nobody. I said, 'Mae Lynn, if you knew just one fourth as much as you thought you did, you'd be a dad-blamed millionaire!' "

If Mae Lynn had a fraction of a brain, she wouldn't have married Wilbur, I thought as I dug in my pocket for bills. The man talked as if he were announcing a wrestling match, and my head rang with his hollering. All I wanted just then was to run inside and bolt the door behind me.

Chief McBride had left my bicycle with the bent front wheel propped against the garage, and I maneuvered it inside before going into the house. Rusty Echols had told me about a bike shop in Charlotte that might be able to repair it. Maybe I would be able to get an estimate when I drove over to speak with Mamie Estes.

Mamie Estes! I had completely forgotten about my scheduled visit with the last living member of the Mystic Six! I'd phoned that morning to ask if it would be convenient to drop by, and Tess, her daughter-in-law, said they would expect me around two.

It was after one when I stepped inside and glanced at the kitchen clock, and the doctor had advised me not to drive. Besides, I was too shaky right now to venture anywhere—with or without a lick on the head. At least I would have a chance to telephone my excuses and beg off until another day.

"I'm so glad you called! I've been trying to reach you," Tess said when I phoned. "I'm afraid Mamie's a bit under the weather today, and it doesn't take much to tire her."

"I hope it's nothing serious," I said. (How can anything *not* be serious when you're a hundred and two?)

"A little cold, I expect. Why don't you give us a call tomorrow and we'll see? I told her you were coming, and I know she'd like to see you."

I promised to phone in the morning, hoping Mamie wouldn't take a turn for the worse and join the other five Mystics before I could talk with her. "Just my luck!" I muttered, heading for the living room sofa.

"What's just your luck?" Augusta wanted to know.

I told her about Mamie Estes being under the weather. "I'm afraid if I wait much longer, she might be under the ground," I said.

"Then I'd think that would be her misfortune, not yours," Augusta said in her calm, matter-of-fact voice.

Her inflection was less than angelic, I thought. "You're right, of course. As usual. It was a callous thing to say, but my head hurts and I feel rotten. I'm scared to death, Augusta! I don't get almost tossed over a cliff just every day, you know, and I'd just as soon not get used to it. I don't know why you're so annoyed with me," I said. "After all, you were the one who

146

encouraged me to visit Maureen Foster. In fact, you insisted on it."

"That's correct, and I share the blame, Arminda. I should have been more careful, but so should you. I didn't realize you'd be riding a bicycle! Don't you see how vulnerable that makes you?" She plopped a pillow at one end of the sofa and plumped it up, indicating that I was to rest there. A shadow of a frown crossed her brow. "I'm afraid I didn't grasp the seriousness of the situation. I thought we had more time."

"More time for what?" I put my head on the pillow and closed my eyes. The pillow was smooth and cool, and so were Augusta's fingers when she touched my forehead.

"Time to work things out," she said. "I take my work seriously, you know, and I want to keep you safe, but you'll have to do your part."

"Uh-huh," I said, feeling the pain ebb as she stroked my head with gentle fingers. They smelled of the lemon verbena my mother used to grow. "The doctor said to wake me," I said, just before drifting off. "Something about a concussion."

"I know," Augusta said. And of course she would. Hadn't she been trained by Florence Nightingale herself?

I woke to Augusta's humming something that sounded kind of like "Pennies from Heaven" and wondered how she could sing off-key and still be melodious. A clatter came from the kitchen, and something smelled rich and wonderful.

Augusta had drawn the draperies against the dark, and I felt a little safer for it. But if somebody out there really wanted to harm me, they wouldn't have much trouble getting inside.

"Time to wake up," Augusta said, plucking my coverlet aside. "You've slept the afternoon away, and I've made vegetable soup for supper."

I was relieved to find my headache gone, but my appetite was present in full force. "I hope you made a lot," I said, making my way to the kitchen. When the telephone rang, I almost resented the intrusion and started not to answer it, then thought better of it. Otto was dead, and somebody had tried to put me out of the picture, as well. What if something had happened to Mildred? Or Gatlin or Vesta?

Chapter Sixteen

"WHAT'S THIS I HEAR ABOUT YOUR having to go to the doctor?" Vesta wanted to know. "Wilbur Dobbins said you fell off your bike and hit your head. You're not having blurred vision, are you? Do you need me to come over?"

I assured my grandmother that except for a few scrapes and bruises, I was fine. "Doc Ivey didn't seem concerned," I said, "so please don't worry about it. You have a enough on your mind with Mildred and all."

"That Mildred! Do you know I had a message from her on my answering machine when I got back from the dentist's this afternoon? Said she was visiting *family* and would be home soon." Vesta hummed sort of low in her throat—which to her is equal to a growl. "It's a good thing I wasn't there to take the call! I'd have told her a thing or two. Why, I was *that* close to calling the police!"

I didn't know how much *that* close was, but I could guess. "I didn't know Mildred had any family," I said.

"She never talked about them much, but I knew she had relatives somewhere down below Columbia. Once in a while she'd hear from one of them, and a couple of times she went down there to a wedding or a funeral or something, but I got the idea they weren't very close."

Somehow I had always felt we were Mildred's family. "I'm glad she's all right," I said. "At least we can stop worrying now. Did she say when she'd be home?"

"Well, of course not!" Vesta snorted. "That would be the thoughtful thing to do, but I imagine she'll just show up one day and act like everything's hunky-dory."

If only it were, I thought.

I wished Vesta could have asked Mildred if she still had the pills Irene Bradshaw gave her, and I went to bed that night mulling over the list of people who might have tried to do me in with that nasty little rope trick. I wasn't sure Irene had the strength to pull the rope that tight, but she wouldn't have to keep it that way long— just long enough to send me into a terminal skid.

Irene had seemed unusually interested in Otto's bookshop. And I knew Edna Smith had at one time been a Girl Scout leader, because Gatlin had been in her troop. Not only would she know about the logging road behind the water tower, but she'd be familiar with tying knots, as well. And so would her daughter, Sylvie.

Peggy O'Connor was obviously trying to cover up something, and she owned a car similar to the one that had passed on Water Tower Road. But Gertrude Whitmire and her brother, Hugh, were the two who had access to Holley Hall the night Otto was killed, although

149

Otto did have a key and could have let a third party inside. And the local police seemed satisfied the two had nothing to do with it.

Unable to sleep, I went down to the kitchen to find Augusta brewing hot chocolate. "I thought you might could use a cup," she said.

"You really are an angel," I said, and meant it. "I just can't believe somebody I've known all my life murdered Otto and might be trying to do the same to me. These people are our friends, Augusta. It's awful not to know who to trust anymore."

She set the steaming cup in front of me. "Drink up now," she said. "We'll think about it in the morning."

But I was forced to think about it a little earlier than I intended when Rusty Echols phoned the next day just as I was getting out of the shower. All the students who had been absent the day before were accounted for during the time I was thrown from my bicycle, he told me. Except for one.

"We haven't been able to locate Duncan Oliver," Rusty said, "and frankly, I wouldn't be too surprised if the little devil might've had something to do with it. It wouldn't be the first time he's pulled a dangerous stunt like that. I know he was the one who threw that rock from an overpass and damaged some tourist's fancy foreign job, but we never could prove it. Even his own mama can't seem to keep up with him."

"You mean she doesn't know where he is?" I asked.

"I mean nobody answers when I call their place. Checked with the neighbors, and they said Duncan's mom quit her job at the mill and went to work somewhere else. None of them seemed to know where. Hadn't seen either of them for a couple of days."

"What about his father?"

150

"He's not in the picture," the policeman said. "As soon as we locate them, I'll get back to you on this. Meanwhile, I'd stay close to home if I were you.

"By the way," he added, "Chief McBride went back to that place where you said the rope was tied and found fiber strands embedded in the tree bark. It's not much, but at least it's something to go on."

When the phone rang just after breakfast, I hoped it was Rusty or his uncle calling to tell me they'd arrested whoever was making my life miserable, but it was Tess Estes phoning to let me know Mamie was up to having a visitor if it still suited me to come. I told her I'd be there in a couple of hours, and had started out the door when I remembered it might be a good thing to let Vesta know where I was going. There wasn't room in the doghouse for Mildred and me both.

"I don't suppose you've heard from her," I said.

"Not so much as a mumblin' word," my grandmother told me. "And how is your head this morning?"

"Got a lot of straight yellow hair on the outside and not much in the inside," I said. "Other than that, it's okay."

"Ha. Ha." She didn't sound amused. "If that's the best you can come up with, you do need to take it easy today. And just why are driving to Charlotte?"

"I'm going to see Mamie Estes," I told her.

"Who?"

"Mamie Estes. The last of the Mystic Six."

"Oh. Mama always spoke of her as Mamie Trammell," my grandmother said. "You don't mean she's still alive?"

"A hundred and two," I told her. "And every minute counts. Gotta run!"

But before I left, I telephoned the Better Health Clinic

151

and left a message for Dr. Ivey. "Just tell him I called to let him know I'm okay," I told the receptionist.

"If you'll hold a minute, I think I can chase him down for you," she said.

"No, that's all right. Thanks. I'm fine, really. All patched up."

If we spoke on the phone, Harrison Ivey might ask me out. Or maybe he wouldn't, and I wasn't sure which bothered me more. But I couldn't deny that I was attracted to him. The thing that puzzled me the most, I think, was that he wasn't one bit like Jarvis.

Augusta seemed unusually quiet during the drive to Charlotte, but I was reassured by her company, especially after what happened the day before. I tried not to think about where I might have ended up if Augusta hadn't warned me to jump, but I found myself glancing in the rearview mirror every few minutes to see if I recognized the car behind us.

"I don't think we need to worry any more about the idiot who tied that rope across the road," I said, more to myself than to Augusta. "Paddington Bear seems to think it was a local delinquent who's done this kind of thing before."

"Paddington Bear?" Augusta was concentrating on the traffic in the other lane and didn't look at me.

"Officer Echols. He said the boy wasn't in school yesterday, and they haven't been able to locate him."

The angel spoke softly. "Vigilance, faith, and determination—they will see us through."

"Glad to hear it. Those are powerful words. Who said them?"

"I can't remember," Augusta said with a perfectly straight face. "But I think it might have been me."

The Esteses lived in a blue Cape Cod with white trim in an older part of Charlotte, and Tess Estes, a plump, graying woman who looked like she should be on the cover of a *Mother Goose* book, met me at the door. She wore an apron that read, PAY THE COOK . . . FORGET THE KISSES! and a smudge of cocoa on her chin.

"You're just in time! Come join us in the kitchen. Coffee's hot, and I've a batch of molasses cookies ready to come out of the oven."

"It smells wonderful in here!" I trailed happily after her past a living room furnished with overstuffed chintz and velvet Victorian, through a dining room featuring Danish Modern, and into an Early American kitchen, where a child-size old woman sat at a table sprinkling unbaked cookies with red sugar.

"We're trying to get a head start on our Christmas baking," the lady in the apron said, "and please excuse my poor manners." She stuck out a floury hand. "I'm Tess, and this is Mother Estes, cookie decorator extraordinaire. The pastry chef on that TV cooking show's been trying to hire her away from me, but I'm not letting her go."

Mamie Estes completed a ginger snowman's attire with a row of raisin buttons and looked up at me with eyes almost as blue as the gingham curtains behind her. She wore no glasses. "You're Lucy's granddaughter." It was more of an announcement than a question.

"Great-granddaughter," I said, and took the hand she offered. It was so tiny and delicate I was afraid I might crush it in my larger, stronger one.

Tess scooped spicy brown cookies from the baking tin and piled them on a blue spatterware plate that she set in front of us. I bit into a nut-encrusted Christmas

153

tree and thought of Augusta, who was looking on, no doubt, with her mouth watering.

"I came to ask you about the Mystic Six," I said to the woman sitting next to me. "I need your help, Mrs. Estes."

A small blue blaze flared in her old eyes, but only for a second. "What kind of help?" she said.

"I need to know about the quilt, what happened to it."

Mamie Estes broke a cookie in two and it crumbled into her lap. "That's all over and done with. Nobody left but me."

"I know," I said. "Still, it could be important."

Tess looked at me across the table and her eyes signaled, *Don't go there.*

But what else could I do? "I'm sorry," I said to both of them, "but . . . well, things have happened that might have been prevented. Bad things." I couldn't tell her about Otto! What if she dropped dead from the shock of it? However, even in her frail condition, Mamie Estes looked as if she could handle a bombshell or two.

"There's something about that quilt you made back then that might help us to work through a difficult problem now," I told her.

Mamie looked at her daughter-in-law and slowly shook her head. "What does it matter now? I can't see the harm—but why? What good would it do?"

She was reluctant to let the old quilt go, and I didn't blame her. She was the last member and had earned the right to keep it. "If you could just let me see it, that might be enough. I'd understand if you'd rather I not—"

"I don't have it," Mamie said in a voice that didn't seem frail at all. "I'd give it to you if I could." She fumbled in the box of cookie cutters until she found one she liked. It was an angel. "I don't care if I never see the blamed thing again."

"Then who? There's nobody else. You were the last one." I glanced at Tess with what I hoped was a "help me" look, but Tess, upper arms jiggling, thumped dough onto a floured board and rolled it into a plate-size circle.

"Flora had it last." Mamie patted the tabletop with pale twig fingers. "I sent it to her just before she died. We were the last, you see."

"Then it should've come to you. Her granddaughter didn't mail it back?"

She closed her eyes, and I could see I was tiring her, but my guilt was laced with purpose. This woman was my last link to something that happened over seventy-five years ago.

"Didn't think to ask her. It's not something I like to remember," she said.

Ignoring Tess's warning look, I knelt beside Mamie's chair and spoke as firmly and as evenly as I could. I didn't want her to miss my meaning. "Mrs. Estes, what is it about that quilt? Why did you pass it from one to the other?"

Her mouth turned up in a halfway smile. "Hot potato," she said.

I remembered a party game we played as children where we passed an object from one to the other until the music stopped. If you were caught holding the "potato," you had to drop out of the circle.

"You mean nobody wanted to keep it?" I asked.

"It was Annie Rose's quilt," she said, and began to cut out Christmas angels in the dough. I could see she wasn't going to tell me any more.

I was surprised to see by the kitchen clock that it was after twelve noon, and apologized for staying so long. "I didn't mean to intrude on your lunch hour," I said,

155

rising to go. "And I can't tell you how much I appreciate your taking the time to see me."

"Bosh! We don't go by a schedule here," Tess said, wiping her hands on a blue-striped dish towel. "We eat what and when we want, don't we, Mother Estes?"

The old woman grunted something that sounded in the affirmative. "Why don't you and your friend stay for lunch?" Mamie said to me. "Maybe we can play some bridge."

"My friend?" I glanced at Tess, who shrugged.

"That pretty thing over there! She looks just like an angel." Mamie finished a row of angel cookies and smiled at a point near the kitchen doorway.

I thanked her and stammered excuses, then stooped to kiss her cheek as I said good-bye.

"Guess it's time to take a break from Christmas baking," Tess whispered as she walked with me to the door. "She's got angels on the mind!"

"She saw you, didn't she?" I asked Augusta once we reached the car.

Augusta held up a crisp molasses Santa and smiled. "Not only that, but she slipped me a cookie!"

"You certainly don't seem disappointed about the quilt," I said. "Mamie Estes was number six, Augusta. We've run out of members. It looks like none of these people knows what happened to it, and I don't know where else to look."

"What did I tell you about determination?" Augusta said.

"But can't you see we've reached a dead end?"

Augusta's necklace winked violet-gold-plum in the sunlight as she ran the stones through her fingers. "We've only come in a circle, Arminda. Now we have to find out which one isn't telling the truth."

Chapter Seventeen

"I'M PRETTY SURE I KNOW WHICH ONE," I
SAID.

Augusta didn't say anything.

"It has to be Flora's granddaughter. Remember how she reacted when I mentioned the emblem on Flora's gravestone? Downright hostile!"

"Peggy O'Connor. She obviously didn't want to admit her grandmother had any connection to that group. Why, I wonder." Augusta watched traffic whiz past at a busy intersection. "Where do all these people come from? And where are they going in such a hurry?"

"To lunch if they're lucky," I said. "Want to stop somewhere for a bite?"

Augusta said she wouldn't mind if we did, so I picked up some pizza to go, and we ate it in a roadside park. It had been sunny and mild when we started out, but now the air had turned brisk, and a chilling wind sent paper napkins tumbling across the grass. I watched openmouthed as Augusta stood and held out her hand. The napkins did a bobbing little ghost dance and sailed into the nearest trash can.

"I so dislike litter," she said. Then took her time searching for a piece with pepperoni before taking a dainty bite.

"Do you think Mamie's daughter-in-law, Tess, knows why the quilt was so important?" she asked.

"She seemed to be aware that the subject was disagreeable to Mamie, but she'd seen it, of course, said it looked innocent enough to her. Like folk art, Tess said. I don't think Mamie talked much about it. Tess said she didn't remember her ever using it on a bed or anything."

"Then I suppose you'll have to make another trip to Georgia," Augusta said. "There must be some way to make Flora's granddaughter realize the seriousness of the situation."

"You mean *we*, don't you? I don't want to have to face that horrible woman alone. Acts like she has a pole up her ass!"

Augusta let that one pass with an almost imperceptible twitch of her eyelid. "It might be nice if your cousin kept you company this time. I should think she'd want to know what's going on. After all, Otto was her kin, too, and he did remember her in his will."

"If you mean Gatlin, I wouldn't count on it. She's all wrapped up in her own world right now."

"Do I detect a faint hint of resentment here?" Augusta sipped coffee from a paper cup.

I shrugged. "I know she's busy and worried about money and the bookshop and all, but she doesn't seem too curious, either. I hate to drag her into this, Augusta. I haven't told her about finding the pin. I'm not sure she'd want to know. After all, Otto's murder might not have had anything to do with the Mystic Six, and Gatlin doesn't seem to think the quilt is important to what's been going on."

Augusta gathered up the debris from our lunch and tossed it into the trash. "We're not absolutely sure that it is," she said, "that's why it's necessary to learn just what Annie Rose's pin was doing on that bathroom floor."

"I think it must've fallen out of Otto's pocket when

he pulled out his handkerchief." I said. "The police found a handkerchief in his hand . . . But why would Otto be carrying around a pin that belonged to somebody who died before any of us were even born?"

Augusta hurried to the car and wrapped herself in her downy cape until only her face peeked out. "Perhaps you and Gatlin should take time to talk," she suggested.

"About what?"

"Arminda, why don't you tell me what's really bothering you?"

"I miss her," I said. No use trying to keep things from Augusta. "Gatlin's always been there for me, and when Jarvis died she was wonderful. Now she doesn't seem to have time anymore. I'm lonely, Augusta. I don't have anybody."

Two sea-blue eyes looked at me over a puff of silvery cloud. The warmth from them zapped me about midchest.

"I know I have *you*, Augusta, but you aren't here to stay. You said so yourself. One day you'll leave me, too—just like Jarvis and Mama."

I hated how I sounded. Childish and selfish. And jealous. I was jealous of my own cousin, my best friend, because she had a family to come home to at night and I didn't. I didn't like myself at all.

My head began to throb, and Augusta touched it with the tips of her fingers, leaving my temples cool and refreshed. "It's been a rough few days, Arminda Grace Hobbs, but you've endured it well. And I, for one, think you have true grits."

I giggled all the way home.

The light on my answering machine blinked red at me from the table in the hallway, and I almost knocked over

159

a lamp in my rush to push the play button. Maybe the police had found out who had meant to send me tumbling off Water Tower Hill, or it could be Vesta calling to say the errant Mildred had returned at last.

"Arminda, Harrison Ivey. Sorry I missed your call this morning. Just thought I'd check and see how you were . . . " The young doctor hesitated, as if searching for words. " . . . Well . . . I'm glad you suffered no long-lasting effects from your fall. But if you need to get in touch, you can reach me here at the clinic or at home. Just leave a message, and I'll get back to you." And he left his home telephone number.

Augusta stood at the foot of the stairs, listening to every word, and if angels could smirk, her expression would come close. "It does one good to know there are still such caring physicians," she said. "I wonder if he makes house calls."

"For goodness' sake, Augusta, he's only being thorough."

"Of course he is. But aren't you going to call him back?"

"What for? There's nothing wrong with me. My head's just fine."

"I wasn't thinking about your head," she said, and with a flounce of her skirt, she left me standing there.

But Harrison Ivey wasn't my priority just then, and when Augusta disappeared into the attic—to prowl around, she said, and see what might turn up—I did the same downstairs. The day was gray and misty and did little to lift my spirits. I wandered from room to room trying to shrug off the feeling of something missing, something left undone. Augusta had prevented me from falling into a void in the physical sense, but I would have to be responsible for taking care of the other.

160

I put on my all-weather jacket with a hood that had survived since college and set out walking for town and Papa's Armchair. It was time for my cousin and me to talk.

I found her sitting at Mildred's desk in the back of the shop with an apple in one hand and a calculator in the other, and if her face drooped any lower, she'd be under the rug.

I nodded toward the apple. "What's the matter? Find half a worm?"

"Worse than that. I can't even afford half a workman at the prices these contractors charge. I've called just about everybody in the area who would even consider the job, and the three who bothered to give me an estimate are out of the ballpark as far as we're concerned."

I sat on the stool across from her. "Exactly what do you need to have done?"

"For starters, an opening in the connecting wall between the bookshop and the tearoom, restrooms installed and a counter to divide the kitchen space from the eating area." Gatlin clicked off the calculator and tossed it aside. "Dave and I can do the rest ourselves."

"I can help," I told her. "I took a course in wallpapering one time."

My cousin laughed. "But can you knock one down?"

"No, but I might know of somebody who could." I told her about Maureen Foster's husband, R.T. "The contractor he was working for went out of business, and he's looking for a job. From what his wife told me, I think he'd like to go out on his own."

"Do you know if he's any good?" Gatlin asked.

"I wouldn't be surprised," I said. "At least it won't hurt to give him a call." If Augusta had anything to do with this setup, the man came with credentials of the highest order.

I gave my cousin the number and waited while she explained to Maureen Foster exactly what she had in mind. But after a few minutes I found her looking at me strangely.

"Why, yes, she's fine," Gatlin said. "No, she didn't say anything about it . . . and when was this?" Looks as dark as swamp mud came my way. "Thank you for telling me," she added, speaking to Maureen but glaring still at me. "We thought it would be safe to let her out of her padded cell for a while, but I can see we're going to have to double the security."

I was glad Maureen had a sense of humor. I was beginning to lose mine. "You don't believe somebody tried to send me down the hillside by the short route?"

"Of course I do, silly! What's hard for me to believe is why you didn't tell me."

"You have enough to worry about with starting this business and a family to take care of."

"Dear God, Minda, you are my family! Didn't you think I'd care?" Gatlin jumped up from her seat and grabbed both my hands.

"It's just that—well, I didn't think you'd take it seriously. I've been trying to discover what the Mystic Six and the quilt they made had to do with what happened to Otto. I think it might be connected to the way Annie Rose died. You sort of blew me off, Gatlin."

"I'm sorry." She gave my hand a squeeze. "I didn't mean to. I guess I just don't understand why you think there's a connection."

"That's because I didn't tell you everything," I said, and told her about finding the flower-star pin in the bathroom stall next to Otto's. "I was afraid it might put

162

you in some kind of danger if you knew. Guess I should have told you sooner. It's scary without you, Gatlin. Damn it! Dave, Lizzie, and Faye will just have to share!"

"My shoulders are pretty wide," she said, but I couldn't miss the troubled look in her eyes.

"Hey, guess what? I have shoulders, too," I said.

Over coffee at the Heavenly Grill, I told Gatlin about my suspicions concerning the group of young women who made a quilt nobody wanted, and the not-so-heavenly happenings in present-day Angel Heights.

"Obviously somebody thinks you're getting too close to the truth," she said. "Do you think they know you found that pin? You've got to be more careful, Minda. Why don't you stay with us until we get to the bottom of this?"

I thought of the "rock" in her pullout sofa and graciously declined. "I'm fine, really. Keeping the doors locked, and the police are good about checking the house. (Naturally I didn't mention Augusta.) Promise me you won't say anything to Vesta."

Gatlin nodded and frowned at me. "Tell me about the quilt. Why do you think it has something to do with the way Annie Rose died?"

I told her about my visit to Mamie Estes. "She said it was Annie Rose's quilt. Said she didn't ever want to see it again, and her daughter-in-law told me Mamie never talked about it, kept it put away.

Gatlin turned her coffee mug in her hands. "What about the others?"

"You were there when we spoke with Martha Kate, Pluma Griffin's niece, when she told us Mamie Estes was still alive," I reminded her. "And you know about Irene Bradshaw's mother. Aunt Pauline, Vesta called her. You'll have to admit Irene acted kinda spooky about your buying Dr. Hank's building. Maybe there's something in there she doesn't want us to find."

I was surprised to see Gatlin smiling as she shook her head.

"What's so funny?"

"Vesta finally told me why Irene wanted Hank's side of the building left alone." She leaned forward over the table and lowered her voice. "She thinks Bonnie's medical records are in there."

"So?"

"According to our grandmother, Bonnie Bradshaw was what they referred to as 'hot to trot.' In other words, she slept around. Rumor has it she had an abortion when she was in college, and Dr. Hank took care of it." Gatlin shrugged. "Oh, it was all on the up and up. A legal abortion. Bonnie claimed she was raped, and Dr. Hank cleared the way for it, only Vesta says nobody believed it."

"I didn't know Queen Victoria was still on the throne," I said. "All this must've happened close to twenty years ago. Why would Irene even give a fig? Why would anybody?"

"Because of the judge," Gatlin said. "Bonnie's husband, Robinson Sherwood. Strict Baptist upbringing, and you can bet your Sunday shoes he doesn't know about the abortion. Bonnie's never been able to conceive, and I don't know this for sure, but I've heard it's probably due to a pelvic infection from her earlier flings. Vesta says they've applied for adoption, and if this got out, it might ruin their chances for that as well as cause a rift in the marriage."

"But even if the records are still there, they'll be destroyed. Besides, it sounds like a lot of people already know it. It's old news, Gatlin. If Bonnie's husband hasn't heard it by now, I doubt he ever will. Poor, silly Irene! I can't believe she'd worry about something as unlikely as that." And then I remembered that it had been Irene Bradshaw who had given Mildred the over-the-counter anti-acid pills the night she got so sick.

"What about that woman in Georgia?" Gatlin asked. "Flora . . . somebody's granddaughter."

"It all comes back to her," I said. "Mamie says Flora had the quilt when she died, and her gravestone is engraved with that six-petaled flower with the star in the center—just like the pin they wore, but Peggy—that's her granddaughter—denies knowing anything about it. Got right testy about it."

Gatlin sighed and shoved her cup aside. "Spooky."

"I know. I dread facing the witch again, but it looks like I don't have a choice."

As we left, I noticed Sylvie Smith in line behind us waiting to pay her bill. I nodded, but she didn't seem to recognize me. Edna, who was putting on her coat, waved when she saw us. How long had they been there?

I opened the restaurant door to a blast of cold air as we stepped outside.

"First I think we should check out the place where it all began," my cousin said.

"What do you mean?"

"I mean Minerva Academy," Gatlin said.

Chapter Eighteen

"**N**OW?" I LOOKED AT MY WATCH. IT WAS almost four o'clock, and the sky was that dirty dryer lint color that on rainy November afternoons, suddenly wraps you in gray. Daylight was almost gone.

"What better time? My two are spending the afternoon at Vesta's," Gatlin said. "I'll have to make it kinda fast, though. I need to pick up some things for the church Thanksgiving basket on the way home. Monday's the last day, and Vesta will have my head if I forget."

The idea of going back inside that building made me wish I'd stayed at home. I dragged my feet. "But—"

"Mrs. Whitmire should still be there if we hurry," Gatlin said, grabbing my arm. "Come on, get the lead out, Minda!"

The grounds of the old academy had been preserved pretty much as I imagine they were a hundred years ago, and it was easy to visualize young girls in long dresses strolling arm in arm along the curving paths. I always considered that period in history an innocent time, and in my mind, the schoolgirls are usually whispering, laughing over some benign secret. Even though the huge oaks had shed most of their leaves, the campus was shadowed by tall hollies clustered along the paths; wind ruffled the spreading cedar that almost concealed the arched entrance.

A light shone from the hallway, and I could see someone moving about in the dimly lit parlor. Holley

Hall had been built of dark red brick that had become even darker with time, and the mock Gothic arches along the porch seemed too heavy for the building. A wisteria vine, now bare of leaves, twisted to the third story, where Otto had sometimes worked in the school's library, and above that squatted a cupola that was said at one time to have housed a bell.

"My goodness, you startled me! I was just getting ready to close up for the day." Gertrude Whitmire switched on a lamp beside her desk and dumped her tan leather purse into a drawer. "I didn't expect visitors this late on such a dreary afternoon, but there's still time to look around, if you like. Is there something you girls would especially like to see?"

I'd seen enough of that place to last me a lifetime, but I wouldn't mind having another look at our great-grandmother's hand-stitched alma mater, and said so.

"Of course, Arminda. I believe you know where to find it," our hostess said.

"Is it all right if we look around upstairs?" Gatlin asked. "I'd like to see where Otto spent so much of his time. I promise not to bother anything."

"You're welcome to browse as much as you like," Gertrude Whitmire said. "I hope you won't mind if I don't give you a guided tour. I'm afraid my ankle's still a bit swollen, and I'm trying to avoid stairs if I can."

The bruise on Gertrude's cheek had yellowed, and the scrapes on her hands hadn't quite healed. The cane, I noticed, leaned against the desk within easy reach.

"I'll be up in a minute!" I called as Gatlin started up the heavy oak staircase.

The door to the parlor was closed, but a light still burned on a table by the window. The room was damp and stuffy, and I pulled my jacket closer about me and

167

hurried to where I knew the needlework hung on the other side of the fireplace, hoping to find something I might have missed. From all I'd learned, the Mystic Six had been a tightly knit group, and it looked as if the secret or secrets they harbored would die with Mamie Estes—unless Lucy Westbrook had stitched a message somewhere on the sampler.

But only a pale rectangle marked the place where it had hung.

"It's gone! It's not here!"

I don't know how long I stood there staring at the spot where the framed needlework had hung, as if I could make it reappear.

"Did you say something, Arminda?" Mrs. Whitmire paused in the doorway, magazine in hand, and I had the distinct notion I had disturbed her reading.

"The alma mater. It's not here."

"What do you mean, it's not there?" Even hobbling, the woman almost bulldozed me in her haste to cross the room. "Why, I can't imagine where it would be. I could almost swear I dusted that frame this morning . . . or maybe it was yesterday . . . well, sometime this week."

"Maybe your brother had it reframed," I suggested, hoping I was right.

"Hugh? I doubt it. That costs money, and there was nothing wrong with the frame it was in. But you know, there was a woman here yesterday who seemed unusually interested. I wonder . . . " Gertrude Whitmire twitched a window drapery, glanced behind a chair as if she thought someone might have hidden it there, and then—apparently seeing my disappointed expression—put a hand on my shoulder. "I'm sure it will turn up. Someone might have accidently broken it, and I expect Hugh has put it away somewhere. You'd be surprised at how some parents let their children run wild in here!"

"That woman," I said. "The one who was here . . . Do you remember what she looked like? Maybe she signed the guest register."

Gertrude frowned, hesitating. "You know, she might have. Why don't you take a look? The register's on that stand in the hallway."

I riffled hurriedly through its pages, but the last visitors to sign the book had been there over a week before.

"Would you say she was sort of fiftish—neat, with graying blond hair?" I asked.

Gertrude considered that. "Well, yes, now that you mention it, she did look something like that. Is she someone you know, Arminda?"

"I'm not sure," I told her, wondering if Peggy O'Connor had been here before me.

Upstairs I found Gatlin examining old photographs and yellowed mementos from the early days of the academy on a glass-enclosed table in the center of the library. She turned when I came in. "Can you believe this, Minda? The class of 1913 had only eight members. When did Lucy graduate?"

"Several years after that I think. Vesta said she and some of the others stayed on as teachers' assistants and took advanced courses for college credit."

"I'm shocked. I thought Great-grandma already knew everything!" Gatlin made a face. "Here's a first edition of those little animal books the professor wrote."

I told her about the missing alma mater, and we looked to see if Hugh Talbot had put it away somewhere in the library. I wasn't surprised when we didn't find it. "Do you think Wordy Gerty would mind if we looked through some of these old yearbooks?" I asked.

"Can't. The case is locked. We can ask, though. Maybe she'll let us have the key."

"Want me to ask?"

"That's okay. Besides, she kinda likes me. I was one of her better students." My cousin flung out her arms and twirled in what she must've considered a boastful dance. "Also, I have to go to the bathroom. Need to come?"

"Are you kidding? I'd tie my legs in a knot before I'd go in that room again!" In fact, I wasn't too comfortable waiting upstairs alone and wished I'd told Augusta where I'd be.

I was glad when I heard Gatlin's quick, light steps on the stairs. "Gert says make it snappy," she said, holding up a small key. "She has a meeting tonight and has to run by the grocery store on the way home."

The yearbooks were greenish brown and the binding was nothing but string. The title, *The Planet*, and a likeness of something that looked like Saturn were embossed in gold on the cover. We each took one and placed them carefully on a table by the window. Mine opened to a pressed flower—a rose, I think—and I wondered who put it there. I was surprised to see that a lot of the posed photographs weren't all that different from the ones you find in annuals today—except, of course for the clothing.

A group of young women in dark bloomers and middy blouses posed with tennis rackets. Members of the Equestrian Club—ten in number—sat sidesaddle on their mounts.

"Here's our Lucy," Gatlin pointed out. "Class president, of course. She must've been a senior that year . . . and would you look at her list of credits! There's hardly room for them all: editor of the school paper,

170

member of the student council, Minerva Singers, lab assistant . . . blah, blah, blah! Was there anything she couldn't do?"

"Doesn't sound like she did such a bang-up job of looking out for her younger sister," I said, and was immediately sorry for saying it.

Lucy Westbrook's pretty young face smiled out at us from an oval in the center of the page. Her hair looked as if it might have been the same auburn as my mother's and Gatlin's, and her eyes were large and dark, but her mouth and the set of her chin could have been my own. "I didn't mean that," I whispered aloud more to myself than to her picture.

"I wonder if there's a copy of the school newspaper somewhere," I said. "Says here it was called the *Minerva Minutes*. Lucy was editor. Be interesting to see what she wrote."

"I'll look again, but I didn't see anything like that in the case. Could be somewhere else . . . "

I think my cousin continued speaking, but I didn't hear what she said because I had just found a picture of the young girl who died, and I couldn't pinpoint it exactly, but something practically jumped out and conked me on the noggin, shouting, *Look at me!* Annie Rose Westbrook reminded me of someone else, someone I knew: not my mother, or Gatlin, or even Vesta. It was in the tilt of her eyes, the tiniest hint of a widow's peak, and a smile that even now looked like a token gesture for the photographer. I felt as if I were looking at a younger version of Mildred Parsons.

"Gatlin, look at this and tell me what you think!" I held up the book for my cousin, but she quieted me with a raised hand.

"Wait a minute! Is that Gert calling?"

171

I listened while Gatlin rose and went out to the landing. I could hear Gertrude Whitmire yelling from below.

"Somebody wants me on the phone," Gatlin called from the doorway. "I can't imagine who!"

I hurried after her downstairs to find Mrs. Whitmire standing beside her desk while speaking to someone on the phone.

"Yes, she's coming. She's right here," she said. "Hold on just a minute.

"Something about a dog," she whispered, handing the receiver to Gatlin.

"Oh, Lord—that bad Napoleon! Don't tell me he's gotten out again!" Gatlin reached for the phone. "Yes, this is Gatlin Norwood. Is there a problem with Napoleon? Hello . . . " She shrugged and frowned. "Oh, dear! I see. Is he still out there? Can you see him?" My cousin made a face and rolled her eyes. "Right. Of course. I'll get there as soon as I can.

"That was Mabel Tidwell from across the street. Good grief, does the woman have built-in radar? Wonder how she tracked me down Anyway, gotta go. Seems Napoleon's taken a liking to her azalea bed."

"Uh-oh! Is he still there? Want me to help you chase him down?"

"If I hurry, I think I can corner him. Mabel was watching from the window, trying to keep track of the silly beast. Poor woman just moved in this fall and already my dog's destroying her yard. Guess we won't be on her Christmas cookie list!"

Gertrude stepped from the bathroom, purse tucked under her arm. "I hope it's nothing serious. Can I give you a ride somewhere?"

"Thanks. I left my car at the bookshop, but you can

drop me there if you don't mind." Gatlin sighed. "This is the second time this week! Looks like we'll have to build a higher fence."

The older woman dug in her purse for keys and jangled them impatiently. "I really have to run if I'm going to make that meeting. Arminda, I'm sure you won't mind locking up?"

I was sure I would, but how did you argue with the queen of routine?

"Just be sure you lock that case before you leave and turn off the lights upstairs. You can leave the key in my desk, and the front door will lock behind you." Gertrude shifted her weight to favor her injured ankle, and I could see she was trying to hide her pain. "I wouldn't mind waiting, Arminda, but Gatlin doesn't have much time—"

"No, it's all right. You go on. I'll only be a few minutes." *Just long enough to see if I can find more in the academy yearbook about my long-dead aunt.*

I switched on every light within reach as soon as the door closed behind them and practically raced up the stairs to the third floor. *The Planet* lay where I had left it, and this time I went through it page by page from start to finish, making note of any mention of the girls who had belonged to the Mystic Six.

Flora and Annie Rose, decked out in flowing white and trailing garlands, were featured as members of the May Court. Irene's mother, Pauline, with dark curls and dimples, presided over the French Club. Pluma Griffin and Mamie Trammell belonged to the Happy Hikers and the Watercolor Society, the latter of which, had Lucy for treasurer.

I became so fascinated with the girls' various activities, I almost forgot what I came to look for. How did they have time to fit studies into their busy

173

schedule?

If the yearbook was anything to go by, these were six normal girls enjoying the privilege of a select private academy before marriage and family set them upon a plotted course for life. Except for the secretive group they belonged to and the "hot potato" quilt, I could see nothing unusual about them.

Other than copies of *The Planet*, the glassed-in case held a couple of textbooks; a composition book open to an essay on "Choices," written in a graceful, flowing script; a small handbook listing the rules of the academy (I planned to come back to this one later); a maroon felt cap monogrammed with an *M* and the year *1915*, and several class photographs taken in front of Holley Hall.

The building settled about me as tired old houses seem to do at the end of the day. *Don't you know it's time to go home?* It seemed to say. *I'm tired. Leave me alone!*

Somewhere below me a stair squeaked. Old timbers popped and groaned at the onset of evening, and I had to fight the instinct to crawl into a corner and hide. Only there was no place to hide, and imagination or not, I knew it was time to get out of Holley Hall.

I heard the clock in the hallway downstairs strike five and hurried to put the yearbooks back into the case and lock it before leaving. And as much as I disliked the idea, I turned off the overhead light before pulling the door shut behind me. The lights I had left burning earlier should give me more than enough illumination from below.

But the stairwell was as dark as the thoughts I was having, and the only light came from a street lamp somewhere outside. Too late I heard the muffled step behind me, then heavy fabric, musty and smothering, came down over my face and arms, and before I had time to struggle, pain ricocheted through my head. I felt myself pitching forward, and this time there was nothing to grab on to.

Chapter Nineteen

*I*NSTINCT TOLD ME TO GO LIMP—WHICH WASN'T a problem, since I didn't have the strength to struggle, and every time I tried to move, the Fourth of July exploded in my head. Whatever had been thrown over me had been collecting dust for at least a hundred years, and I coughed and gasped for air, making the situation even worse. Somebody standing over me grunted as he tugged at the fabric, and I cried out as what felt like a foot came in contact with my back, rolling me into a close, suffocating shroud.

I fought to free my hands, but they were pinned to my sides, and I was being dragged like a bundle of dirty sheets over creaking wooden floors.

And where was Augusta? No wonder she was a temporary guardian angel! She probably couldn't hold a permanent job.

But she had warned me, hadn't she, about doing my part? About not allowing myself to become vulnerable. And what had I done? I had left the house without telling her and ended up in the very place where my cousin Otto met his end.

The person push-pulling me grunted and panted, and thankfully stopped to rest now and then as he hauled me inch by inch across the floor. If only I could delay him until somebody came! Augusta had told me angels don't usually swoop down and rescue people, but this time I think God might allow just a little swoop. After all, this seemed to be a matter of life and death. *My* life. *My* death.

If only I could see! I struggled to move my arms, tear the smothering cloth from my face, but I couldn't work them loose. My breathing came too fast, and my heart beat so loud I thought it would explode.

Jarvis, how could you let this happen to me!

But Jarvis was gone, dead, and it looked as if I might soon join him. I wasn't ready.

This person was going to kill me, and Augusta wasn't going to fly down and snatch me up. The only one who could save me was *me*.

Save your strength, Minda!

The direction came from somewhere within me, and I let myself go lax. If only Gatlin would come back! Or Gertrude Whitmire. Anybody! My head struck something hard, and I yelled out. That would definitely leave a bruise—if I lived that long. I had been struck in the hallway, and if I wasn't completely turned around, we must be near the stairwell.

The stairwell. Whoever had waited for me in the dark hall meant to pitch me over the railing!

I couldn't free my arms, but I had enough leverage to bring my knees to my chin. I tucked in my head, doubled into a ball, and heaved myself toward what I hoped was the opposite direction. It might only delay at best, but I would snatch whatever time I could. By damn, I wasn't going to make this easy!

The person who had been dragging me made some kind of hissing noise, and what must have been the toe of a shoe grazed my shin. I squirmed into a sitting position, inching backward until I was braced against the wall, and prepared myself for a fight.

In silence I waited for the inevitable jerk or the prod of a heavy shoe, my muscles tensing in expectation. The quiet became more threatening than the sound of someone moving about, because I didn't know what to expect or when to expect it, and so I sat, almost afraid to breathe. What were they waiting for?

My nose began to itch, and I couldn't free my hands to scratch it.

Your nose does not itch, Arminda Hobbs! Think of something else . . . something pleasant . . . like that good-looking young doctor whose call you didn't return . . .

A door opened, and heavy footsteps thumped in the hallway below, then hesitated on the stairs. Someone was coming. "Dear God in heaven, what's this?" A man spoke; his footsteps grew louder, closer.

I felt a hand on my shoulder and kicked out, wriggling from his grasp.

"Hey! Watch it! I'm not going to hurt you."

I heard him groan and strain as he stooped beside me. "How in the world did you get all trussed up like this? What's been going on here?"

Now I recognized the voice. Hugh Talbot. You might know he'd try to blame me for almost becoming a victim in his precious academy.

"Wait a minute now—they've got the blasted thing tied with a cord or something!"

I stiffened as clumsy hands pushed and tugged at me, took long breaths as the dusty cloth loosened.

I sat up and shook off the last of the mummylike wrappings: thick velvet draperies that looked as if they'd once been blue, and stared into the owlish eyes of Fitzhugh Talbot.

They blinked at me. His hairpiece bristled like a worn hairbrush, and his face was a dusky gray. In fact, the whole place was gray because no one had turned on a light. "Arminda," he said, looking closer. "Is that you?"

Before I could reply, the front door slammed open

below and I heard somebody taking the stairs at least two at a time. "Minda! Are you in here? Is everything all right?" Gatlin called. "Why is it so dark up there?"

My legs weren't so shaky, I found, that I couldn't run to meet her.

Again we sat in the dismal front parlor of Minerva Academy and waited for the police. And this time, out of consideration (or fear of a lawsuit?) for what I'd been through, Hugh Talbot had turned up the heat. Still, I shivered as I sat in the burgundy velvet chair pulled close to a gas fire that hissed and curled, then hissed again.

"I thought something was wrong when I got home and found Napoleon still in his pen," Gatlin said. "Then Mabel Tidwell said she'd just come home from her sister's in Greenville and hadn't called me about the dog or anything else.

"I tried to phone you here, Minda, but all I got was voice mail." My cousin stood beside me, her hand on my shoulder. "You're going straight to the emergency room as soon as we leave here. Are you sure you feel like waiting for Chief McBride?"

"What's another knot?" I tried to shrug, but it hurt too much. "It'll match the one on the other side of my head." I was so glad to be alive and out of those awful wrappings, I didn't mind waiting for medical attention if it would bring us closer to finding out who was in such a hurry to send me out of this world.

"At first I thought it was somebody playing a joke," Gatlin said. "One of Dave's students, maybe. I could just imagine some of those clowns watching from a parked car somewhere and laughing while I made a fool of myself yelling for Napoleon."

179

"What made you change your mind?" I asked.

Her hand tightened on my arm. "I don't know. Something. Sounds kinda crazy, I know, but it was almost like a voice whispering in my ear, telling me to get over here in a hurry."

Hugh Talbot had been standing quietly by the window, watching, I assume, for the police. Now he turned to me. "Arminda, I wouldn't have had this happen to you for anything in the world. We're going to get to the bottom of this. I promise."

"I'm sorry I kicked you," I said. "I thought it was—whoever hit me over the head coming to finish me off."

"Do you have any idea who it might've been?" Gatlin asked. "Did they say anything? Could you tell if it was a man or a woman?"

"All I heard was a lot of grunting and panting," I said. "Whoever it was is probably soaking in a hot bath right now."

I said that without looking at Hugh Talbot because I wasn't completely sure it hadn't been him. He had happened on the scene just before Gatlin came bursting through the door and charged up the stairs. How could I be sure he hadn't been there all along, and had seen her coming from the window in the upstairs hall, then saved his skin (and mine) by playing the hero?

Gertrude Whitmire and Chief McBride reached the academy at the same time, but Gertrude, being the pushier of the two, had the first say.

"Arminda, please tell me you're all right!" she demanded, descending on me with cane in hand and Hershey on her breath. "I was carrying my groceries inside when Hugh phoned to tell me what happened! And I was the one who asked you to stay. I feel terrible, just terrible!" And she stationed herself across from me

180

as if she meant to make herself my permanent guardian.

"Let's take a little walk," the chief suggested after noting the stories from Hugh and Gatlin. "I imagine you're about ready for some fresh air."

And I was, although I realized he wanted to question me away from the others.

"Now, tell me," the chief said as we paused where the pathway curved away from the building. "Who knew you were coming here today?"

"It was sort of a spur-of-the-moment thing," I told him. "Gatlin and I decided to browse around the old library as we were leaving the Grill this afternoon. Nobody knew we were coming."

"Was anyone else with you? Or could somebody have overheard?"

We sat on a cast-iron bench that felt cold all the way through my pants, and yellow light from a lamp behind it made shadows loom on the walk. "Sylvia Smith was there with her mother, but I don't think they were listening to what we said," I told him.

"Maybe Gatlin or Mrs. Whitmire mentioned it to somebody after they left here earlier," I suggested. *Or Hugh Talbot might have been waiting for his chance.*

The chief took my elbow to escort me inside just as his nephew and another policeman pulled up alongside Gertrude's car, parked near the front steps. Her groceries—or some of them, I noticed, were still on the front seat.

The boy, Duncan Oliver, they had suspected of causing my bicycle accident, had already been living in Columbia at the time, the younger policeman told me.

"We'll question everybody in this blasted town if we have to!" Chief McBride said, glaring at the ground as we walked. "You get on over to the doctor now and

181

have 'm take a look at you, and if you think of anything else that might help us, give me a call, all right?"

I nodded. He was a kind man, and I was close to tears—if I tried to speak, there would be no stopping them.

Harrison Ivey wasn't on duty at the emergency room—thank goodness! The poor, helpless victim is not the image I like to project, and I'd just as soon he not learn about my recent misadventure. The staff nurse checked me over and gave me something for my headache, and at Gatlin's insistence, I went home with her for the night, stopping by the Nut House only long enough to grab a toothbrush and pajamas.

While inside, I sensed an atmosphere of—dare I say it—annoyance of a most unangelic nature and found Augusta stewing over a basket of needlework in the upstairs room that had been my grandmother's. Her long fingers moved almost faster than the eye could see as the needle wove in and out of what seemed to be a pile of old socks.

"I thought you hated darning socks," I said.

Augusta didn't look up. "I said I *dislike* mending things," she said. Two red spots the size of fifty cent pieces burned on her cheeks. "I also *dislike* it when someone goes back on her word."

"Look, Augusta, I'm sorry. I know I promised to be careful, but I only meant to stop at the bookshop. If I had known—"

"But you didn't know, and I didn't know where you'd gone. Fortunately I was able to get a message to your cousin. I assume she reached you in time to prevent—"

"Minda! Need any help up there?" Gatlin, who had followed me inside, called from the landing.

"No thanks! Be down as soon as I can scrounge up some clean underwear!" I hollered back.

"I don't guess you found anything in the attic?" I said to Augusta in an attempt to get her off my case.

"As a matter of fact, I did: your grandmother's christening dress, your mother's birth announcement, and a composition book that might have belonged to Lucy."

I heard Gatlin's footsteps on the stairs. "Minda? Who are you talking to up here? I do believe you've had too many licks on the head!"

"I told you I had a guardian angel," I said.

"Then if I were you, I'd get rid of her. Her performance of the last few days leaves a lot to be desired."

"I'm thinking about it," I said, making a face at Augusta.

Still, I noticed that she followed me down the stairs and would probably be waiting at Gatlin's. At least I hoped she would.

Chapter Twenty

GATLIN AND DAVID MADE THE ULTIMATE sacrifice of spending the night on the pullout sofa so I could have their bed, but I might as well have been trying to sleep on a truckful of gravel rumbling down a mountain pass for the way I flopped about. Every time I closed my eyes I could almost feel that dusty velvet closing in on me, relive the helplessness of not being able to use my arms.

I rubbed my left forearm where an indentation had

remained hours after I was freed. Gertrude Whitmire said the draperies had been taken from one of the third-floor rooms and left on a chair while the windows were cleaned for the holiday season. "I meant to get rid of those old things," she told us, "but after what happened to Otto, it didn't seem important. I forgot they were there."

Whoever attacked me had tossed the fabric over my head and then hit me from behind with something heavy—probably the metal doorstop—that was meant to knock me out.

"The thickness of those old curtains probably saved your life," the chief told me. "If you hadn't fought back, then gone limp the way you did, they would've pitched you straight down that stairwell."

The rope used to bind me after I was mummy-wrapped in the draperies was the kind found in every hardware store, but the police planned to do a fiber analysis to see if it matched the strands found in the tree on Water Tower Road.

After kicking off my covers for the third time, I looked up to see Augusta standing there with a mug of something hot. I've never liked milk, hot or cold, but I hated to hurt her feelings, so I sat up and pretended to be pleased.

"Don't worry, it's not milk, it's tea," she said. "Lemon ginger. It'll relax you, help you sleep."

I thanked her and chugged it right down.

The telephone woke me, and I could tell from the light outside, I'd slept most of the morning away.

Gatlin stuck her head around the door. "Good, you're awake! How's the head?"

"Full of marbles, but I'll be okay after I've had

coffee." I threw an arm over my eyes to shut out the sun. "What time is it?"

"Almost ten . . . and guess what? The prodigal has returned."

I rubbed my eyes. "Huh?"

"That was Vesta calling. Mildred's back!"

"Did she say where she's been so long? Why she didn't let us know where she was going?"

"She's not saying much of anything, according to Vesta, but she'd damn well better talk to me!"

My cousin plopped on the bed beside me. "Do you feel like going with me? I'm going to find out what all this is about if it kills me."

"Don't say that!" I shivered under the covers, thinking of what had happened the day before. But I didn't want to miss out on this. "Where is she?" I asked.

"In her little rooms behind the shop. Where else?" Gatlin stood to examine her reflection in the mirror and made a face. "Yah! Bad-hair month! Dave's taking the girls to Sunday school and church, and he'll pick up sandwiches or something and meet us at the bookshop for lunch. That should give us at least a couple of hours to worm something out of Mildred. Coming?"

"Wouldn't miss it," I said.

On the way to Mildred's, Gatlin told me she'd spoken with Maureen Foster's husband, R.T. "He called last night and promised to come by and look at my disaster, see if he thinks it's worthwhile."

Although she tried to make light of it, I knew Gatlin's hopes were riding on this project. Under Otto's management, Papa's Armchair barely turned a profit. Vesta had said as much. Incorporating a tearoom would fill a need in the community as well as bring in more customers, but I wasn't sure it was worth the expense.

185

My cousin must have been reading my mind. "Sometimes you have to spend money to make money," she said, pulling into a space in front of the shop. "Anyway, it's too late to turn back now. Dr. Hank's promised to have all those old records removed tomorrow."

"What's he doing with them?" I thought of Irene Bradshaw's paranoia about her daughter's secret.

"Don't worry, they'll be destroyed. Told me he should've had it done long ago, but nobody wanted the storage space, so he just left 'em there."

"I hope he reassures Irene," I said. "And speaking of Irene, did Vesta find out about those pills she gave Mildred?"

"She didn't say anything about it. We can add that to our list."

Gatlin had a "don't mess with me" look on her face as she unlocked the door of the bookshop, and just then I wouldn't have wanted to be in Mildred Parsons's shoes.

But Mildred, though frail, was up and ready for us. We hadn't called ahead on purpose, but I guessed she must have expected us.

We found her at her desk in the tiny back office, and she looked up, adjusting her bifocals, when she heard us come in. "Good morning," she said, as if she'd been there all along.

"Mildred, where on earth have you been?" Gatlin stood, arms folded, in front of her. "We were worried to death, and you can imagine how we felt when we learned you lied about visiting Lydia Bowen!"

Mildred flinched. She tried to cover the expression, but I saw it. *Lie* is a strong word.

However, she didn't deny it. "I had my reasons," Mildred said. "I'm sorry if I caused concern, but this is something I had to do, and I had to do it alone."

And I had thought only John Wayne talked like that. "Are you going to tell us what that was?" I said.

"You know, of course, I have family down in Brookbend. There were certain things there I needed to look into."

Obviously seeing my puzzled expression, Mildred went on to explain. "I doubt if either of you've ever been to Brookbend. There's not much there, and it's out of the way—a little farming community about fifty miles below Columbia, but I still have relatives there. It's where I was born and raised, and my parents are buried there."

I waited for her to continue. She didn't.

"I don't understand why you couldn't have let us know where you were going," I said. "We were more than *concerned*, Mildred. Vesta was about ready to call the bloodhounds out on you."

"Was it really so important that you couldn't tell *us*?" Gatlin asked. "Why all the mystery?"

Mildred thumbed through papers on her desk and picked up a pencil. "I'd rather not discuss that just now, and I'd be grateful if you didn't pursue it." Her announcement had a period as big as a grapefruit at the end, and I knew there would be no use in questioning her further.

I glanced at Gatlin, who looked as if she might spew cinders, but she only shrugged and turned away. I followed her to the front of the shop.

"It won't do a bit of good to keep after her when she's like this," my cousin muttered. "Might as well leave her alone for now."

I remembered that we'd forgotten to ask Mildred about the stomach medicine Irene had given her, and

187

mentioned it to Gatlin.

"I'm about ready to slip her some arsenic myself!" she sputtered, "but go on and ask her if you think you'll get a civilized answer."

Mildred Parsons doesn't scare me, I told myself. After all I'd been through, I was prepared to stand up to the devil himself! After all, I had an angel on my side. I marched back to stand beside her.

Mildred raised an eyebrow at me and went on scribbling.

"Do you remember Irene Bradshaw giving you some kind of pills for your stomach the night you got so sick?" I asked in a voice too loud to ignore.

"Of course." She didn't look up.

"Do you still have them?"

She sighed and folded her hands in front of her. "A few I think. I took most of them in Brookbend . . . a most unsettling experience."

"And they didn't make you sick?"

"Certainly not! Why would Irene give me something that would make me sick? Frankly, they were most helpful. I wish I'd known about them earlier."

"Do you think you might spare a couple? I think I ate something that disagreed with me last night. My stomach's giving me fits."

"My goodness, Arminda, why didn't you say so? They're over there in my purse . . . Let me see . . . I'm sure I didn't take them all." Mildred dug in her pocketbook and brought out a flat cardboard box. "Here they are! Good, I thought so. You may have the rest."

I thanked her and tucked the box into my pocket, then turned to find Gatlin holding up two fingers in a victory sign behind Mildred's back. Surely the medication was harmless if Mildred had continued taking it with no bad

188

results. Also, the pills were the kind you punch out from a foil packet, and I didn't see how they could have contained anything like a strong narcotic, but it wouldn't hurt to have the remaining ones checked out.

"I don't guess Mildred knows about Otto's leaving his share of the shop to you?" I whispered as I helped Gatlin sort through boxes.

She shook her head. "I'm letting Vesta take care of that. And we had talked about adding a tearoom, so that's no surprise. Also she'll be getting an annuity, so financially, she'll be okay."

"From Vesta?"

"Well, yes, but as far as Mildred's concerned, Otto arranged it in his will."

"I never knew Otto was so thoughtful," I said.

My cousin laughed. "Neither did Otto." She stood and stretched. "So what now?"

"About the bookshop or Mildred?"

"Neither, silly! What do we do about you? About somebody who obviously doesn't have your welfare at heart. It's all because of that pin you found when Otto died—I know it is! Somebody thinks you're getting a little too close, and they want you out of the way before you find out any more."

"It's the quilt," I said. "I keep coming back to that old quilt."

"Then let's find the damn thing! What about that woman in Georgia? The one whose grandmother had it last?"

"Peggy O'Connor. She pretended she didn't know what I was talking about, but she was lying through her pearly whites."

Gatlin thought about that. "Then let me have a go at her. I'll set her straight."

"But what if she's the one trying to stop me?" I said. "Come to think of it, all the bad things started to happen after I paid her a visit." But somehow I couldn't imagine the ladylike grandmother lurking in the underbrush until I biked past, or trussing me up like a turkey and dragging me across the floor . . . unless she had an accomplice.

I remembered a car like Peggy O'Connor's on Water Tower Road the day I was forced to jump from my bike, and, according to Gert, a visitor fitting her description had been nosing around Minerva Academy the day the framed alma mater came up missing. "There's something peculiar about that woman," I said.

"What can she do over the telephone?" Gatlin said, and held out her hand for the number.

I stood and watched while my cousin made the connection. What if Peggy O'Connor *was* behind Otto's murder and all the rest? What if she was outside right now, looking in the window, waiting for just the right moment to strike again? "She's probably gone to church," I said.

But Gatlin waved me quiet. I listened while my cousin introduced herself in her "sorority rush" voice, then explained why she was calling.

Her expression changed from tea party polite to an icy pre-attack calmness. "I don't think you understand, Mrs. O'Connor. We have an urgent situation here, and we're appealing to you for help . . . "

Gatlin shook her head at me. The "urgent situation" didn't look hopeful. "I can understand why your grandmother didn't want to talk about the quilt, but it's only a bed covering—it isn't cursed! That was a long time ago, and now we need to put those secrets to rest . . . " Gatlin's voice could cut stone. "I'm sorry you feel that way, but we know from Mamie Estes that Flora was the last one to have it. Can't you at least tell us where it is?"

When Gatlin held the phone away from her and stared at it as if it might explode in her hand, I knew our last hope had hung up. "Still cranky from Halloween," Gatlin said. "Broomstick splinters up her ass."

I giggled, although our predicament wasn't a bit funny. Gatlin always could make me laugh at the most inappropriate times, like when old Mr. Scruggs used to get up to lead the singing at Sunday night church services, and Gatlin would grab her neck and cross her eyes. Poor Mr. Scruggs had a prominent Adam's apple and his eyes were a little off focus. Vesta got to where she finally quit making us go.

We were still laughing a few minutes later when David came in with the sandwiches, the two girls trailing behind him. He shoved books aside on the table for our lunch and pulled up a chair for Mildred.

"I'm hungry. Let's eat!" Faye grabbed for the food as her dad unfolded the sack and handed out the sandwiches, tucking a paper napkin in his younger daughter's dress. Gatlin poured milk and coffee from thermoses she'd brought from home.

"I'd like to contribute to the meal," Mildred said, "but I'm afraid my cupboard is bare. I haven't had a chance to go to the store yet."

"We'll have to take care of that," I told her. "If you'll make up a list, we'll go right after lunch."

Mildred nodded agreeably. She didn't know, of course, that my offer came with strings attached. I had a question for Mildred Parsons I didn't think she could dodge.

Lizzie dipped a french fry in ketchup. "Did they find the person who tried to hurt you, Minda?"

"Not yet, honey, but I'm sure they'll find them soon," I said, wishing I could believe it.

"Hurt you? Why? When did this happen?" Mildred had started to take a bite of her sandwich and now held it in midair. "Are you all right?"

"I'm fine except for a few bumps on the head," I assured her. "Tell you about it later."

"I wish they'd hurry and lock up the maniac who's doing this," my cousin said later as she dropped me off to get my car. "I'm afraid to turn my back on you!"

"Sounds like it was the same person who tried to flip me over the cliff," I said. "And Hugh Talbot was after something that day I found him checking out the window on the back porch." I reminded her about the man's suspicious visit.

Gatlin pulled beside my car in the driveway of the Nut House and looked around as if she expected somebody to jump out at us from behind the nandina bush. "Do you think Hugh might've killed Otto?"

"The police don't seem to think so. He's over at the academy almost every day, but he swears he wasn't there the night Otto was killed."

"How about Wordy Gerty?" Gatlin turned to me, eyebrows raised.

"Come on, Gatlin—Wordy Gerty? She was at that Movies 'n' Munchies thing at the church. Even Mildred remembers seeing her there. Besides, how could the woman try to run herself down? Even Gert couldn't manage that."

"Could've been Hugh . . . " Gatlin drummed on the steering wheel. "I'm sure it has something to do with that old school."

But Hugh had stepped in to save me from a nasty free fall. Hadn't he? And I didn't really think he'd try to run

192

over his sister, no matter how badly she got on his nerves.

"It could've been just about anybody," I said, digging my car keys from my purse. "I think I'm going to live in a closet—one with thick walls and no windows. You can slip food under the door."

"We're going to find that quilt, Minda," Gatlin said. "If that O'Connor woman thinks I've given up, she needs a refresher course in Bitching 101. I'm holding Vesta in reserve."

"God help her," I said. "But don't send Vesta in just yet. First give me a chance with Mildred."

"What would Mildred know?"

"More than you think," I said. *A lot more than you think.*

Chapter Twenty-one

J WAITED UNTIL WE HAD FINISHED GROCERY shopping to throw my firecracker into the furnace. Mildred sat in the passenger seat while I piled her groceries into the trunk.

"Don't let me forget to set aside some of those canned goods for the church cornucopia," she said when I slid in beside her. "They're supposed to collect them for the care center sometime this week."

I said I wouldn't.

"And when are you going to tell me about those 'bumps on your head,' as you describe them? What happened, Arminda? Why was someone trying to harm you?"

"In a minute," I said. "First tell me about your visit to

193

Brookbend. Did you have a nice time with your relatives there?" I glanced at her as we waited to turn out of the parking lot.

"It was all right. Watch that truck, Arminda! Some people don't seem to know how to use a signal."

"Tell me about your mother, Mildred. What was she like?"

"My mother?" Mildred opened her black leather purse—the only one I'd ever seen her carry—then snapped it shut again. "Well . . . she was just . . . my mother," she said. "Why do you ask?"

"I've never heard you say much about her. What was her name?"

She turned and looked at me, shifting the purse on her lap. "Ann. Her name was Ann."

I felt her eyes on me as I maneuvered into the left lane of traffic. The Presbyterians were already returning from lunch at the Dine Rite Cafeteria a few miles down the road. The Methodists would be next, and finally, the Baptists.

"I know who she was, Mildred." I smiled. "*Cousin* Mildred. Is that why you made that mysterious trip to Brookbend?"

For a minute I thought she hadn't heard me, or if she had, she was going to deny it.

"I wish you hadn't found that out, Arminda. I'm afraid it could be a dangerous thing to know. There's something dreadful going on here, and I don't want anything happening to you—although it sounds as though my warning might be a bit too late."

In a rare gesture of affection, Mildred put a hand on my arm and, I think, came close to patting it.

"You have a point there," I said, and told her about the two attempts on my life.

194

"Great mercy's sakes alive!" This was as close as Mildred ever came to cursing, and she did it with a flair Sarah Bernhardt might've envied. "Could Gatlin place the voice of the person who phoned? The one who pretended to be her neighbor?"

"Not really. Said she sounded like she had a cold. Or it might've even been a man."

"How did you know—about my mother, I mean?" Mildred spoke in little more than a whisper.

"I saw her picture yesterday in an old yearbook at the academy, and it reminded me of a photograph I'd seen of you taken when you were younger."

"Where on earth did you find that?"

"Came across it when Vesta and I were looking through your things—"

"You and Vesta went through my belongings? Why?"

"We needed to know what you packed when you left for your *destination unknown* so we'd have some idea of how long you planned to be gone." Irritation edged my voice, and I didn't try to sugarcoat it. "We were worried about you, Mildred. We didn't know where you were."

"I'm sorry about that." Mildred stared down at her lap and looked solemn—and more or less remorseful.

"So, are you going to tell me now?" I glanced at her. "About your mother, Annie Rose. Where did she go when she left here, and why did she let everybody think she drowned?"

My passenger studied about that for a minute. "Gatlin will probably be at the bookshop for a good while yet. Why don't we go back to the home place where we can talk? These groceries should be all right for a while in the trunk, don't you think? And I'll tell you what I know."

"Fine. But first I think I have something that might belong to you," I said.

A welcoming lamp burned in the back hallway of the house on Phinizy Street, and the kitchen had a faint, spicy smell that made me think of happier times.

Sniffing, Mildred followed her nose to the apple-shaped cookie jar on the counter and lifted the lid.

"Why, Minda, I didn't know you had the recipe. These were always your favorites. Remember? Your mother made them every Christmas."

"Elf krispies!" I bit into a thin, nut-filled cookie, zippy with cloves and allspice. "Mom said this is what Mrs. Claus made for Santa's elves," I said, filling the kettle for tea.

Mildred smiled as she helped herself to another. "You know, I expect she still does," she said.

I left her waiting for the kettle to boil while I hurried upstairs for the pin I'd found in the bathroom stall at Minerva Academy. It was fastened just where I'd left it weeks before on the inside of a hideous orange toboggan cap Gatlin had once given me during her (thankfully) brief knitting stage.

"Where did you find this?" Mildred asked when I placed it on the table in front of her. She turned the pin in her fingers and examined the initials on the back. "I was afraid it was gone forever!"

I told her how I had found the star-flower pin on the floor of the women's restroom and had put it in my pocket, then forgotten it during the grim events that followed. "It wasn't until Gatlin and I discovered the minutes from what must have been a meeting of the Mystic Six that I remembered it," I told her. "The emblem on the paper was the same as that on the pin, and it's on the alma mater, too—the one my great-grandmother stitched that was hanging at the academy."

Mildred frowned and shook her head. "The Mystic Six?"

"It was a club—a secret society, I think, and there were six members. Your mother, Annie Rose, was one, and so was her sister, Lucy. The others were Mamie Trammell Estes—who, by the way, is the only one still living; Pluma Griffin; Irene Bradshaw's mother, Pauline; and Flora Dennis."

Mildred nodded. "I remember Pauline. She came here once just before Lucy died. And Flora . . . "

Mildred stood and reached for the kettle. "There are several kinds of tea bags. I didn't know what you wanted—"

"What about Flora?" I snatched a tea bag from the closest box and took the kettle from her.

"She and Lucy corresponded—seemed to be close friends. I wrote to her when Lucy died."

I sensed there was more, but Mildred wasn't going to share it. Not yet, anyway. "Then you know about the quilt?"

I watched her face, waiting for her answer. Earlier she had claimed she'd never heard of it.

Mildred sighed. "Lucy kept an old quilt in a trunk, but I didn't know of its significance until I hung it out to air once. She demanded I take it down. Something amiss there, I thought, but of course I didn't know what! I only saw it two other times: once when it arrived in the mail, and again when she asked me to box it up and send it to somebody else."

"Do you remember who it was?"

"I wouldn't if you hadn't mentioned her, but I believe her name was Mamie . . . Yes, I'm almost sure of it."

"The members of the Mystic Six made that quilt," I told her, "and passed it from one to the other. Mamie Estes said it was Annie Rose's quilt, but I think they made it after she died—I mean, left, and it's looking more and more like it has something to do with Otto's murder."

"Yes, I'm afraid you're right." Mildred tucked the little pin inside a zippered pocket in her purse. "Arminda, promise me, please, that you won't say anything about finding this pin to anybody else. Otto must have had it with him when he died. Why, I don't know, but apparently someone wants it badly enough to kill."

I didn't tell her that Gatlin already knew. Why double the worry? "What will you do with it?" I asked. "It isn't safe to keep it around—especially after what happened to you earlier."

Mildred made a face, remembering, no doubt, her trip to the emergency room. "Don't worry. I'll put it in a safe place. No one will think to look there." She took a sip of tea and held the cup in both hands. "I don't want to let it get away from me again. It belonged to my mother, you know."

"Have you always known that Annie Rose was your mother?" I asked. "The pin has her initials, *A.W.*, on the back."

But Mildred shook her head. "I've suspected, of course, and over a period of years, my suspicions became even stronger, but I was told my mother's maiden name was Waters—Ann Waters—and that she was raised somewhere near Greenville. I had to go back to Brookbend to find the truth." Her voice quivered. "If I had only gone sooner, perhaps Otto would still be alive."

198

"How could your mother's true identity have anything to do with Otto's being murdered?" I asked.

"I think Otto found out something that somebody wanted to remain a secret," Mildred said. "And he let it be known to the wrong person."

She turned and looked at me, and her smile made me want to cry. "I loved that boy as though he were my own—still do, but Otto had a way of twisting things about to suit his own needs. He may very well have brought about his own death."

"How do you mean? Do you think he was blackmailing somebody?"

Mildred stood and turned on the burner under the kettle. This was to be a multi-cup discussion, and if the situation hadn't been so serious, I would've smiled. "I don't like that word," she said, "but yes, I think he might have been.

"You asked why my mother left the way she did, and I think I know. She let everyone think she had drowned in the Saluda because she was pregnant. With me."

"But that's a terrible thing to do! Can you imagine the grief and pain that caused her family? And to never see them again—"

"Arminda, this was 1916. My mother wasn't married. Things like that weren't accepted then. I suppose she felt if she returned and they learned the truth, it would dishonor her family."

"So she left her shawl beside the river and made her way somehow or other almost two hundred miles away to Brookbend?"

Mildred jumped up to turn off the steaming kettle and poured water into our cups. I stayed seated and let her do this, knowing the small, everyday tasks were probably helping her deal with the struggle of sharing

199

her story—a story that had obviously shaken her. Now she smiled. "She even took the name of the place where she was supposed to have drowned," she said. "My mother told me her maiden name was Ann *Waters*. She must have taken a bit of amusement from that!

"My father—or the man I always thought was my father—raised me as his own. His first wife had died in childbirth, and his own mother was getting along in years and in poor health. Mama came to live with them as sort of a housekeeper and caregiver to the little boy, Jake, who was about three at the time. And the two of them married—Ben Parsons and my mother—not long after she came there to live."

"But how did you come to stay in Angel Heights? And with your own aunt, Lucy? Didn't you have any idea who she was?"

Mildred shrugged. "I was told all my relatives were dead and that Lucy was an old school friend of Mama's. You see, when I was growing up, my mother would let her name slip from time to time."

"What do you mean?" I stood and brought the cookie jar to the table. Tea was fine, but for this I needed nourishment.

"She'd say things like, '*Lucy had a coat just like that!*' Or '*Lucy and I used to play this game . . .*' And of course, I wanted to know who Lucy was."

"What did she say?" I asked.

"Told me she was a close friend and that they'd gone to school together. Eventually, stories about Lucy and the things they did back in Greenville became a familiar part of my life. It was only when she was close to death that Mama mentioned Angel Heights."

Absently, Mildred ran a finger along the rim of her cup. "She was delirious some of the time, talked about

Lucy a lot. And somebody named Augusta. I never did find out who she was. Anyway, I asked her if she wanted me to contact Lucy, thinking of how wonderful it would be if she could only see her again. 'Lucy *who*?' I asked, because she'd never mentioned her last name . . . and Mama said *Westbrook* because of course she didn't know her married name.

"But as ill as she was, my mother was still conscious of what she considered proper morals," Mildred said. "I asked her if Lucy still lived in Greenville, and she looked at me so funny—like she'd never heard of such a thing—and said, 'Not Greenville! Angel Heights.'

" 'Wouldn't you like to see her again? Do you want me to try and find her?' I asked, and my mother became so agitated I thought she would bolt right out of bed. And her eyes, Arminda . . . her eyes looked almost wild! And she talked—well, she said crazy things. It nearly frightened me to death."

"Do you remember what she said?"

"I don't think I'll ever forget it. She drew herself up and clutched my sleeve. *'No! No! You mustn't tell! Mustn't ever tell! Promise me . . .'* "

Mildred shivered and clasped her hands together. " 'Tell what?' I asked. I had no idea why she was so worked up or what it was she wanted me not to tell."

She paused, and a slight frown wrinkled her brow. " *'Lucy must never know about me!' Mama said, and her eyes locked into mine, wouldn't let me go. Oh, my dear Lucy! I'm sorry . . . so sorry! You must give me your word, Mildred. Don't tell. Please don't tell!'* "

"Did you ever know what she meant?" I asked.

"Not really. Not until I'd lived here in Angel Heights for a while. A long while." Mildred dipped a cookie into her tea and nibbled at the edges.

"So why did you come here?"

"After my mother died, things seemed to go from sour to just plain rancid. Jake, my older brother—or I thought he was my brother—and his wife, Estelle, were living with us at the time with their daughter, who was then about seventeen. You see Ben, the man I knew as my father, had died a few years before, and after Mama passed away, the house went to Jake." Mildred took a deep breath and drew herself up. "Estelle made it clear I wasn't welcome there—resented me, I guess.

"Angel Heights was the last place my mother mentioned, and of course her friend Lucy lived here. Since I had no family of my own—except for Jake, who let that silly Estelle tell him how to put on his drawers in the morning—I decided to find out for myself why Mama got so hysterical about my mentioning her to Lucy. There was nothing to hold me in Brookbend, and she'd made me beneficiary of a small insurance policy, so I quit my job as bookkeeper for a greenhouse there and came here to Angel Heights." She smiled. "That was before you were even born, and I only meant to stay long enough to see if I could learn why this woman, Lucy Westbrook, was so important to my mother."

"And did you?"

"Not until just before Lucy died, and I began to suspect who my mother really was," Mildred told me. "I asked her once if she'd gone to school with anyone named Ann Waters, and she claimed she'd never heard of her. She hadn't, of course. I know that now."

"Do you think she knew who you were? That you were her sister's daughter?"

"Oh, no! I'm sure she didn't. Lucy was convinced her sister drowned, never questioned it. It wasn't a subject she discussed—nor did she like anyone else bringing it up."

Mildred stood and rinsed her cup in the sink. "I probably wouldn't have stayed here if it hadn't been for Otto," she said, still with her back to me. "He was nine years old then, and his mother had more or less deserted him—gone back home to Texas without so much as a by your leave!" She wiped her hands on the dish towel and turned to face me with a sound that was first cousin to a snort.

"When I first came here to Angel Heights, it didn't take long to learn Lucy's married name was Alexander and to find out where she lived, and I dropped by the house on some pretext or other. Told her I was new in town—which of course I was—and asked if she needed any sewing done. I'm a fairly good seamstress, you know. I'd brought my portable sewing machine from home and had taken a room at Bessie Overton's. You don't remember her—dead now, but she used to take in tourists."

"So, did she?" I asked.

"Did she what?"

"Want any sewing done?"

"Well, of course she did," Mildred said. "Lucy was a clotheshorse from the word go. Invited me right in, and that's when I learned about the boy. She said they were looking for a housekeeper—somebody to keep an eye on Otto. I could see that she didn't want to be bothered with the child, and Vesta was busy with her own interests. Your grandfather was still alive then, and they stayed on the go a lot."

"And you took the job. Didn't they ask for references?"

"I told them up front I didn't have experience in that area except for the time I spent with Jake's daughter, Julia, when she was a child, but I learned from my

203

mother how to take care of a house and cook. The greenhouse where I'd worked before gave them a reference, and that seemed to satisfy them." Mildred shrugged. "Guess they were desperate. I meant to stay only a few months—a year at the most—until I could decide where I wanted to go from there, but of course by then I knew I couldn't leave Otto."

Somehow it always came back to Otto.

"Does my grandmother know what really happened to your mother?" I asked.

"Good heavens, no! She never knew her, of course, but Vesta's always enjoyed telling about her beautiful aunt, Annie Rose, who died so young and so tragically in the Saluda River. It makes a good story."

"She's never seen the pin with your mother's initials on the back?"

"No one has—except for Otto, and I never showed it to him. It was one of the few things left to me by my mother, and I kept it in a special place. Not special enough, I guess, to keep hidden from Otto.

"Lucy had a pin just like it," she added. "I found it just after she died, and that was what convinced me the two were sisters. That and some pictures I came across in the family album."

"Mildred . . . ," I began, and then hesitated. How do you ask a question like this? I took a deep breath and plunged in. "Mildred, do you have any idea who your father was?"

She stood at the window looking out on the backyard already layered in the gloom of late afternoon. "Does it matter? Whoever he was, he's long dead now."

"Do you think it had anything to do with Otto's death?"

Mildred turned, and I was surprised to hear her laugh.

"You mean the fact that I'm illegitimate—or would've been if my mother hadn't married when she did?" She shook her head. "People don't kill for that kind of thing in this day and time, Arminda."

"How can you be sure Ben Parsons wasn't your natural father?"

"Because I found my mother's marriage license to him. It was dated five months before I was born." Mildred crossed her arms and looked at me. "I'm sure she didn't know him before she came there. And her name on the license was *Annie Rose Westbrook.*"

I felt a shiver go through me. "Is that what you learned when you went there this last time?"

She nodded. "I should've done this long ago, but Estelle said there was nothing of my mother's there, said they'd thrown out her things years ago. Hateful to the end, Estelle was, but Julia is more like her father. Wrote me a week or so before Otto died and said she was putting the old place on the market and had discovered some things of my mother's in the attic. Jake died not too long after I left there, and Estelle's been gone four or five years. Julia and her husband are moving into a smaller place."

"Have you told anyone else about this?" I asked.

Mildred sighed as she sat across from me. "Not yet. I just wish I'd known this sooner! Everyone who knew my mother is gone now, and I have so many questions to ask."

I reminded her about Mamie Estes. "Her mind's still good for somebody as old as she is, and she remembers your mother."

"Do you think she would talk with me? I wouldn't want to frighten her."

"Why do you say that?" I said.

205

"When Lucy died all those years ago, I felt I'd lost my last link, and then I remembered Flora Dennis." Mildred looked away, but I could still see the hurt on her face.

"What about Flora?"

"She used to correspond with Lucy, and I knew they'd gone to school together, so I thought perhaps she'd remember my mother, Annie Rose. I wrote to her telling her of Lucy's death and enclosed a copy of a photograph of Mama. It was made in our backyard in Brookbend when she was still a young woman, and I asked Flora if she remembered her."

"Did you tell her it was a picture of Annie Rose?" I asked.

"No, no. It was kind of a test, you see, to discover if my mother was really who I suspected, but Flora never answered my letter."

"Maybe she was sick," I said. "Or just forgetful. I don't think she lived too long after that."

"It was more than that, Arminda. When I didn't hear from her after a few weeks I became concerned that perhaps she hadn't received my letter, and I telephoned there. When Flora answered the phone, I tried to explain who I was and what I wanted, but I couldn't get any response from her. The woman never said a word! After a few minutes, her granddaughter came to the phone and was most unpleasant to me. Accused me of trying to pull a cruel joke and warned me to never call there again. So of course I never did."

"I can see why she reacted that way, Mildred. Flora thought your mother was dead—drowned. She never knew you existed, and now you were sending her a photograph of a dead woman."

"I certainly didn't intend . . . I suppose I went about it

in the wrong way. If only she'd have let me explain!"

I told her how Peggy O'Connor had responded when I mentioned the emblem on her grandmother's gravestone. "Must be an emotional family," I said. "You'd have thought I'd dug up a body in the garden."

"I don't know about a body," Mildred said, "but something mighty queer's going on with her, and I think I know what she's hiding."

I looked at her, and she answered my unspoken question.

"The quilt. I believe the O'Connor woman has the quilt, and for some reason she doesn't want us to see it."

Chapter Twenty-two

I GROANED, THINKING OF ANOTHER LONG DRIVE to Georgia only to have a door slammed in my face. "Maybe if you go with me, Mildred, we can convince this woman we don't have some evil plot against her. We have to track down that quilt!"

"She's had a few years to mellow since I spoke with her last." Mildred said, starting for the telephone in the hallway. "Let me speak with her first—won't hurt to give it a try."

"Gatlin didn't have any better luck than I did," I told her. "You'll just be wasting your time."

"Don't worry, I'll be diplomatic," she insisted, waiting by the phone.

Diplomacy is not one of Mildred's greater traits, and I tried not to make a face. Still I dug up Peggy O'Connor's phone number from somewhere in the depths of my purse and stood by as she punched in the number and explained to the person who answered exactly who she was and what she wanted. Mildred looked at me as she spoke in her usual calm, no-nonsense voice, and her expression never changed.

"Mrs. O'Connor, I'm eighty-three years old, have never had much of an imagination, and doubt if I ever will. I'm telling you the truth, and I hope you will believe me when I tell you that your grandmother's friend, Annie Rose Westbrook, didn't die as she believed in the Saluda River. I've only recently learned that Annie Rose was indeed my mother. She left Angel Heights when she was pregnant with me and never returned . . .

" . . . Oh, but Mrs. O'Connor, it *should* concern you because that quilt your grandmother had . . . "

Mildred came very close to rolling her eyes at me. "Yes, I'm sure your grandmother had it last because Mamie Estes mailed it to her. Mamie's a hundred and two but she still remembers your grandmother, and she's the last surviving member of that little group of friends—they even had a name for themselves, I hear."

Mildred raised an eyebrow at me and I mouthed the answer she wanted. "The Mystic Six, I'm told," she told her, then, frowning, listened quietly to whatever was being said.

"Please don't hang up, Mrs. O'Connor. I wish we could convince you of the importance—"

I held out a hand for the receiver, and Mildred gave it to me with a world-weary sigh. If it had been Peggy O'Connor's neck, I would gladly have wrung it.

"Here's the thing," I said. "One person has been murdered here, and several—including me—were attacked. We believe the quilt may give us the key to the reason behind it. If you know anything about this, Mrs.

O'Connor, your life may be in danger, as well. Won't you help us, please, before someone else is hurt?"

For a few silent seconds I thought she had gone away, and then she cleared her throat. "I can't help you," she said.

"Can't or won't?"

"I don't have the quilt, and I don't know where it is."

"Do you know anyone who might help us find it?" Why was this woman being such an impossible, rigid ass?

"I'm sorry," she said, and hung up.

It was dark when I drove Mildred back to her place a few minutes later, and I think both of us felt as dismal as the damp November night. Regardless of her protests, I insisted on going inside to carry in her groceries, but I really wanted to be sure everything was all right. Gatlin, I noticed, had left a light burning in the front of the shop, and we found a note from her under the connecting door to let Mildred know that R.T. Foster would be by in the morning to take a look at the bookstore and its adjoining building.

Mildred brightened when she read it. "I do hope this works out for Gatlin. It's been difficult for them financially, I know, and if there's one good thing that's come from Otto's death, it's that Gatlin will have a chance to do something with this place."

"You knew then—about the will?"

"Of course I knew! Otto and I discussed it before he made it out, and I was the one who suggested he name Gatlin. After all, she should be next in line." Mildred smiled. "Good heavens, Minda! You didn't think it would upset me that he didn't leave his share to me, did you?" She shook her head. "I wasn't supposed to outlive

209

him. Besides, the amount Vesta sets aside for me each month more than takes care of my needs."

Now it was my time to smile. "We thought . . . that is, we knew Otto would have wanted you to have something."

"Yes, I imagine he would if he'd thought of it—but he didn't." Mildred lowered her voice to a hoarse whisper. "There's no need in saying anything about this to your grandmother, Arminda. Just let her go on believing that I think Otto provided for me. She's glad to share, and I'm glad to accept it—so let's just keep this between the two of us."

I agreed. Annie Rose, I thought, would be glad as well.

Driving home, I thought of what Mildred had said about her mother's mentioning Augusta, and knew then what Augusta's unfinished business here had been. As far as I was concerned, it was still unfinished. The angel claimed not to know any more than she had told me about what happened to the Mystic Six after Annie Rose supposedly drowned, but still I wondered if she was keeping something back.

Augusta had kept out of sight during my visit at the Nut House with Mildred, yet I could sense her presence there, and even though she wasn't beside me in the car, I thought I got a whiff of her "angel essence." Tonight it was a combination of strawberries and mint.

Coming from town, I usually drove straight down River Street and turned left on Phinizy, but now I found myself going out of my way. *What now, Augusta?* I thought. *I'm really tired, and it's been a long day.*

Hank and Edna Smith's rambling Dutch barn of a house stood on a corner two blocks over, and with all that had happened, I supposed the time had come to speak openly with Sylvie. If she knew something about Otto that might help us clear away some of the clutter, we needed to know it now.

The house was dark except for a light burning in the kitchen, and Sylvia's car was parked in the driveway with the door behind the driver's seat open.

Good! This would solve my problem of dropping by without first calling—always a no-no in Vesta's book. I pulled up to the curb and waited for Sylvie to come out, explanations ready on my tongue. *Just happened to be in the neighborhood and saw your car . . . and did you kill my cousin Otto?* Well, that certainly wouldn't do! I'd have to think of a better way to wade in than that. I decided on honesty. *Something's very wrong here, Sylvia, and it seemed to have started with Otto. Do you know if he was involved in anything that might have led to his murder?* When I'd overheard her at the cemetery, she had told Otto—dead though he was at the time—how sorry she was. Sorry for what?

I sat there for almost ten minutes waiting and wondering why Sylvia Smith didn't come back outside and finish carrying in her luggage or her groceries, or whatever she had left in the car. I could see the empty backseat in the light of the open car door, but there didn't appear to be anyone or anything inside. Maybe Sylvie had forgotten to close it, in which case, the light would eventually drain the battery.

Okay. I would close her car door and go home—deed done. I really didn't want to confront Sylvia alone in her house without either of her parents there. For all I knew, she was the one who had tried to dump me down the stairwell from three floors up.

Except for a bag of groceries on the floor, the car was

empty as I had suspected, but curiosity—or something else—drove me to glance in the kitchen doorway which had been left partially open, and what I saw was a foot.

The foot wasn't in a normal position such as standing, walking, or sitting. It was splayed out on the floor with a leg attached. Sylvie Smith's leg.

She was breathing—thank God—but her face was pale, and blood matted her pale hair and puddled on the blue vinyl floor. I touched her wrist and found a weak pulse; her eyelids fluttered.

"Help is coming, Sylvie," I told her. "You're going to be all right." I didn't know that at all, but that's what they always tell people in situations like this and I hoped it might help. I called 911 from the kitchen phone and begged them to hurry, praying the whole time that Sylvia wouldn't die right there because I didn't know what else to do other than kneel on the floor beside her and let her know she wasn't alone.

A paper sack filled with what smelled like hamburgers was on the floor beside her, and she still wore a jacket and gloves. I looked about for a pocketbook of some kind but didn't see one. Had Sylvie surprised a burglar? I opened her coat to check for a bullet wound or any sign of bleeding there, but the only injury appeared to be to her head.

Could the person who did this still be inside? *Don't think of that, Minda! Just don't think at all!* I wanted to bolt out the door, run to my car, and drive away as fast as I could, but I couldn't leave her here. Sylvia shivered, and I remembered reading somewhere that you should keep people warm to prevent them from going into shock, so I took off my jacket and covered her, listening all the while for an approaching ambulance. And I ran out to meet it when it came.

"What were you doing at Sylvie Smith's?" my grandmother wanted to know. She dropped by the home place the next day—along with just about everybody else in town—when she learned I'd been the one to find Sylvia.

I told her about seeing Sylvia's car in the driveway with the door open and how I only meant to do a small good deed before moving on.

"Thank goodness you did!" Gertrude Whitmire added, "or else the poor girl would've probably bled to death right there on the kitchen floor!"

I suppressed a shudder, seeing again the gory gash in Sylvia's head. "I hope I was in time," I said. "The last time I checked with the hospital, Sylvia was still in intensive care after an 'iffy' night."

"Iffy, yes." Irene squeezed my arm before I could dodge. "I heard they found the weapon. Of course, they won't say that's what it is, but why else would a heavy oriental vase be lying out in the yard? And with blood on it, too!"

Vesta looked interested. "Edna always kept sea oats in that vase. Sneaks them from the beach. I told her that was illegal." She pulled off her gloves and sank into the chair that had belonged to her husband, nudging it a little closer to the fire. "I left you some of that lemon cake you used to like back in the kitchen. Had one of my rare baking spells yesterday—don't know what came over me, but I hope it won't come again!"

"And I brought some of my carrot muffins," Gertrude said, setting a napkin-covered plate on the coffee table. "Thought you could use something nourishing after all you've been through. Hope they're up to par."

"Oh, I'm sure they will be," I said, trying to ignore

213

the glances Irene and Vesta exchanged. Everybody in Angel Heights knew that Gertrude Whitmire didn't bake, but bought sweets on sale from the bakery, kept them in her freezer, and when needed, passed them off as her own.

I lifted the napkin and touched a muffin. It was still cold. "Looks good," I said. "Thank you both. When I gain another five pounds, I'll let you take me shopping for my new wardrobe."

Irene walked to the fireplace and stood looking down at the flames. "I don't see how anybody can even think of food with all that's been going on around here. I've just about lost my appetite."

"I've lived here all my life," my grandmother said, "and until recently I've never felt unsafe, rarely locked a door—but now I'm constantly looking behind me." She looked up at me. "I never thought I'd say this, Minda, but I wish you wouldn't stay here in this old house alone. There's room at my place, you know."

Irene saved me from answering. "I'd think you'd be nervous, too, Gertrude," she said, "living out there so far from town—especially after that maniac tried to run you down. Aren't you afraid he'll come back?"

"He hasn't so far, and I'm hoping that was an isolated incident." Gertrude picked up a sofa pillow and plopped it in her lap. "But I've had my alarm system updated, and then Hugh checks on me regularly." She gave the pillow a squeeze. "Surely they'll find out who's responsible and put an end to all these atrocities soon!"

"Yes, soon. I do hope poor Sylvie will be all right," Irene said. "Why in the world would anybody want to do such a thing?"

"Looks to me like she interrupted a burglary," Vesta said. "Her purse was taken, but they found it in a

214

Dumpster later with the money still inside. It had to be somebody from around here—somebody who knew Hank and Edna would be out of town for the night. Hank wouldn't miss that medical convention in Charleston—goes every year."

"Doesn't seem like we're safe anywhere," Gertrude said. "Look what happened to Mildred, and she lives right in the middle of town!"

Irene left the fireside to sit beside Gertrude. "Did they ever find out what they were looking for, Vesta? I heard somebody just about tore that bookshop apart. They didn't bother any of Mildred's things, did they?" She shuddered. "I mean, they didn't actually break into where she *lives*?"

"I don't think so," my grandmother told her. "If they did, we didn't notice it. You know how Mildred is; she doesn't care for a lot of extras, and probably wouldn't wear expensive jewelry if she had it. I can't imagine what a burglar would hope to find, and I doubt if she knows either, but the idea is appalling. Mildred is a very private person, and I've always respected that."

"I'll bet I know what they were looking for," I said to Vesta later in the kitchen. Augusta had brewed a pot of coffee with a reach-out-and-grab-you nut-brown smell, and the two of us were arranging cups on a tray.

"You mean Otto's old zebra?" my grandmother whispered. "What do you suppose Mildred keeps in there she doesn't want the rest of us to know about?"

"Why don't you ask her?" I said. But Vesta was busy pouring cream into a pitcher and either didn't hear me or pretended not to. I think it was the latter.

"Gatlin tells me she's thinking of making a tearoom of

215

Hank's old building if she can find someone to do the work," Irene said as coffee was served.

Vesta nodded. "Someone's supposed to look at the building today, now that it's empty. Hank finally had all those old records in there destroyed. Should've done it years ago."

I noticed that she didn't look directly at Irene as she spoke.

"And does Mildred plan to stay there with all that remodeling going on?" Gertrude asked.

"I don't think she'd miss it," I told her. "In fact, she's looking forward to it."

Gertrude nodded. "Probably feels a lot safer with all the hustle and bustle about."

Irene gathered her coat about her and rose to leave. "As safe as any of us can feel until we find the bad apple among us," she said.

"An apt description if I ever heard one," Augusta said as she stood at the window watching the three women leave in their separate cars.

"What do you mean?" I asked. I knew she had been eavesdropping when Vesta and the others were here. Even though I didn't see her, there had been a strong "Augusta current" in the air.

"Bad apple. *Rotten* apple would be even more fitting." She frowned. "Did the police find any evidence at the Smiths' that might help in their investigation?"

"The vase, of course," I said, "and they dusted for prints. They didn't find a forced entrance, but Vesta says Edna and Hank just about always left a side door unlocked."

"I wonder if whoever it was found what they were looking for," Augusta said. "Do you think Sylvia has something of Otto's? Could that be what they were after?"

"Only Sylvia could tell us that," I said. "And she's not talking right now."

I stood at the window beside her. "You brought me there, didn't you? You wanted me to find her."

"Find who?"

"Sylvie. I didn't plan to go there. It's like I was led."

Augusta spoke softly. "She needed help, Arminda."

"And so did Annie Rose," I said. "You helped her stage that drowning. You were the one who sent her to Brookbend."

"The drowning would have been a reality if I hadn't convinced her not to take her own and her unborn baby's life," Augusta said. "Annie Rose was planning to put an end to her life and her child's, as well."

"But why Brookbend?"

"I knew the Parsons there. Had been assigned to Ben's mother, Ella, for a while. Ella was dying, and she accepted that, but she worried about her widowed son and the child, Jake, who had no one to care for them. They were good people, and they agreed to take her in. Annie Rose left her shawl beside the river and found a ride to the next town, then took a train for Brookbend, where Ben and his mother waited." She smiled. "He came to love her, you know, and she, him."

"Do you know who Mildred's father was?" I asked, but Augusta shook her head.

"She never told me. Wouldn't talk about it at all."

I was going to ask Augusta what she thought we should do next when the telephone rang and answered my question for me.

It was Peggy O'Connor calling to tell me she had thought about what Mildred and I had said and had a change of heart.

Chapter Twenty-three

"THAT'S WONDERFUL!" I SAID, OOZING GOOEY relief all the way to Cornelia, Georgia, via Ma Bell. "And I promise we'll take good care of your quilt and return it promptly. In fact, if you'd rather, we could examine it there."

"But I told you, I don't have the quilt. I sold it."

"Sold it? Then who—?"

"There was always something depressing about that old quilt," Peggy O'Connor said. "Gram never told me what it was, but I know she felt that way about it, too. After she died, I got in touch with a collector, thinking, of course, that my grandmother was the last member to go. I felt just terrible when you told me about Mamie Estes, and I've torn this house apart looking for the receipt, but I must've thrown it away because I can't find it anywhere. If I could only remember the name of the person who bought it, I'd be glad to buy it back and deliver it to Mrs. Estes myself."

I smiled at the thought of the pristine O'Connor household being "torn apart."

"Mamie Estes doesn't want it," I assured her. "I think she was as glad to be rid of it as you were, but I believe you're right in your feelings about it. That quilt could hold the key to a grim secret—one someone doesn't want us to learn."

"It has something to do with that society they belonged to, doesn't it?"

I could hear Peggy O'Connor tapping the receiver with a well-manicured nail. "My grandmother wouldn't talk much about it, but it had a serious influence on her life. Did you know she wore that pin until the day she

218

died? I had her buried in it."

I remembered how she'd carried on when I'd questioned her about Flora's unusual grave marker. You'd have thought I'd insulted her ancestry all the way back to Adam. This, however, was not the time to remind her, I decided.

"Look, I'm . . . sorry . . . for the way I acted . . . when you were here that day." The woman drew out each word like it was stuck to her tongue with superglue. "It's just that the elderly lady who called earlier . . . "

"Mildred?" I offered.

"Right. Well, when she sent that snapshot to Gram all those years ago, it nearly frightened her to death. Withdrew into herself for days and wouldn't even talk about it. I didn't know what was going on—still don't— but it made me uneasy somehow."

I told her I didn't blame her—which I didn't—and that I was sorry for troubling her—which I wasn't. "I don't suppose you remember where this person lived? The one who bought the quilt?"

"Somewhere up in the mountains. Dahlonega maybe, or it could've been Toccoa, even Gainesville. She advertised in a catalog, came here and saw it—bought it right off. Said she entered them in shows—kind of like artwork, I think.

"Anyway, I'm sorry I can't help more. Got to thinking about what you said, about it being important. And a little voice just whispered to me to tell you what I knew. Maybe it was Gram's."

I thanked her and hung up, making a face as I did. I wish Gram had whispered sooner. Heck, I wish the old woman had hollered!

"Well, I suppose that's that." Mildred spoke in Eeyore-

219

like tones. "Only the good Lord knows where that quilt is now."

"Not necessarily," I said. "I think I know somebody else who might help us find it, or at least lead us in the right direction." And I told her about Maureen Foster.

Maureen wasn't familiar with the quilt we were looking for, but she referred me to Louise Starr, the woman who ran the gift shop she sold to in Charlotte, who in turn directed me to Alpha Styles.

Alpha Styles owned a folklore museum up near Blowing Rock in the North Carolina mountains, and it must've been blowing that day because she bellowed at me over the telephone as if she were trying to speak over a howling wind.

"HATTIE CARNES!" the woman told me.

"Hattie Carnes. Yes. And where—?"

"HATTIE BROUGHT THAT QUILT IN A COUPLE OF YEARS AGO. I'VE NEVER SEEN ANYTHING LIKE IT! SHE LET ME SHOW IT FOR A SEASON, BUT WOULDN'T SELL IT FOR LOVE NOR MONEY. I TRIED, BUT I COULD TELL I WAS JUST HOLLERIN' INTO THE WIND."

Which in her case must have been a familiar experience, I thought as I held the receiver away from my ear. Hattie Carnes, I learned, lived in the foothills near Lenoir. She had a phone, Alpha said, but rarely answered it. I took a chance and drove up there anyway, hoping to find her at home. Mildred went with me, and at the last minute, my grandmother decided she, too, would go along for the ride.

For once, I was in luck. A hound dog—friendly, thank goodness—greeted us in the yard, and the whole place, I thought, had a serene feeling about it. Hattie's home, a two-story frame building with a low-columned

220

porch extending across the front, had at one time been a tavern, Alpha had told me, and was supposed to be one of the oldest buildings in the area. It had never had a coat of paint as far as I could tell, but the weathered gray house looked down on the road below from a screen of stately cedars, much as a revered matriarch might peer from an upstairs suite. We could smell corn bread baking as soon as we got out of the car, and I heard the sharp sound of pounding coming from somewhere out back.

Hattie Carnes was cracking black walnuts with a rock on the back steps and didn't seem surprised to see us. She wasn't as old as the home she lived in, but she couldn't be too far behind, and she didn't look a whole lot bigger than Gatlin's Lizzie.

"You'd think with a family as big as mine, somebody would learn to make black walnut cake besides me," she said, wielding a rock about as large as her own head. "All of 'em gotta have it, but you don't see 'em standing in line to crack these nuts, do you?"

I said I sure didn't and offered to help, but she said she thought she had enough, and kicked the shells off the steps with a dainty, boot-clad foot, picked up a large, chipped coffee cup full of nut meats, and invited us into her kitchen.

I introduced myself, Vesta, and Mildred while our hostess took two huge pans of corn bread from a stove that must have dated back to the 1930s. I guess she saw me staring because she gave it a fond little pat. "Tappan gas range—belonged to my mama. My girls want to buy me a new one, but nothing cooks like this!"

I glanced at Mildred. We were going to have a hard time convincing Hattie to let go of anything!

She shooed us to the long oak table and served us

apple pie and coffee, ignoring our protests. "I've got twenty-seven folks coming for Thanksgiving, been cooking all day, and this will give me a minute to sit," she said. "My feet will say thank you, and so will I."

The corn bread, we learned, was for the dressing; Hattie had light bread rolls rising in the refrigerator, she told us, and three kinds of pie in the freezer.

"We came to ask you about a quilt," I said, after I washed down the last bite of pie with coffee that could raise the dead.

"I know," she said. "The Burning Building."

"I don't think so," Vesta told her. "Ours is a family heirloom. It was made by a group of girls who attended an academy many years ago in the town where we live."

Hattie stirred more sugar into her coffee and tasted it. "The same. I call it the Burning Building."

How did she know we were coming? Did the woman have special powers or something?

"Alpha Styles called me," Hattie explained. "Told me what you wanted."

I had almost forgotten she had a telephone.

"I suppose she told you it's not for sale," Hattie added, offering more coffee all around.

I smiled and covered my cup. "If we could just see it, take a few pictures—"

Vesta spoke up. "It belongs in Minerva Academy," she said. "That quilt should be on display there. It was sewn by academy students; my own mother was one, and I think my aunt worked on it, too."

"Your mother?" Hattie Carnes had turned back to the stove with the coffeepot. Now she stood with it in her hand. "You say your mother worked on that quilt?"

I could tell she didn't believe my grandmother, thought she was just making up a tale to convince her to

222

give up the quilt, but Vesta barreled on in her usual bull-headed manner.

"That's right. There should be a small insignia in one corner: a six-pointed star within a flower. It was a replica of the pin they wore."

Hattie set the pot on the stove. "And you brought the pin?"

"Well, no . . . but it's back at the house somewhere, I expect. Minda, you were asking about it, weren't you?" Vesta seemed to realize she had met her match. "I'm prepared to write you a check today, and I'm willing to meet your price."

But Hattie shook her head. "I've never cared for a lot of fluff and comfort in my life. Don't even own a television, and my car's almost twenty years old, but I do love old things—especially quilts. Quilts are my one indulgence, and I don't sell them for profit."

Vesta, for once, was speechless, and we sat in silence until Mildred snapped open her squishy black handbag and dug inside. "Here," she said, putting the tiny star-flower pin on the table. "This is the pin they wore."

Hattie Carnes reached for it, then stopped and looked to Mildred for permission. Only when Mildred nodded, did she pick up the pin to examine it. "Well, I'll be jiggered," she said. "It sure does look the same."

"It is the same," Vesta told her barely lifting an eyebrow. "It belonged to my mother."

"No," Mildred told her, accepting the pin back from Hattie. "It belonged to mine."

Vesta had already turned to Mildred, to ask, I'm sure, how she had come by Lucy's pin. Now she stared at her, her mouth working, but nothing came out. Then my grandmother glanced at me, hoping, I suppose, that I would clear this up somehow. After all, Mildred had

223

been under a lot of strain since Otto's death. But I could only smile.

"Annie Rose didn't die . . . " Mildred struggled to speak. "She had me instead."

She reached out to Vesta, who looked as if she might vault over the table to wrap long arms about her. My grandmother didn't ask any questions, and Mildred didn't give any answers because just then both women were crying, but I could tell that after the initial shock of Mildred's announcement, Vesta was completely at home with the news. Later, after everyone's emotions dwindled, Vesta held Mildred at arm's length and declared that although Mildred definitely had the Westbrook nose, her stubborn streak must've come from her father's side.

Hattie, although thoroughly mystified, seemed to relish every second of the drama before her and insisted on selling the quilt back to us for the price she had paid years before.

"But it would be worth much more than that now," Vesta argued. "Please let me make it worth your while."

"I've had over ten years of pleasure from that quilt," Hattie said. "And if that wasn't enough, what went on in my kitchen today more than made up for it!"

And the two cousins, Mildred and Vesta, sitting together in the backseat as we drove home that evening, talked nonstop, trying to piece their lives together, pausing only for barbecue sandwiches so big they fell apart in our hands, when we stopped in Lexington, North Carolina, for supper. Naturally I listened.

As far as I could tell, Mildred told my grandmother essentially the same story she had told me, and the two of them agreed that the quilt might possibly have

224

something to do with what happened to Otto—and to Sylvie Smith, and what almost happened to me. But I still felt that Mildred was holding something back. I guess she was waiting to see what secrets the old quilt would unfold.

Hattie had tucked it tenderly into a large muslin pillowcase and it sat on the front seat beside me for the ride home. Since it was late when we arrived back in Angel Heights and we wanted to examine the quilt in the daylight when we were all rested—except for a quick peek, which none of us could resist, we put our project on hold until morning. Mildred, without so much as a feeble protest, agreed to stay that night with Vesta, and the two planned to drive over for breakfast in the morning.

"You can treat us to some of that cranberry bread," my grandmother said.

"What cranberry bread?" I asked.

"Somebody's surely been baking," Mildred said. "The whole house smells of it. In fact this old place has a calmness about it, a comfort. Don't you sense it, Vesta? I declare, I feel like I've come home."

"You have," my grandmother told her as they went outside together.

I watched the two of them walk down the back steps and into Vesta's car; then I went inside and locked the door, taking the quilt up to my room with me for the night. Augusta had to be somewhere close by—cranberry bread doesn't appear by itself—yet I would be glad when daylight came and we would finally have a chance to learn what the Mystic Six had to say for themselves. I hoped we wouldn't be disappointed.

Chapter Twenty-four

"IT REALLY IS PRETTY," VESTA SAID THE NEXT morning after cranberry bread (compliments of Augusta) and scrambled eggs and bacon (compliments of me). "You know, I don't think I've ever *looked* at it before."

We had spread the quilt on the double bed in what had been my great-grandmother's room, and although it smelled of mothballs and was somewhat dingy in places, the colors were still bright. It seemed to be sort of a patchwork replica of the old Minerva Academy campus with Holley Hall in its center. Tiny evergreens dotted a calico lawn that was intersected by a tan linen path meandering much as it does today. A gray stone wall surrounded the grounds, and a bright blue river zigzagged past.

Vesta put her finger on a slender tree in the corner of the campus. "This must be that huge red oak that shades the street. Some of these hardwoods weren't tiny even when I was growing up, but I know they've replaced a lot of them."

We counted three smaller buildings scattered about the campus that were no longer there. Vesta remembered the larger one as the old dining hall that was torn down after being badly damaged in a tornado.

"It cut a path through the edge of town, then veered and hit that part of the campus," she told us. "Fortunately no one was hurt, but it did a lot of damage. The academy closed its doors as a school a few years after that."

"Did you go there?" I asked.

Vesta shook her head. "No, Mama didn't want to

226

send me to Minerva. I went to the public schools here, then went off to college, but I remember that storm. I must've been about eight at the time. It destroyed a wooden classroom building, too—ugly, two-story thing that was built to replace the one that burned, but it happened on a Sunday morning, thank goodness, when everybody was in church."

"I can see why Hattie Carnes called this quilt the Burning Building," Mildred said. "It seems to be the dominant theme."

I had to admit it kind of gave me the creeps. Red and orange flames, so vivid they looked as if they would singe you if you touched them, curled raggedly from the upstairs windows, dark puffs of smoke billowed from the roof.

"It is a strange theme," I said. "With the variety of quilt patterns to choose from, why on earth would they want to devote their time to making this?"

"It tells a story," Vesta reminded me. "A tragic story, true, but it involved a place and an event that had a great impact on their lives. Fitzhugh Holley, the young professor, died in that fire. They said he went back inside to save one of the girls."

"So I guess he was a hero of sorts." Mildred touched the worn applique, then abruptly drew back her hand.

"They named the main building after him," Vesta told her. "And I understand there was a huge demand for his children's books, although he didn't live to see them in print. "Yes, I'd say he was a hero."

"What did your mother say about him?" I asked.

My grandmother shrugged. "She didn't talk about him. It was too close to her, I guess."

"Who was the girl he saved from the fire?" I asked her.

Vesta smoothed a wrinkled corner, looking at it all the while. "Good heavens, I have no idea! And after all this time, I don't suppose anyone else would, either."

"Maybe Mamie Estes would," I said. "I'll call her."

But Mildred put a delaying hand on my arm. "Never mind, I know who it was. It was Irene Bradshaw's mother. Irene told me once."

"Aunt Pauline?" Vesta leaned on the foot of the heavy Victorian bed. "She never mentioned it to me."

"Maybe she didn't like to talk about it," Mildred said, "but Irene seemed quite proud of it. Said her mother had gone to take the professor his tea—seemed he always enjoyed a cup in the late afternoons—and she found the office filled with smoke and Professor Holley asleep in his chair. She managed to wake him, help him to the stairs . . . the office could only be reached by an inside stairway, I understand, but by that time Pauline became overcome herself. Fitzhugh Holley was said to have carried her down the stairs and outside."

"So why did he go back?" Vesta wanted to know.

"Irene seemed to think he believed there was another student still inside," Mildred said.

"But there wasn't." I looked at the dreadful building and could almost smell the scorch of burning wood. "What a waste!"

Vesta lifted the quilt and held it to the light. "Did you notice the angel a little to the right above the building? She's almost hidden by a cloud, but she seems to be smiling on the whole scene."

"She? *He*, you mean. That must represent the professor." I examined the tiny angel. It did seem to have definite feminine characteristics.

I looked closer at the quilt. Beneath a grove of patchwork trees a distance from the flaming building,

228

five figures stood watching. They were primitive figures, such as the kind a child might design, but they were most decidedly female, and each wore a different color scrap of fabric for a dress.

Even the bright morning sun couldn't warm the cold that came over me. Somehow I knew the crude doll-like characters represented the five woman who made the quilt, and each wore a tiny piece of material from her own dress.

"What a morbid lot they were! They've even included a teapot in here." I showed the others a square in the corner of the quilt.

"And what about the little tree with yellow flowers?" Vesta pointed out. "I've never seen one like it. Do you suppose it has any significance?"

"It looks something like a golden chain tree," Mildred said. "A neighbor had one when we were growing up; we used to call it a bean tree because it has long clusters of beanlike seedpods. The flowers look something like yellow wisteria."

"Like these," I said, patting a sunshiny square. "Aren't they beautiful?"

"Beautiful but deadly," Mildred said. "The seeds are extremely poisonous. Mama wouldn't let us play close to that tree." She sank into the little maple rocking chair by the window and closed her eyes. "I'm getting a bad feeling about this."

Mildred looked like a life-size apple doll sitting there in her crisp blue checked housedress with the lace-trimmed collar and stockings the color of strong tea rolled (I knew) just above the knees and held in place with worn elastic. I went over and knelt beside her. I had a bad feeling, too, and the more we delved into the story behind the quilt, the darker things seemed. Suspicions whirled in my mind like

229

worrisome gnats clouding my vision. These innocent-seeming young women—my own great-grandmother among them—had done something horrible, and I didn't want to focus on it.

"This is upsetting you," I said, taking her hand. "We can put the quilt away for a while."

Did we really want to uncover the reason for this ghastly quilt? Now I knew how Peggy O'Connor, Mamie Estes, and all the others had felt. I wanted to send it as far away as possible and never see it again.

But then we might never know.

Mildred looked at my grandmother, who nodded to her with a barely noticeable squint that I knew meant she was worried. "Minda's right. This can wait," Vesta said.

"No, it can't." Mildred took my arm and let me help her to her feet. "Can't you see what happened here?"

I glanced at my grandmother and could tell by her expression that even if she did see, she'd rather not discuss it.

Mildred stood looking down at the quilt. "I think I know who my father was," she said. "I've wondered all along, but I'm almost certain of it now. My father was Fitzhugh Holley, and those girls set that fire on purpose. They meant for him to die."

"Oh-h, Mildred . . . " The words slid from Vesta's mouth with such a final sound it seemed she'd never speak again.

She did, of course. "What makes you think they would do a thing like that?" she asked. "That doesn't make any sense at all." Her words weren't too convincing, I thought, since she backed away from the quilt as she spoke.

"They did it for revenge and probably for self-preservation. Look." Mildred placed a finger on the angel. "This isn't the noble professor looking down, it's supposed to be my mother, Annie Rose."

My grandmother shook her head. "But how—?"

"They thought she drowned in the river, you see. They knew about the pregnancy and who was responsible for it. They thought she took her own life."

"How can you be sure?" I asked. "Mamie's the only one left, and she stops short of admitting it."

"And you said yourself he saved Pauline Watts," Vesta said. "Carried her out of that burning building. Didn't Irene tell you that?"

"Irene told me," Mildred said, "and I'm sure her mother *told her* that was what happened. That was their story."

"But that's a hideous thing to do—even if he was responsible for—what you said!" Vesta laced her fingers together as if she meant to pray this away.

"There's more." Mildred ran her hand over the quilt, traced the telltale designs with her fingers. "There was a letter."

"What kind of letter? Who wrote it?" I moved to her side to see what she was doing. Was the letter inside the quilt?

"The letter was from Flora Dennis. She and Lucy corresponded, you know, and just before Lucy died, a letter came from Flora." Mildred turned to Vesta. "Your mother didn't feel up to reading it, so she asked me to read it to her.

"There were things in that letter that would lead one to believe Annie Rose wasn't the professor's only victim, and that Flora herself might have been one, as well."

"What things?" Vesta asked. "What happened to the

231

letter?"

"Your mother asked me to get rid of it, tear it up and throw it away."

"Oh, no!" Vesta and I groaned together.

"But I didn't, of course," Mildred said, standing a bit straighter. "I think I must've wondered then if there was a connection between something that happened here and my own mother, and so I kept it."

"What did Flora say that was so awful?" I asked. "Can you remember?"

"You don't forget things like that," Mildred said, looking at both of us in turn. "She said she hoped that horrible man would burn eternally in hell, said she wasn't one bit sorry for what they did, and Lucy shouldn't be, either."

Vesta picked up a corner of the quilt and looked at it closely, as if she could read something further there. "Did you ask my mother what it was that they did?"

"Yes, but Lucy evaded the question, said Flora was getting senile, talking nonsense with all that rambling, but I could see the letter bothered her. She must have known she didn't have much longer to live, and I think she might have been having some regrets about what they did. Of course at the time, I had no idea what that was."

"And we can't be sure about it now, either," Vesta said. "What would keep the professor from escaping once he knew the building was on fire? How could they be sure he would die so obligingly?" My grandmother folded her arms.

"The girls have told us how—right here in this quilt." Mildred directed our attention to the teapot, the tree with yellow flowers. "Irene said her mother took the professor his afternoon *tea*. It must have been a daily

232

custom. The seeds of the laburnum, or golden chain tree, are toxic. Ingested they cause weakness, drowsiness. I believe they made a brew of them and added it to his tea."

"So he wouldn't wake up when they set the fire." Vesta absently fingered the edge of the quilt. "The man must have been a monster! But why couldn't they go to their parents? Surely somebody—

"Wait a minute. What's this?" She held up a small bulge, covered with a scrap of green. "It feels like something's under here . . . Minda, get the scissors!"

I pressed the cloth between my fingers. "It's just a wad of padding. I hate to ruin an heirloom, even if it is depressing."

"But look what's covering it," Mildred pointed out.

I looked. "A leaf. Okay, so—"

"A *holly* leaf," Mildred said, hurrying to the closet. "There should be scissors on the second shelf."

A few minutes later we discovered how the five girls made certain Fitzhugh Holley didn't wake from his drugged sleep and escape. They had locked him in his office, then later sewed the key into the quilt.

"Do you think this has anything to do with what happened to Otto?" I asked Mildred.

"It certainly doesn't put Fitzhugh Holley in a very good light, but then it wouldn't do much for the other families, either—the ones involved in setting the fire. And there's no way to prove it either way." Mildred frowned. "The quilt tells a story. I feel it's true, and so, I think, do you, but who would believe it—or even care— after all these years?"

"Gert would, and probably Hugh," Vesta said. "Even the suggestion of lewd behavior would knock their sainted granddaddy off his pedestal, but I honestly can't

233

see them killing for it. Illegitimate babies don't seem to be a big deal these days—no offense, Mildred."

"And none taken." I was surprised to see Mildred smile. She held out the key, which had been wrapped in cotton batting. "What do we do with this?"

"Throw it away," I said, and my grandmother nodded in agreement.

"My mother led me to believe that Annie Rose helped make this quilt," Vesta said, "but it's only initialed by the others." She held a corner of the quilt under the bedside lamp to show the star-flower emblem and the neatly stitched initials of the other five members of the Mystic Six.

"I believe she started out making it with the other girls before things began going wrong," Mildred said. "Except for the fire, the rest of the quilt is almost festive, with its winding paths and trees. And look at the main building—there's even a cat curled on the steps. I think it began as a tribute to a place they loved; then when things took a nasty turn, I imagine they put it away."

"Until Annie Rose drowned—or they thought she drowned," Vesta said. "And they took things into their own hands."

"I wonder whose idea it was to hide the key in the quilt," I said. When I'd thought of the quilt as holding the key to a secret, I really hadn't meant it literally.

"I can't imagine," Vesta said, "but I think I do know who thought of the laburnum tea. It must've been Lucy, my mother. She always liked botany, plants, things like that. Did you know she majored in biology in college?"

I helped the two older women fold the quilt and put it away until they decided what to do with it. I didn't think it would be going on display at Minerva Academy.

And since both Vesta and I were curious to read Flora Dennis's letter to Lucy, the three of us drove to Mildred's. Instead of coming in the back way through Mildred's apartment, I parked in front of the bookshop, where we heard sounds of hammering from inside.

Gatlin met us at the door with a wide grin. The place was a mess, and dust and debris were everywhere. "Mind where you step," she said, "R.T.'s doing his thing." She paused to introduce us to the tall man banging on the wall with a sledgehammer, and I finally got to meet Maureen Foster's husband.

"Minda's the one who recommended you," she told him. "Now I guess I'll have to be nice to her."

"So when can I expect lunch?" I asked, stepping over a pile of plaster.

"R.T. says May—April if things go right. Of course we'll have to have a new roof, but he gave me a fair price." Gatlin gave me a shove and grabbed the others by an arm. "Come in the back office where we can breathe. It's awfully dusty in here."

I had noticed that R.T. wore a mask to screen out the dust. "Actually, we were headed for Mildred's," I said. "Just wanted to see what was going on."

"So has everybody else. I think you're the third group to drop by this morning. Hugh was here earlier and Irene Bradshaw just left—came to tell me Sylvie Smith's out of intensive care now."

"That's wonderful!" I said. "Is she out of her coma? Can she remember anything?"

"They say she's come around, but didn't get a chance to look at the person who hit her. When she's a little stronger, Minda, you should pay her a visit. Bet she'd be glad to see you. If it hadn't been for you, Sylvie might not be around."

"It was just luck," I said. It wasn't, but how could I explain a bossy angel?

While we were talking, Mildred had slipped through the connecting door to her small apartment, and now she reappeared with a look on her face that scared even me.

"It's gone," Mildred announced, doling dagger looks equally among us.

"What's gone?" Gatlin asked.

"My zebra. Otto's zebra. It's where I keep . . . Oh never mind! But I need it. There are things in there, important things."

Vesta frowned. "The letter?"

"Yes, the letter. Why would anybody take that old stuffed zebra?" Mildred wailed. "It doesn't mean a thing to anyone but me."

"Oh, dear. I'm afraid it does to Faye." Gatlin clutched my hand—for support, I guess. "She was here with me before school this morning; I had to let R.T. in, and she needed to use the bathroom—you know how Faye is, and they had cut off the water in the bookshop, so I let her use yours.

"I saw her playing with the zebra as we were getting ready to leave for school. She said Tigger needed a playmate, but I told her to put it back."

Gatlin smiled. Mildred didn't. "Mildred, honestly, I'm so sorry. I thought she'd put it back where it belonged."

"Maybe she misplaced it," Vesta said. "Let's look around and see if we can find it. I expect Faye just dropped it somewhere."

But the old stuffed animal containing Flora Dennis's condemning letter wasn't in Mildred's tiny apartment.

"She must have taken it to school with her," Gatlin said, now close to tears. "I was in a hurry and didn't pay

236

close attention, just assumed it was Tigger."

"It's all right," Mildred said, although I could tell by her face it wasn't. "I'm sure it will be fine with Faye at school, and you can drop it off when you pick her up from kindergarten after lunch."

But a few minutes before Gatlin planned to leave to collect her daughter, the school called to tell her Faye had disappeared from the playground.

Chapter Twenty-five

"SHE WAS HERE, AND THEN SHE WASN'T," THE young teacher said, her voice trembling. "We were on the playground for only about fifteen minutes because we planned to rehearse our Thanksgiving skit before being dismissed for the day. Faye and Cindy Emerson were playing pilgrim over by that big oak tree. Had some kind of stuffed animal with them." She took out a tissue and blew her nose. "They insisted on wearing their pilgrim hats outside."

Not Faye, no! Please, not Faye! I felt cold inside and empty, like I had when Jarvis died, but falling apart wouldn't help Faye or anyone else. Since Gatlin was in no condition to drive, I had insisted on taking her to school, and Mildred wouldn't be left behind. My grandmother had left earlier to pick up groceries for Thanksgiving dinner.

Dave, who had arrived a few minutes after we did, turned from the window that overlooked the playground in the principal's office, where we gathered. "Did Cindy notice where she went? Did Faye say anything?" His face was like stone except for a slight twitch under one eye. Gatlin was trying hard not to cry, and she clung to her husband's arm as if it might keep her from toppling over.

"Cindy said she saw Faye speak to a man," Mrs. Grimes, the principal, told us, but she didn't think she went with him. Soon after that the children were called in from play, and Faye wasn't among them. Her coat is gone, and we couldn't find the stuffed animal, either, so she must have taken them with her."

"What man?" Gatlin asked, her voice growing louder with each word. "What did he look like? What was he doing here?"

"We're looking into that right now, checking volunteer records." Mrs. Grimes spoke with an "in charge" voice. "I'm sure Faye's just playing somewhere, hiding probably. You know how children are at this age. We'll find her soon. Try not to worry."

"Not worry? A five-year-old is missing, and we're not supposed to worry?" Mildred, in her twenty-year-old coat and smushed hat with a pink feather on it, stepped up to face the principal. "If she's not on the grounds, then she's outside them. Possibly with some strange man. How did you let this happen?"

"We're searching the grounds right now," Mrs. Grimes said, "and the buildings, inside and out. If she's here, we'll find her."

"And if she's not?" Dave reached for the phone. "I'm calling the police."

The young teacher, whose first name, I think, was Nancy, put a hand on his. "We've already called them."

Gatlin looked at me. "Do you think it's about that zebra? She took it after I told her not to, and now she's run off somewhere, afraid she'll be punished."

"Maybe she felt sick and went home," I said. It

238

wasn't far, only a few blocks, and Faye could have walked it easily. Had done so, in fact, with her mother. "Did she feel all right this morning?"

"Faye wouldn't do that," Gatlin said. "She knows I'll come for her if she's sick, and she was fine this morning as far as I know."

"I'll check the house again," Dave said. "I went by there first, and she wasn't there."

"I'll go with you," Gatlin said.

"No, stay here. One of us should be in case she turns up." Her husband gave her a brief kiss on the forehead.

"Call," she said, and he nodded, leaving.

Gatlin went to the window. "I'm going to check the grounds, and if she's not there, I'm turning this building upside down."

"I'll help," I said.

"No, please!" Mrs. Grimes stood. "I assure you we've searched the place thoroughly. The police should be here any minute, and I'm certain they'll conduct one as well. Faye's morning kindergarten class has been dismissed for the day, and I can't have you disrupting the others."

"I don't care what you want or don't want!" Gatlin said, her voice breaking. "I want my child back. I want my baby! I have to do *something*!" And she threw herself on my shoulder and sobbed.

"Mrs. Grimes?" A slender, rather colorless young woman crept in with a note in her hand, and the principal introduced her as Betty Ann Harris, an assistant in the media center. "Our volunteers are all accounted for, and none of them were on the playground when the little girl wandered."

Wandered away? But I suppose I hoped the woman was right, that Faye did wander away on her own.

239

" . . . but one of the fourth-grade girls said she saw a child talking to that man who helps with the newsletter," she continued. "You know, the one who prints it all out for us once it's put together."

"You mean Hugh Talbot? My goodness, is it already time for another issue?" Mrs. Grimes turned to us. "He's been such a help to organize our little newsletter. No one else seems to have time for it. They're going to republish some of his grandfather's animal stories, he tells me, and I hear one of the children's networks is interested. They're timeless, those little tales."

"Where did she see them?" Gatlin asked. "And when?"

"I believe it was during their playtime," Betty Ann Harris said.

"You believe? Well, for goodness' sakes, let's get the child in here and find out. Who is she, and who's her teacher?"

Mrs. Grimes conferred with her secretary, and the little girl was promptly summoned, but she didn't remember seeing Faye leaving with the man in the brown overcoat.

"If she didn't leave with him, where did she go?" I asked her, trying to sound calmer that I was.

"I don't know, but I think she ran away. I was looking out the window, sharpening my pencil, you know, and the teacher said I'd been there long enough and to come and sit down."

Mrs. Grimes picked up the phone. "I'll call Mr. Talbot at his office, see if he can help." But after what seemed like a century, she shrugged and hung up. "Nobody answers. I expect he's at the academy."

I could almost feel Mildred's bright eyes boring into me, and I turned to find her trying her best to give me some kind of silent message while inching toward the door.

"Why don't Mildred and I see if Mr. Talbot's at the academy, then look around while we're there?" I suggested to Gatlin. "I know it's hard for you, but I think you should stay right here so we'll know where to find you." I know she was thinking of what had happened to me at Minerva Academy, and worse, what had happened to Otto. I remembered the smothering smell of the dusty drapes over my head, the helplessness of being pulled along the floor. Surely no one would do something like that to a child!

I felt the tears on her cheek as I gave her a hug, but managed to hold in my own until we were outside.

"Stop that. We don't have time for tears," Mildred said. "We have to find this child, and I'll be willing to bet Hugh or his sister is behind it."

She sounded so much like Augusta, she might have been taking lessons. Still, I snuffled, imagining my small cousin shivering under a hedge somewhere or curled beneath a bush—hiding. From whom? At least she'd been wearing a coat, and this was one of our milder days, weatherwise. But if anything happened to Faye, I didn't think we'd be able to bear it.

The police pulled into the parking lot as Mildred and I started to drive away. The chief's nephew, Rusty Echols, was behind the wheel, and I waved them down and told them where we were going.

"After your last experience over there, I'm surprised you'd even consider going back to that place," he said. "You just sit tight until we've checked out the school, and we'll see if anything's going on at the academy."

"I don't have time to sit tight. My little cousin is missing, and she was last seen talking to Hugh Talbot. If

I were you, I'd get on the radio and tell your uncle or somebody to meet me there," I said. And I didn't give him a chance to answer.

"What makes you so sure it's Hugh or Gert?" I asked Mildred, hoping I was far enough away from the police car that they couldn't tell how fast I was driving.

"Hugh was at the bookshop this morning, remember? Gatlin said he'd dropped by earlier. Hoping nobody would be there, no doubt, so he could get his hands on my zebra! What a shock it must've been for the old fool to see Faye walking off with it."

"But we don't know for sure that Faye did walk off with it," I reminded her. "And how would Hugh Talbot know you hide things there?"

The words were barely out of my mouth before I remembered who told the secret of Mildred's hiding place. My grandmother and I had talked about it in the kitchen only the day before. *And Gertrude Whitmire had been . . .*

"Oh, dear," I said. "I'm afraid Gertrude might have heard us whispering in the other room when she dropped by yesterday morning."

"Whispering about what?"

"The would-be burglary at the bookshop, and that you hide things in the zebra," I said. "Of course, Vesta didn't know what was in it."

"So I suppose Gert passed the information along to Hugh." Mildred made a funny noise in her throat and dug in her purse for a hankie. "I can't believe they'd hurt that child, Minda. I just can't let myself believe that. They would be my niece and nephew, you know, if what I suppose is true, but I'll be darned if I claim them!"

I almost ran off the road. Mildred Parsons said *darn!*

242

"Minda, I'm sure it must have been Gert who slipped something into my drink the night I got so sick after that meeting," she said.

"I thought you said she wasn't there."

"Well, she wasn't at the meeting, and to tell you the truth, I'd forgotten she was even there because she just ran in for just a minute—or hobbled in, rather. Janice had taken her a casserole when she hurt her ankle so bad, and Gert dropped by to return the dish. Came in the kitchen door and must've left the same way, I guess, because nobody saw her but Janice and me, and I wouldn't have noticed her, either, if I hadn't had to use the bathroom. That's down the hall from the kitchen, you know."

"But how would she know which cup was yours?"

"Oh, the rest of them were having that punch Janice makes. I don't ever drink that stuff. Too sweet. Everybody knows I just take coffee straight and black."

"So the drinks must have already been poured, and Gert—or somebody—just put the stuff in yours."

Mildred shook her head. "Now is that any way to treat a relative?"

Holley Hall looked almost festive with shocks of cornstalks by the steps and pumpkins on the porch. We arrived to find Hugh Talbot fastening a decoration of dried gourds and Indian corn on the front door.

He turned when he heard us approaching. "Does this look all right? Gert was supposed to take care of all this, but she's run out on me."

"Gatlin's little girl is missing," I said. "Faye. She's only five, and I understand you were talking to her on the school playground this morning."

"Is that who that was? Yes, I did speak briefly to a

243

little girl as I was leaving. And she's missing, you say?" He opened the door and motioned for Mildred and me to come inside. "Do they have any idea where she might've gone?"

"No. That's why we're here. We thought she might have said something to you," I said.

"Did you notice anyanything that might give us an idea where to look for her," Mildred said. "You can imagine how frantic her parents are—we all are. Was she holding anything when you saw her, a toy or something?"

Hugh Talbot shook his head and wouldn't meet our gaze. "Not that I remember."

"Are you sure?" Mildred jammed her face right into his, pink feather quivering atop her hat. "Her friends say she was playing with a stuffed animal, one I believe you had some interest in, Hugh Talbot. Now Faye's disappeared, and so has the zebra."

"What's this all about?" Hugh took a few steps back. "I can assure you I don't have any interest in a child's teddy bear. My goodness, why—"

"Not teddy bear, a zebra!" I said, flanking his other side. "We don't have time for games, Mr. Talbot. A five-year-old is missing. If you have any idea where she might be, you've got to tell us *now!*"

"We know about your grandfather and his extracurricular activities," Mildred said. "We've seen the quilt, and we know all about the fire, so if you're trying to protect your grandfather's reputation, you're a bit too late."

"Quilt? What quilt?" He seemed genuinely confused.

"Never mind the quilt," I said. "I'm sure you must have suspected that Annie Rose Westbrook, my relative who was supposed to have drowned in the Saluda, was pregnant with your grandfather's child. He forced himself on her as he did others, but Annie didn't die. She went away, married and had her baby . . . "

Hugh took another step sideways, his eye on the door. I blocked him.

"How on earth could you know any of this is true?" he said.

"Because *I'm* that baby," Mildred told him. "My mother was Annie Rose Westbrook, a student here at the academy, and a member of the Mystic Six. I have her pin."

Hugh Talbot tried to laugh. "That doesn't mean a thing. The girl probably wasn't wearing it when she . . . Well, what does it matter now, anyway? This happened years ago."

"Oh, but she was wearing it," Mildred said, holding the pin in the palm of her hand. "This pin belonged to my mother. It has her initials on the back. She always kept it in a box in her dresser drawer, but I didn't know what it was until lately. Lucy had one just like it, and so did the other members."

"I really don't give a damn about your mother's pin, or any of the rest of this! Can't you see that?" The man's face turned red, and sweat broke out on his forehead, even though it was cold in Holley Hall. "What my grandfather did was his business. I couldn't care less."

"Then why were you so interested in the stuffed zebra Faye was playing with?" I asked.

"I didn't care about—I only asked her where she got it. But it seemed to frighten her, and she ran away. I didn't hurt the child, didn't mean to scare her. Look, I really don't know where she is, but if you're concealing something important in that toy, you might want to call

245

the police. I'm afraid the little girl could be in danger."

"We've already called them," I told him as I saw Chief McBride and another policeman pull up out front. "Why do you think she's in danger?"

"I—I can't be sure . . . "

"Tell me!"

A brass paperweight in the shape of a monkey sat on the desk only a few inches away, and my hand moved instinctively toward it, but Mildred grabbed my wrist firmly. "For heaven's sakes, don't bean him now, Arminda! He won't be able to talk."

Hugh Talbot sank into a dainty Queen Anne side chair that seemed almost too fragile to hold him, and put his head in his hands. "It's Gert," he said. "My sister's the one who wanted that zebra. She thinks there's something hidden in there, something incriminating that might hurt us, hurt the family.

"I was just going to look at it, that's all. I guess the little girl thought I meant to take it away from her. She ran away before I had a chance to explain."

"Does your sister know what happened?" I asked.

He nodded. "I was supposed to bring it here, and when I came back without it, she tore out of here like a bat out of hell. God knows where she is now."

"Do you think she would harm Faye?" I had to ask.

He sighed. "Not deliberately, but she's obsessed about our grandfather, our heritage, she calls it. At this point, I don't know what she might do; I really don't."

Chapter Twenty-six

I HONESTLY THINK HUGH TALBOT WAS GLAD to see the police. He started to stand; then sat down again. "Have they found the little girl?" he asked the chief.

"Not yet. They're still searching the school, but Dave didn't turn up any sign of her at the house."

Where in the world could she be? Wherever Faye was, she had to be hungry. She rarely ate much breakfast, and she hadn't had any lunch. I looked at my watch. It wasn't quite one o'clock, yet I felt it should be late afternoon, that Faye had been missing for hours. I told Chief McBride what Hugh Talbot had said about Gertrude Whitmire.

"Mrs. Whitmire? You think *Mrs. Whitmire* could be responsible for the child's disappearing?"

You'd have thought I'd said Jesus Christ drowned kittens and tied tin cans to puppies' tails.

"And what makes you think that?" the chief wanted to know.

I wanted to dash out the door and search the town for Faye, but I didn't trust Hugh to give the account correctly. And I wanted this crazy woman stopped. "Mrs. Whitmire's been having a few problems lately," I said. "I'll let Mr. Talbot tell you about it."

While Hugh gave the police the story, I phoned Vesta and left a message about Faye's being missing. "Has anyone checked my place or my grandmother's?" I asked when I was through.

"I believe Dave went by there earlier, and we have

volunteers right now lined up to search everywhere between here and the river. I'll ask them especially to be on the lookout for Mrs. Whitmire's car. A blue Lincoln, isn't it?" He asked her brother. "Don't suppose you know the license number? Well, never mind, I'll get it."

The river! Oh, dear God, I hadn't even thought about the river! "I have to go," I said. "I have to look for Faye."

"Ma'am, we're doing everything that can be done." The chief's voice was gentle. "I honestly believe the little girl is hiding somewhere. She ran away from school, and now she's afraid to come home. She's going to be all right, just you wait and see."

Yeah, that's easy for you to say, I thought. *She's not your little girl.* Heck, she wasn't mine either, but if I ever did have one, I'd like one just like her, and when they did find Faye, I was going to buy her all the hot dogs she could eat!

"If you don't mind, I'd like for you to stick around awhile," Chief McBride said. "Since you were the one who found your cousin Otto, maybe you can help us out here." He nodded to Mildred. "Charlie here can run Miss Parsons home if you like."

"I don't want to go home, but I would like for you to take me by the school while they look for Faye. I think Gatlin and David might need some help when Lizzie gets out of school."

The chief and I agreed that was an excellent idea, and after the two of them left, moved into the musty, grim parlor, where Hugh suggested we might be more comfortable. The three of us sat around the feeble gas fire, and it reminded me of my recent nasty experience, as well as the day weeks before when we had waited here after I had found my cousin's body.

The thought of it made me shudder and draw my coat closer about me. The chief must've been thinking the same thing, because he turned to Hugh Talbot, who sat next to the mantel, leaning forward with his hands clasped between his knees. "All this has something to do with Otto Alexander's death, doesn't it, Hugh?" Chief McBride asked.

Hugh didn't answer. Why wasn't I surprised?

"Yes, it does," I said. "There's something I haven't told you. The day I found Otto's body, I also found a pin—about the size of a sorority or fraternity pin. It was in the shape of a flower with a star in its center, and it had belonged to my aunt—great-great-aunt really, who was supposed to have drowned in the Saluda over eighty years ago."

Hugh made sort of a rumbling noise and shifted in his chair. "You say you found that here? Where?"

"In the bathroom, in the stall next to Otto's. It was on the floor, and I almost didn't see it. I think he had it wrapped in his handkerchief, and when he pulled it out, the pin rolled under the side of the stall—just before *somebody* smothered him." I looked at Hugh Talbot, and this time he met my eyes.

"It wasn't me," he said. "I'm not taking the blame for that."

"Mr. Talbot, you're in and out of this place all the time. As far as I know, you, your sister, and Otto were the only ones who had a key." The chief stood and leaned on the mantel. He was not a tall man, but he looked tall then. "I know you announced a football game that night, but the game was over by a little before ten. Where did you go then?"

"I've already told you, I went home! We've gone over this before." Hugh slapped his knee, and his

249

hairpiece slid a little to the side. "I want a lawyer."

"Fine, call one, but if you had nothing to do with this, it will make it a whole lot easier for you and for us, too, if you just cooperate," the chief said calmly.

The man sat there so long I didn't think he was going to answer. Finally he sighed and rose to his feet. "I need a drink. Do you mind?"

He moved to a small cupboard that looked like part of the wainscoting and took out a decanter and several small glasses. "Anyone care to join me?" he asked.

Of course the chief said no thank you and so did I, although to tell the truth, I could've used a belt about then.

He downed one drink in what seemed like a gulp, poured another to sip, and then sat again in the chair by the fireplace. "I was at the bookshop—Otto's shop—that night."

Hugh Talbot spoke so softly I could barely hear him. "I knew Otto would be at the academy then, and there was something I wanted to find."

"And what was that?" the chief wanted to know.

"It has no relevance to what happened. It was just something I knew Otto had, and I thought perhaps it was somewhere in the bookshop."

So Mildred's pencils really had been moved!

Chief McBride leaned forward. "Man, how can you say it has no relevance? A man is dead, this young lady here has been attacked, and now a child is missing." He did everything but wave a finger in the man's face, but still Hugh wouldn't tell us what he was looking for.

"I don't suppose you found it, then?" the chief said.

"No." Hugh slumped in his chair and stared at the feeble fire. He didn't move, rarely blinked.

"Is that what you think is concealed in the stuffed

250

animal you wanted from the little girl?"

"That was stupid of me, I know. It was just something my sister asked me to do."

"And why would Mrs. Whitmire want this child's toy?" Chief McBride asked.

"She thinks there's something in there that would put our family in a bad light. My sister is very proud of her heritage."

Chief McBride sat and closed his eyes for a minute, as if the whole thing were just too much for him. "So, you didn't go to the academy the night Otto Alexander was killed?"

"No." Hugh Talbot shook his head.

"But you knew he was going to be here. How was that?"

Hugh Talbot sighed. "Otto had called me at the academy, left a message on the machine. He said he'd be here that night—he volunteered in the academy library, you know—and that he had something I might be interested to see. He'd hinted—well, more than hinted, really—that he could ruin me. Wanted money, of course."

"So Otto was blackmailing you?"

"That was his intention, yes, but I wasn't planning to take the bait."

"The pin," I said. "He told you about the pin." I knew Otto had taken the pin from Mildred's hiding place.

Hugh nodded. "That was part of it." He turned to the chief. "My grandfather, I'm afraid, wasn't as squeaky clean as he was stacked up to be. A bit of a ladies' man, I think. At any rate, he got one of the young women in the family way, and she was supposed to have drowned in the Saluda—only it turns out she didn't. Now her daughter has come back to haunt us for his sins."

251

"Don't you dare make light of it!" I jumped to my feet and would have clobbered him, I think, if the chief hadn't cleared his throat really loud. "Your grandfather forced himself on those girls—students who were supposed to be in his care! He should've been locked away.

"You killed Otto, didn't you? You got him drunk, then smothered him to keep him quiet."

"No, I did not. I'm sorry my grandfather was a lech and that he caused grief to those young women—if indeed he did—but that's not my fault. I wouldn't kill a man for that."

"Otto met somebody here that night," I told the police chief. "He had that pin in his pocket just before he was killed, only it rolled into the next stall, and the murderer didn't see it."

Chief McBride frowned. "Why didn't you tell us this earlier?"

"I forgot I had it. Didn't even realize what it was for a while; then I guess I was afraid. Otto might have been killed for that pin; I didn't want the same thing happening to me."

The chief turned to Hugh. "And you say these things weren't important to you, yet you searched Otto's bookshop for *something*. Was Otto already dead?"

"Certainly not! I knew nothing about that. But I had to look there while Mildred was at that church movie thing, and I knew Otto would be waiting to meet me at the academy. Look, I was only trying to spare us both a lot of trouble."

"So if what you say is true, someone else must have known about that telephone message. What happened to that tape, Mr. Talbot?"

Hugh Talbot shrugged and stared into his empty

glass.

There was only one other person who could have heard Otto's message on that tape. Gertrude Whitmire. And she was somewhere in this town hunting for a five-year-old with a stuffed zebra.

"I have to go," I said, and didn't stop until I reached my car.

I drove straight home, keeping an eye out for both Faye and Gertrude Whitmire along the way, pulled into the drive, and ran into the house. I needed some heavenly help, and fast.

"Augusta!" I called her name over and over again, checking every room, but she wasn't there. I knew she wasn't there as soon as I walked inside, but I had to hope.

"How could you do this? How could you leave me when I need you most?" I yelled aloud to an echoing house.

Pausing in the hallway, I called the school to see if Faye had turned up. The police had completed their search there with no success, the principal told me. And Gatlin and Dave had collected Lizzie and gone back to their place with Mildred.

Mildred answered when I phoned there and told me she was staying with Lizzie while her parents were out scouting for Faye.

"Do you have any idea where they've looked so far?" I asked.

She hesitated. "The school, of course, and the neighborhood around it, and I think they went to your place, too."

"What about the shop?"

"That's the first place Dave checked," Mildred said,

sounding more like Eeyore than ever.

I felt like Eeyore, too. "I'll keep in touch," I said, and then went out and sat behind the wheel of my car and closed my eyes.

"Think blue," Augusta had advised me once when I got all worked up about something. "It calms you, helps you think straight." I could almost sense her beside me now.

I pictured a sky with clouds drifting, misty blue mountains framing a crystal sapphire lake. Where would I go if I were five years old, cold, hungry, and scared?

I would go home, of course, but obviously Faye hadn't done that. For some reason she was afraid to go So what would she do then?

Knowing my little cousin, I was almost sure she felt guilty for taking Mildred's zebra, and perhaps felt she would be punished for not returning it. Yet Mildred had said they had already checked the shop.

Checked it first!

R.T. Foster was getting ready to leave for another job when I pulled up in front of the bookstore, but the door was still unlocked.

"Any news about the little girl?" he asked, loading tools into his truck.

I shook my head. "Not yet. I was hoping maybe you'd seen her."

"No, they came by here earlier looking. Of course, I've been busy on the other side trying to get rid of some of this clutter, but good Lord, I would've called if I'd have seen her!"

I told him I thought I'd hang around for a while just in case Faye might turn up, and before driving away, he showed me how to lock up without a key using the entrance to the empty building.

The books that remained in the bookshop were shrouded in sheets to protect them, and the floor was littered with plaster dust and jagged pieces of wood. The place would have given me an eerie feeling even if I weren't already scared out of my skin.

Still I searched the rows of empty shelves, boxes of books, lifting covers to peer underneath, hoping to glimpse a frightened, runaway child. I even wandered into the empty room where R.T. had been working but found only sawdust, brick fragments, and dirt. The place smelled of damp and mildew, and I couldn't imagine it ever being a restaurant, but if R.T. Foster said it was possible, then we'd have to hope he knew what he was talking about.

The restaurant seemed unimportant now. I didn't even care anymore who murdered Otto or tried to dump me over a railing. The only thing that mattered was finding Faye alive and safe.

Back in the bookshop I noticed R.T's large footprints in the snow of plaster. He had made a trail going back and forth, in and then out to his truck. And then I saw something else. Small footprints. Very small footprints leading to the back of the shop. In my hurry to look under covers, I hadn't noticed them before.

I also hadn't noticed the scent. Strawberries—faint at first, and then stronger as I followed the footprints to the door of the small back office. Augusta was here, and so, I hoped, was Faye.

But when I opened the door, the office was empty. And so was my heart. Was this some kind of rotten trick? I could almost visualize the missing child curled up in the old armchair that had belonged to my grandfather. But the chair was empty. The office was empty. Yet the smell of strawberries remained.

255

"Don't play with me, Augusta Goodnight!" I said, stamping my foot. And since that didn't get results, I stamped it again.

"Minda?" A sleepy voice spoke from underneath Mildred's big old desk, and Faye, clutching the celebrated zebra, crawled out, dragging a fringed throw behind her. "Did you bring me anything to eat?" she asked.

Chapter Twenty-seven

"IT LOOKS TO ME LIKE YOU'VE ALREADY eaten," I said, noticing the chocolate on her face and the candy wrapper under the desk. It was all I could say for the moment. I held her on my lap in the big armchair and let the tears flow.

"Why are you crying, Minda?"

"Because I was worried about you, you silly! We didn't know where you were. Why did you run off like that?"

"That man—he was mad at me for taking Mildred's zebra."

"What man?"

"The man back at school—on the playground."

"What makes you think that, honey?"

"He wanted to know where I got it; I think he wanted to take it away from me."

"Why didn't you tell your teacher? You know she wouldn't let anyone do that?"

" 'Cause I was scared . . . " Faye rubbed her eyes and began to cry. "Mama told me not to take it, and I did anyway. I was afraid I'd get in trouble, so I hid in the bushes until the man left, and my class had already gone inside."

"Don't cry now, it's all right. And then where did you go?"

"Home. Well, I started home, and this lady came up in a big car and asked if I wanted a candy bar."

"Faye! You know better than to take candy from strangers!"

"But she wasn't a stranger, Minda. I've seen her lots of times. Besides, it was chocolate."

"So you accepted the candy?"

"Yeah, and then I ran away and hid."

"Where?"

"In Mr. Thompson's garage. He's got lots of neat stuff in there, but I didn't bother any of it. Besides, it was cold. I just hid in there till that lady left. She wanted my zebra, too," Faye said, snuggling closer.

"She said that—that she wanted the zebra?"

"Yeah. That's why she gave me the candy. She said she'd give it back, but I didn't believe her. It's Mildred's zebra, and she'd be really mad if I lost it!"

"She be even madder if we lost you," I said. "Is that why you came back here, to return the zebra?"

"Uh-huh. I wanted to, but I didn't know the way. And that lady with the big car kept driving by real slow. I was so afraid she'd see me, Minda! I hid behind a wall once, then got under a tree. I wanted to go home, but she kept going past, and I didn't know how to get there. I cried."

I drew her close and kissed her. "Oh, baby, I'm so sorry! But she's not going to find you now. How *did* you get here?"

Faye sat up straighter and bounced in my lap. "Why, the pretty lady brought me here."

257

"What pretty lady?" I asked.

"I don't know her name, but I was sitting under this tree crying, and oh, I wanted my mama—but I wanted to get Mildred's zebra back first. The lady smelled nice, made me feel good—warmlike, you know. She showed me a shortcut here through people's backyards. I crawled under the desk so the bad people couldn't find me, and she covered me up real warm and cozy and told me to wait for you."

"The man who was working here didn't see you?"

"I was real quiet. I tiptoed. He didn't see the lady, either. Guess he was too busy."

Still holding her close, I reached for the phone. "Everything's going to be all right now, and your mama and daddy are going to be so glad to hear you're safe and sound!"

"Will Mildred be mad, do you think?"

"Mildred will be so happy to see you, I'll bet she'll forget all about that silly zebra," I said.

"But I haven't."

I looked up to see Gertrude Whitmire standing in the office doorway, and she had a revolver in her hand. "I'll take that now," she said.

"No!" Faye clutched the animal closer and grabbed me with a choking hold. "It's not yours, it's Mildred's."

"Mrs. Whitmire, I don't think you realize what you're doing," I said. "You're not well, and you're frightening this child." *And scaring the hell out of me!* Cautiously, I reached again for the phone. "We can get you some help." I spoke as softly, as evenly as I could to reassure Faye and to keep Gert from completely freaking out. Somebody had to be calm—or pretend to be calm. I wanted to throw up.

"I wouldn't touch that telephone." Gertrude stepped

closer. Her eyes were abnormally bright. Scary bright. She wasn't Gertrude Whitmire, the longtime teacher students joked about but always respected. She was someone else, someone—something—cruel and loathsome, and I didn't know how to deal with her.

Then, although I couldn't see her, I knew Augusta was there. Her essence was all around me, and I took a deep breath, feeling her presence, sensing her goodness.

"Give her the zebra, Faye," I said. And the child silently put the stuffed animal into Gertrude's outstretched hand.

Did Gert mean to kill us now that she had what she wanted? I couldn't let that happen. Slowly I eased Faye off my lap, meaning to shove her under the desk while I tried to disarm this madwoman. She was bigger, taller than I was, but I had youth on my side. And I had Augusta.

I watched as she snatched up the zebra, clawed at the threadbare fabric, and the sleeve that had been concealing part of her weapon became dislodged. Gertrude's revolver was a hairbrush!

Gertrude Whitmire was so intent on ripping apart the zebra, I had telephoned 911 before she knew what I was doing. The hairbrush slipped unnoticed to the floor. Putting Faye behind me, I braced myself for what this woman might do when she realized what had happened. I knew now it must have been Gertrude who attacked me on the bicycle and at the academy. This person was definitely out to get me, but what could she do now? Shoot me with a hairbrush?

She picked it up and threw it at me instead, missing my head by inches.

Faye peered from behind me. "Minda, what's wrong with that woman?" she asked, crying.

259

"She's sick, Faye; she's not going to hurt us." I gave her a little shove. "But I want you to crawl under the desk again—just for a little while, okay?"

"You've caused me more trouble than you're worth!" Gertrude Whitmire's words clattered like ice cubes dropped one at a time, and I watched Faye roll under the desk and out of her reach as the woman lunged at me, her hands at my throat.

Instinctively, I threw up my arms in a defensive maneuver I'd learned years before on the grammar school playground, and kicked her in the stomach. Kicked her *hard*.

The breath went out of her with a *whooshing* sound, and she sank to the floor and moaned. Maybe she would be out of commission for a while.

I held out my hand to Faye and pulled her into my lap, then grabbed tissues from Mildred's desk and wiped away her tears. "I'm going to call your mama now. Don't you want to talk to her? Tell her you're all right?"

"Mrs. Whitmire, would you like me to call your brother?" I asked after Faye had spoken to both parents, who were on their way, she said. Faye had curled up in the armchair, and I wrapped the throw around her. Now I stood between the child and the woman who had threatened us—but not too closely. I didn't know what she might do.

Gertrude had quieted now, but still sat on the floor, tugging persistently at the stuffed animal's puckered seams.

"Would it help if your brother were here?" I asked again.

"That Hugh? What for? He's already botched things

260

up. If you and your family had stayed out of this, everything would've been all right."

"You mean Otto would still be alive?"

"He was going to tell everything. *Everything!* It would've ruined us! Otto left that message for Hugh, but I heard it first. Hugh wanted to take the easy way out—"

"Like search the bookshop until he found what he was looking for?" I said.

"That wasn't the way! I knew it wasn't the way, so I just took care of things myself. What Hugh didn't know wouldn't hurt him. Everybody thought I was at that church movie thing, but I sat near the back and left well before it was over."

Gertrude laughed. "Otto had so much to drink, he didn't even know what was happening."

"But I thought Otto had quit drinking."

"Otto thought he had, too, until I put vodka in his orange juice. By the time he realized it, it was too late. He kept the juice in a little refrigerator off the library up there. Came in early that night and fiddled around some, had a few glasses while waiting for Hugh to come." Gert smiled and gave the zebra a punch. "But Hugh didn't come. I came. By that time he was drunk as a skunk. It doesn't take much, you know, if you haven't imbibed in a while."

"And he didn't suspect?"

"Not at first, and then he tried to hide. He joked about it, you know. Made light of my grandfather. Why, he said awful things! Guess he thought I wouldn't look for him in the ladies' room, or maybe he was so drunk and confused he wandered in the wrong room. Oh, it was so easy! The fool didn't even fasten the door of his stall!"

Poor Otto! "But the door was fastened when—"

"Oh, I did that afterward. Stood on a chair. Took a little stretching, but walking keeps me fit, you know."

This woman had absolutely no conscience, no regret.

"And then you came! As soon as I got rid of one nuisance, here came another! You and that Mildred dredging up old lies. You just couldn't let it go, could you?"

"But why Sylvie Smith? What has she ever done?" I took a step away from her and reached for Faye's hand. The woman had long arms and a shifty look.

"Sylvia happened along at an unfortunate time," she said, watching me.

"What were you looking for there?" I asked.

"You know." The look she gave me could split a redwood tree. "You know very well."

But I didn't.

Dave, Gatlin, and the police all arrived at about the same time a few minutes later, and after collecting Lizzie and Mildred, my cousins and I had a late lunch of hot dogs (at Faye's request), at the Heavenly Grill.

Later, over ice cream, I told them what Gertrude had said. "I know she was the one who tried to flip me off my bike, then later meant to do me in at the academy," I said, "but how did she have time to get back there after dropping Gatlin off at the bookshop to get her car?"

"I imagine she parked somewhere close by and walked back to the academy," Dave said.

"If Hugh hadn't come when he did, I might have been part of the flooring!" I said, wishing I hadn't eaten all those fries. "Gertrude must have heard him coming and hidden in another room, then sneaked down the back stairs while he was 'unwinding' me. I guess she meant to make it look like a suicide . . . but she had groceries

262

in her car, remember? How could she have had time to go to the store, then get back to the academy in time to pretend to be so shocked?"

"Those groceries were for the church Thanksgiving collection," Gatlin said. "She probably already had them in the trunk. It wouldn't take a minute to move them up front to look like she'd been shopping. I'll bet if you looked at the date on the receipt, it would prove it."

"Too late now," I said. "But I still don't see how she could've called you on the phone pretending to be your neighbor."

Gatlin frowned. "I think I know. If you'll remember, she went into the bathroom while I was actually talking to the 'neighbor.' I think she called the academy on her cell phone, summoned me downstairs, and then disappeared into the ladies' room to continue the conversation. She didn't come out until I was off the phone."

Mildred, who had been silent, finished her coffee and looked at me. "I really don't believe Gertrude cared for you, Arminda."

I laughed along with everybody else. "I don't think she liked you much, either. And to think I felt sorry for her because her husband died."

"He didn't die," Gatlin said. "Amos Whitmire ran off several years back with a topless dancer from Atlanta. Poor Gert hasn't been the same since."

"I don't guess we'll ever know what she put in your coffee that night," I said to Mildred.

"I don't think I want to know," Mildred said. "But she sure turned the bookstore upside down! We were getting just too close to something that made Gertrude Whitmire most uncomfortable."

"But didn't somebody try to run over Mrs. Whitmire

263

with a car?" Lizzie asked. "She hurt her ankle real bad, remember?"

"Gertrude Whitmire *said* somebody had tried to run her down," her mother said. "She probably got all those cuts and scratches staging her fake accident."

"So everyone would think she was a victim," Dave said. "Looks like the wordy one will be put away for a long time. Wonder how long this has been coming on."

"I don't know, but I hope they put her someplace where she can't hurt anybody else. Do you think she knows about the quilt?" Gatlin asked.

"I'm not sure," Mildred said. "Perhaps not. But Otto must have told her about the group of girls and their pin, as well as the letter from Flora. I think she knew what her grandfather had done, and I'm certain she felt threatened by me, as well."

"I can't help but feel there's something else," I said as Mildred paid the bill. She insisted on it being her treat. "Hugh never would say what it was, but he was looking for something other than that letter. I'm sure of it."

Vesta came rushing up as we were leaving the restaurant and demanded a full account. "Why didn't you get in touch with me? Had to go to three stores to find that stone-ground cornmeal I like, and had no idea what was going on! You can imagine my shock to come home and find my own great-grandchild missing!"

I told her it was a little difficult to get in touch with somebody when you didn't know where they were, but she was so busy hugging and kissing Faye, she didn't even hear me.

The day had turned to dusk by the time we all ended up back at Gatlin's. Vesta heated spiced apple cider while Dave built a fire in the fireplace, and we all sat around, not saying a whole lot, but thankful to be together. The frenzied panic of the morning seemed a bad dream.

I was getting sleepy just sitting there with Napoleon's head in my lap when Chief McBride came to the door. "I've brought you some company," he said, ushering in Dr. Hank.

Of course, we all wanted to know how Sylvie was and were told her condition had been upgraded and they thought she might even be able to go home soon.

"That's one reason I'm here," the doctor told us. "She thought you might like to have this. It was in Sylvia's safety deposit box, but I believe it belongs to you."

"What in the world is it?" Vesta asked.

"Something Otto asked her to keep," the chief said. "He must've realized he was in danger and gave it to her for safekeeping."

"Sylvie thought it was a rare manuscript that Otto planned to sell," Dr. Hank said. "He was a good friend and had helped her purchase such things for her library collection in London, so she agreed to keep it for him, not knowing, of course, what it was.

"But when Otto was killed," he continued, "Sylvie says she became frightened and suspected that somebody might have been after the manuscript. That's when she rented the safety deposit box. She planned to leave it there until whoever killed Otto was safely in jail." He gave the portfolio to my grandmother.

"Hank, I'm sorry, but I have to ask," Vesta began. "What happened between Sylvie and Otto? Were they— engaged, or something?"

"Not hardly. Just friends. Both of them loved books—especially old books, so they had that much in common. And Otto was helping Sylvie with a collection

265

for the museum in London. To be honest, I doubt if Otto cared in that way about the opposite sex."

"Oh." Vesta glanced at Mildred, who seemed to agree.

"Have you seen what's in here?" Vesta turned to Dr. Hank, and he nodded, grinning.

"Hell, Vesta, you know how curious I am."

Inside were several composition books, yellowed with age, a sketchbook filled with drawings of the characters Doggie Dan and Callie Cat, all signed by Lucy Westbook, and a manuscript in the same handwriting, unsigned and wrapped in oiled paper.

"Where did Otto find these?" Vesta asked.

"In the attic, I suppose," Mildred told her. "Don't you remember how he combed that attic when we moved out of the old place?"

My grandmother leafed through the papers almost reverently. "Why, these belonged to my mother. She drew these pictures herself . . ."

"And wrote the stories, too," Gatlin said, glancing through one of the composition books.

The folder had also contained a sheaf of letters Lucy had written to my great-grandfather before they married and the handwriting was the same as that on the other written materials.

"I've seen this old manuscript before," Vesta said, holding the bound papers wrapped in oiled paper. "It was in the showcase at the academy, the one in the library. It's said to be an original manuscript of one of the first stories."

"Looks like Otto helped himself to that one, too," I said.

"And it looks like Fitzhugh Holley was a plagiarist," Mildred said. "Good gracious, couldn't the man do anything right?"

"He had you," Vesta reminded her.

The next day was the Wednesday before Thanksgiving, and I had invited the whole family over for the holiday. Dave had promised to smoke the turkey, and Vesta was making rolls and dressing. Mildred agreed to bring sweet potatoes—the good kind with brown sugar and nuts on top, and Gatlin said she'd contribute a cranberry salad, so I really didn't have that much to do. Still, I should have stayed home baking, but there was something I couldn't get off my mind.

"Why?" I asked Gatlin over the phone that morning. "Why in the world would Lucy let that horrible man take credit for her own creation?"

My cousin was mincing ingredients for the salad: celery, pecans, oranges, cranberries, and I had to wait until she'd switched off the food processor. "I can't imagine, but she must've had a reason. Whatever it was, we know the truth now. Otto must have thought he'd struck gold when he found that sketchbook and Lucy's stories, then matched them with the handwriting on that manuscript."

A production company, we learned, had expressed an interest in reprinting the old stories with the possibility of later introducing them as cartoons, and perhaps a line of children's clothing. The characters, although dated, still had a quaint appeal, and Hugh Talbot, when backed against the wall, had agreed not to contest the rights if it eventually came about.

"What are you making for dessert tomorrow?" Gatlin asked.

"Don't worry. It won't be pumpkin pie." (My cousin hated pumpkin pie.) "I'll let you know when I get back."

"Get back from where?"

"Mamie Estes's. If anybody would know why our great-grandmother let that man put his name on her stories, it would be her."

"But Minda, she's a hundred and two! What makes you think she'll remember?"

"Some things you just don't forget," I said, and hoped I was right.

As it turned out, I was. I hadn't even called ahead, but took along a jar of strawberry preserves Augusta had made earlier, and took my chances. Augusta went along for company, and seemed quieter than usual, I thought, during the drive to Charlotte. She didn't even tell me to slow down or to mind the other traffic.

"I hope she's not asleep when we get there," I said as we turned into Mamie's street. And then I had a horrible thought. After all, the woman was 102! "Ohmygosh! What if she's—"

"She's not."

"Well, I guess you'd know," I said.

Her daughter-in-law met me at the door. "Well, my goodness, look at you! Mamie said you'd be coming today! She's waiting for you in the sitting room. Please come in."

"I see you've brought your friend again today," Mamie said after the younger Mrs. Estes left the room.

I took her hand and gave her the preserves. She looked frailer than before, paler, as if she were fading away. "That's right," I said. "Her name is Augusta."

Mamie nodded. "I know."

I sat beside her and got right down to business. When somebody's 102, you don't dilly-dally.

I told her we had found Lucy's sketches and early

manuscripts. I didn't tell her about Mildred because I knew she had been part of an awful deception, thinking her friend had drowned, and it might upset her to learn the truth.

"Do you know why my great-grandmother let Fitzhugh Holley take credit for her stories?" I asked. "Because if you do, I'd like to know."

Mamie did know, and when she told me, I could understand why the remaining members of the Mystic Six did what they thought they must do.

Chapter Twenty-eight

"HE WAS A HANDSOME MAN, SUCH A HANDSOME man! And pleasant, laughed a lot. Everyone loved him—including most of the girls at the academy." Mamie Estes looked as if she'd swallowed something bitter as she sat there turning the small jar of preserves in her hands. "Just about everybody had a crush on the professor—I know I did—but that was before we knew."

I waited for her to continue, not wanting to interrupt, yet I could hardly sit still in my eagerness to hear the rest. I glanced at Augusta, who stood in the background. She wore a frothy white dress today that almost blended with the lace-curtained windows. The angel, hands folded, smiled at me and waited serenely. But she had an eternity; I didn't. And Mamie—well, I didn't even want to think about that.

"He was a fiend!" Mamie said, speaking louder than I would have thought she was capable. "He never bothered me because I wouldn't give him the chance, but I don't know how many others he . . . well, he raped them is what he did! Led them to trust him, then forced himself on them—all of them so innocent. We didn't know a lot back then, and the poor girls didn't know what to do."

"Flora Dennis was one of them, wasn't she?" I asked.

She nodded. "I don't suppose it would do any harm to tell it now. Yes, Flora was one. She was one of his assistants, so honored at first, flattered to be asked. Later, I think she tried to warn Annie Rose, but was embarrassed to come out and tell her what had happened, and Annie Rose probably wouldn't have believed her, anyway." Mamie smiled. "Girls were as headstrong then as they are now, believe it or not."

"Why didn't they tell someone—their parents or a counselor?"

"Dear child, we didn't have counselors back then. Sometimes, if you were lucky, you had an understanding teacher or parent, but people just didn't talk about things like that. The girls were ashamed—and afraid, I guess, that *they* would be blamed for what happened to them. That they would be more or less marked as bad girls forever."

"That's horrible!" I felt anger rising in me, fueled by the helpless frustration of being unable to change something that had happened so many years before.

"You're right. It *was* horrible, and once poor Annie Rose told us about her pregnancy, it all came out."

Tess Estes came in then and asked us if we'd like something hot to drink, but Mamie waved her away. I was glad she didn't want to be interrupted any more than I did.

"I remember when she told us," Mamie went on after her daughter-in-law left the room. "We were working on that quilt—the six of us." She smiled. "You know about our little group?"

I nodded.

"Annie Rose broke down crying, told us what had happened. She had already missed two periods, she said. Then Flora told us the same thing had happened to her and a couple of other girls, only they were lucky enough not to get in the family way. Professor Holley threatened to ruin their reputations if they said anything, Flora said."

My eyes grew hot, and I felt the first salty surge of tears. I blinked them back. "So what did you do then?"

"Lucy went to see Fitzhugh Holley. She wanted him to arrange to send Annie Rose somewhere to have her baby, to protect her from the scandal. And she demanded that he resign. The professor just laughed. He was a married man, you see, already had a little girl. He was respected in the community. 'Who would believe you?' he said to Lucy when she threatened to tell what he'd done."

"Didn't the professor's wife know what a creep he was?" I said.

"If she did, she didn't let on. Remember, things weren't like they are today. The scandal would've been mortifying.

"Lucy's visit did more harm than good, I'm afraid. Earlier she had let the professor critique her little animal stories, seeking his advice, thinking he might even help her find a market for them, and unknown to Lucy, *he had already found a publisher!* I don't know if the publisher mistakenly thought he'd written them or if Fitzhugh Holley deliberately put his name on the manuscript. At any rate, the vile man threatened to spread awful rumors about Annie Rose—Lucy, too—if

271

she didn't keep quiet about the authorship. Said he'd tell everyone he'd seen them in the company of drummers at the Plenty Good Boarding house, where most of the traveling people stayed." Mamie lowered her voice. "Proper ladies didn't go near there."

"Drummers?"

Mamie laughed. "That's what we used to call salesmen—traveling salesmen. At any rate," she said, "things went from bad to worse in spite of our good intentions. But I must say the other members of the Six stood behind Annie Rose. We were trying to find a place she might go to have her baby in secret, and Pluma—I think it was Pluma—was waiting to hear from a cousin in Augusta when that poor child took her own life."

I was tempted to tell her she hadn't, but Augusta gave me the "Don't you dare!" glare.

We were silent for a moment, and I could see that she had just about used up her strength, and I, my time. "It's too late for Lucy," I said at last, "but there's a good chance the stories will be published this time under the right name, in spite of the late—and despicable— Fitzhugh Holley!"

Mamie Estes gave a feeble wave of her hand. "Oh, him! Don't you worry about that one. He's just where he ought to be. That's all taken care of."

"What will you do about the quilt?" Augusta asked during the drive back to Angel Heights.

"It's not up to me to decide, but if it were, I'd destroy it," I said. "The secret of what those girls did should end with us, and I think Mildred and Vesta agree." And except for the few of us who already knew, I didn't think Mildred meant to reveal her true ancestry.

The alma mater my great-grandmother had written and stitched had been found wedged beneath the spare tire in the trunk of Gertrude Whitmire's Lincoln, and Vesta has promised it to me.

"Ordinarily I don't go along with keeping bones in the closet," Augusta said. "But it's time to turn over a green leaf and start with a clean tablet, if you know what I mean."

I wasn't sure, but I thought I could figure it out. "Aren't you freezing?" I asked.

The dress she wore looked like something you might wear to a summer lawn party—a two-piece white georgette with flowing sleeves and delicate embroidered flowers. The trailing necklace winked at me in sapphire, rose, and gold. Sunset colors. And a scarf, sheer as sunlight, draped her shoulders. She shivered. "You might nudge up the heat a bit."

"Why in the world didn't you wear a wrap? You know how cold you always get."

"I came away in such a hurry . . . " She leaned forward, spread her pink fingers in front of the heater.

"Oh, bosh!" I said. "You just didn't want to hide that new dress! You did that embroidery yourself, didn't you? Augusta, you are so full of it!"

"Enough of that, Arminda!" Augusta turned her face away, but I could see she was smiling.

"Thank you for looking after Faye," I said later at the house. "That was you yesterday, wasn't it? How did you know where to find her?"

"Gatlin and her husband came here searching for her, so I just followed them and looked where they didn't." Shrouded in a huge apron with silly chickens on it that

273

covered her from neck to hem, Augusta concocted a trifle with layers of ladyfingers, custard, and fruit. The next day we would top it with whipped cream flavored with sherry.

"And thank you for everything else, too," I said. I put my broccoli and onion casserole—my mother's own recipe—in the refrigerator to bake the next day.

"You're welcome, Arminda." Augusta covered her masterpiece with plastic wrap and stood back to admire it. She began to take off her apron.

For some reason, I didn't want her to take it off. "Do you think we should make the relish tray now or wait until tomorrow?" I asked.

"Why don't you make it now?" She dropped the voluminous apron over my head, tied it behind me with a gentle tug of the sashes. The sweet fragrance of her reminded me of summer: chasing butterflies through the grass, picking wildflowers for my mother, playing hide and seek at twilight. Happy things.

Still, I didn't like what I was thinking. "Why are you putting this crazy thing on me? You know I don't wear aprons," I said.

"There were times, Arminda Hobbs, when people had to protect their clothing; you couldn't just throw everything in the washing machine. You'll do well to keep that in mind. Besides, I want you to have it."

"But it's yours. You'll need it . . ."

She didn't answer.

I felt like somebody had kicked me in the stomach. "Oh, Augusta! When?"

She pulled up a stool and poured coffee for both of us. Black for her, sweet and white for me. "Soon now. It's time, I think, don't you?"

I wanted to say no. It would never be time. I wanted

her to stay forever, but I knew she was right. Augusta had two missions: mine and one unfinished from years before. I was going to be okay. I sipped my coffee for a minute until I was able to speak.

"You've accomplished what you came for," I told her. "You should be pleased."

"*We've* accomplished what I came for," she said, touching my forehead with a light fingertip.

"And where will you go now?"

Augusta smiled. "As for that," she said, "I'll just have to wait and see."

I smiled, too. "I have to make a phone call," I said, scrambling to find a number I had written down days before.

"Checking the menu with your family?" She lifted a quizzical brow.

"No, I'm calling the doctor."

Augusta put down her cup and frowned. "Are you not feeling well, Arminda?"

I laughed. "I feel just fine," I said, and left a message for Harrison Ivey inviting him to Thanksgiving dinner.

Dear Reader:

I hope you enjoyed reading this Large Print mystery. If you are interested in reading other Beeler Large Print Mystery titles or any other Beeler Large Print titles, ask your librarian or write to me at

Thomas T. Beeler, *Publisher*
Post Office Box 659
Hampton Falls, New Hampshire 03844

You can also call me at 1-800-818-7574 and I will send you my latest catalogue.

Audrey Lesko chooses the titles I publish in Large Print. Our aim is to provide good books by outstanding authors—books we both enjoyed reading and liked well enough to want to share. We warmly welcome any suggestions for new titles and authors.

Sincerely,